Moringa Leaf

GRETA SHELLING

This is a work of fiction. All of the characters, names, incidents, organizations, and dialogue in this novel are either the products of the author's imagination or are used fictitiously.

WestBow Press books may be ordered through booksellers or by contacting:

WestBow Press
A Division of Thomas Nelson & Zondervan
1663 Liberty Drive
Bloomington, IN 47403
www.westbowpress.com
844-714-3454

ISBN: 978-1-6642-5644-6 (sc)
ISBN: 978-1-6642-5646-0 (hc)
ISBN: 978-1-6642-5645-3 (e)

Library of Congress Control Number: 2022901480

Print information available on the last page.

WestBow Press rev. date: 03/03/2022

for my son
and all who aspire to be and have more than they are and have

This story weaves together
historical events and fictitious characters
in such a way that
no one—or anyone—could say,
"That's me!"

Special thanks to
all who contributed to
the historical, literary, cultural, psychological, and religious
aspects of this work.
You know who you are!

Part I

Ani Su-Li Sunatu hated her Chinese middle name. It meant "beauty." Not that she saw herself as ugly. She was fully aware that her rounded shoulders aroused much envy among her peers. But brains, education, and life accomplishments were more valuable to her self-identity than physical beauty. And because the Indonesian government did not recognize Chinese names anyway (even though she was half Chinese), she had everyone call her by her Sundanese name, "Ani."

Ani's third year of college in the city of Bandung was about to begin. She looked forward to learning, yet she dreaded another year of the horde classroom mentality and rote-learning methods of her university. When she mentioned this to her Chinese maternal uncle, Lee Salim, one day, he casually asked, "Why not go to graduate school in the USA? It is different in America. There, professors allow you to ask questions and discuss issues in class."

She almost dropped her teacup. Studying in America had been her dream ever since she was twelve years old, but she had never dared mention it to anyone. "You are an intelligent, diligent student, Ani," her uncle continued. "You have already studied English these past few years. Your best friend in high school was an American, and you spoke English with her all the time, didn't you? With some extra tutoring and a few months of advanced English studies during the next two years, I am sure you will score well on the TOEFL English proficiency test and the GRE's. Then you can go to graduate school at an American university. Any idea what you would like to study?"

"Business, I think," she said with a stammer. She saw herself as a bank manager one day or the owner of a large corporation. Or a small one would be all right, too.

Her uncle walked over to the bookshelf and picked out an atlas. Leafing through it, he turned to the map of the Americas and placed it before Ani. "The university I went to 22 years ago was right here," he said, pointing to the eastern section of the United States, just north of Washington, D.C. "It is relatively small, but it has an outstanding academic reputation—especially in the business department. How would you like to study there?"

A silence fell between them as Ani studied the map. "Sounds great, Uncle," she replied pensively. "There is just one problem. You know my parents can't afford this."

"True. They probably can't," Lee Salim replied, closing the atlas and placing it back on the shelf. "But why not apply for a scholarship? I will pay for all your other expenses. How about it?"

Ani held her breath for a moment. "You think I can do this?"

"Just give it a try, one step at a time. What do I always say? *Dunia tak selebar daun kelor.* The world is larger than a moringa leaf."

"I know. I wonder if they have that saying in America."

"They say it differently, but I can't remember how."

Chapter 1

Three years later, in early September of 1997, Ani Sunatu woke up shivering in a semi dark room. For a moment, she could not remember where she was or why. She sat up, rubbed her almond-shaped eyes, and looked around. The wall was white without blemish—like that of a hospital room. A desk, an empty bookshelf, a chest of drawers, another bed, and next to hers, two large suitcases jolted her memory. She was finally at Newton University outside Baltimore, Maryland, the United States of America!

Ani recollected leaving Jakarta on Sunday at 10:30 p.m., changing planes twice, and reaching Dulles Airport near Washington, D.C. twenty-seven hours later. Because she had gained a day due to the time zone change, her arrival time was Monday at 1:30 a.m. A taxi had taken her to the entrance gate of Newton University in Maryland two hours later, where a muscular African-American security guard greeted her warmly. After driving her to her dormitory in his golf cart and carrying her two enormous suitcases and a shoulder bag up three flights of stairs, he had chuckled and said, "I don't usually do this, you know. But you're the first student who's arrived. All the others won't be coming until Tuesday. Just don't tell anybody I helped you, or else I'll get fired!" When Ani had reached into her purse to give him a few dollars for tip, he waved her off. "Oh no, miss! I don't want nothin'," he said and left. She had locked the door to her room, dropped fully dressed onto her bed, and instantly fallen asleep.

Reddish sunlight filtered into the room around the edges of the window blinds when she got up to use the bathroom. Her watch said

6:30, but she did not know whether it was morning or evening. She would know soon enough, she decided. She fished for a fresh set of clothing and her toiletries, went to the bathroom, and took a shower. The sun rays between the shade and the window frame had become brighter. She concluded it must still be Monday morning. Much too early to get up, she thought, but partly because of excitement, and partly because she had slept long hours on the flight, she felt wide awake.

Wishing for more daylight in the room, she tried to pull up the shades, but she did not know how to. In desperation, she climbed on a chair, carefully removed the shade from the hooks, rolled it up halfway by hand, and hung it up again. She peeked outside. An empty parking lot below, a three-story building across the way, and a barren, carpet-like lawn on either side of the building met her eyes. A pair of small brown birds flew across the window, and a grayish creature with a bushy tail, which she later learned to be a squirrel, scurried across the empty parking lot below. She retreated from the window, half wondering if she were having a nightmare. The eerie quiet in the dorm did not help. No footsteps, no shouts, and no voices in the hallway. No people anywhere. Where were they all? Then she remembered what the security guard had said when she arrived. "You're the first student who's arrived," he had said. "The others are probably not coming until Tuesday."

Ani's growling stomach and dry mouth reminded her that she had not eaten since noon the day before. She had been sleeping and therefore missed the last meal during the flight to Washington. The campus cafeteria was closed, the security guard had told her, but she could take the bus to the nearest shopping center to get food. But which bus, and in which direction? She rummaged through a folder of papers sent to her by the admissions office of the university. There! A timetable of bus runs between the campus and a nearby store. The bus would come every hour from 8:30 a.m. to 9:30 p.m. during the week, but not on Sundays or holidays.

She put on her denim jacket, assuming it was even colder outside than inside. After all, wasn't this September in the northern USA? As soon as she opened the front door of the building, she realized her mistake. It was almost as hot and humid out there as in Bandung!

Not wanting to miss the bus, she stuffed her jacket into her backpack, rolled up her sleeves, and hurried out through the open campus gate. The kind guard was not there anymore. She looked both ways and found a sign that said BUS STOP to the left.

She stood waiting for at least an hour and a half. The soles of her feet burned badly inside the Nikes, and her shirt was soaking in sweat. She wanted to sit down on the ground, but ants were crawling underneath her—the kind that might bite, she thought. Shifting her feet apart for stabilization, she bent her body forward and backward to relieve her lower back. Why did the bus not come, she wondered? "Maybe I will starve in the great, prosperous United States of America," she muttered as she turned her drenched, weary body and headed back to her room.

A water fountain in the hallway caught her eye. It took her a while to figure out how to get water from it. *Splash. Gulp.* She spat out the cold water, which not only smelled like the sulfur in her father's medicine cabinet but also tasted like the stuff her family's servant used for cleaning. Pinching her nostrils together, she took another swallow. And another. The cold air from the vent blowing on her sweat-drenched T-shirt made her shiver as she stumbled back to her room. She grabbed a towel and a fresh change of clothing and retook a long, warm shower.

Once back in her room, Ani flopped onto her bed. Something sharp pressed against her chest. The culprit? A thumb-length golden miniature keris (or dagger) threaded onto her gold necklace. This miniature replica represented her grandfather's meter-long keris, a family heirloom that hung in her parents' bedroom. The top of its distinctive handle was shaped into a frowning face with its tongue sticking out. "Some say it has special powers that will bring you success," her father had told her when he had given her this mini replica as a farewell present. "But *I* say it has no powers of its own.

Its powers depend on what *you* do with your life. You are the one responsible."

Ani gently stroked and kissed the keris pendant. Instead of starving in America, she would keep looking for a solution until she found one somehow, somewhere. This notion felt like it conflicted with her Muslim belief that Allah ultimately decided and guided everything and that she did not have to try so hard to carve out her future. For now, she would accept her uncle's challenge. And just in case nothing she chose worked out, Allah would have to win.

The thought reminded her that it was time for her mid-morning prayer. She got up, prostrated herself before the window facing east, and began to recite a prayer to Allah. Uncle Lee Salim came to mind while she prayed. Had he not handed her a business card of a friend in Maryland just before she left? "If you have a question or a problem, call this woman," he had said. "She is a volunteer for the university's international student office. I met her twenty-five years ago, and I still get Christmas cards from her once a year. She has a big heart."

Ani remembered passing by a public telephone in the hall. Trembling, she rummaged through her purse in search of the woman's business card. She found it and ran out to the hall phone, but a sign said she needed to insert seventy-five cents. She galloped back to her room and grabbed her wallet. Fortunately, it contained a few quarters that she had acquired when she exchanged her Indonesian rupiahs at the airport.

"Hello," the recording of a woman's voice said on the telephone. "We're sorry we're not able to answer the phone. But if this is an extremely urgent matter, please leave a message after the beep." *This is an urgent matter,* Ani told herself. But she didn't know what the word "beep" meant, nor how to leave a message. She hung up. Just as she began to return to her room, the wall telephone rang. She picked it up. "Hello?" she said timidly.

"Did someone just call me from that number a few seconds ago?" a warm, middle-aged female voice asked.

"Yes, I did," Ani replied timidly. "Are you Mrs. Outhouse?"

A soft chuckle preceded the woman's reply. "Yes, but I think you mean Osterhouse. But you can call me Grace. And you are—?"

"I am Ani Su-Li Sunatu, and I am a new student at Newton University. My uncle, Lee Salim, gave me your telephone number. He said he met you when he was a student here twenty-five years ago."

"Oh, yes! Salim! Of course. From Indonesia, right?"

"Yes."

"Oh my! You're stranded on that godforsaken campus on a holiday weekend, aren't you? And I bet you are all alone, am I right? And oh my goodness, no buses, no food! You must be famished."

Ani did not understand the word "famished". But, sensing the woman's empathy, she merely replied with a sniffle.

"How do you want me to call you? Ann? Or Sue?"

"My name is pronounced Ah-nee."

"Can you tell me which dorm building you're in, Ani?"

"One minute, I will look at my papers."

"Never mind, honey," Mrs. Osterhouse said kindly, using two words that Ani could not remember the meaning of. "In about twenty minutes, follow the road away from all the other buildings until you come to a large gate. It's a circular road, so you can't get lost. Wait under the roof of the gatehouse. I'll be there with my blue van in about thirty minutes. Oh, and bring your overnight clothes so you can stay overnight with us. You can eat your meals with us, of course. I will take you shopping in the morning for whatever you need. Did you understand all that?"

"Yes, I think so." Ani was not sure if she'd just heard an invitation or a command. In either case, she felt too hungry to refuse. Would this be one of those kind but religious Americans a friend had warned her about? And what would her father and uncle think if they knew she depended on an American instead of herself? The growl in her stomach loudly admonished her not to care about either question.

Chapter 2

About ten miles east of Newton University, twenty-eight-year-old Tom Hanson's portable phone rang. It was lying on the glass coffee table in front of him, but he decided to let the machine answer. Today was his lazy day—a Sunday, and someone else in his computer repair business was on call. Besides, he was busy rolling up his socks while watching a baseball game on television.

A melodious female voice piped through the answering machine. It was from pretty, pliable, plastic Dora. "Listen, sweetie," it said, "I gotta cancel our date tonight. I just don't feel good. Can we have a rain check? But I want you to know that I'd still like to see you another time. When would . . ."

Tom sighed in relief and turned off the volume to the rest of her message. He leaned back and placed his bare feet on the coffee table. The Baltimore Orioles were up at bat in the top half of the third inning, and so far, neither team had scored. Their batter hit a ground ball, ran to first base, and kept running to second. The outfielder threw the ball to the second baseman, who caught it and tagged the batter two seconds before he could touch the base. The score was still 0-0. *Just like my love life,* Tom mused with a sigh.

He turned on the answering machine volume and listened to the whole message. As usual, Dora had nothing significant to say. She only made him look good in public. She was shapely. Her green eyes pierced like a cat's under her perfectly lined eyebrows and wavy auburn hair. But he certainly could not imagine spending the rest of his life with her. She seemed to have no other interests besides getting pampered by his attention, and for him, the sum of his expenditures on their dates far outweighed any pleasure gained.

As Tom rolled the last clean pair of socks and stuffed them into a drawer, he suddenly felt tired. Very, very tired. Up until now, a string of light-hearted, bubbly women who liked to snuggle up to him like purring kitty cats had kept him feeling wanted, but never satisfied. Now at age 28, he had simply had enough of temporary parking places.

And there was his mother. She would pester him with questions about every girlfriend he ever had, not hiding her wish that he would marry soon and provide her with grandchildren. He wondered how long he could go on disappointing her.

But disappointing his mother was nothing compared to an underlying question that had plagued him ever since his puberty days: Would he ever be or feel worthy of someone he truly loved and admired? His self-worth, he thought, had to be measured by dollars and cents. "Without enough dough to your name," his father had said many times, "you'll be worth nothing to a woman." So if his father was right, rich meant valuable, and valuable meant rich.

So Tom felt he was neither.

As a successful contract computer technician for a small firm in the greater Baltimore area, Tom Hanson enjoyed a decent salary. However, he was still paying off a considerable college loan debt every month. His brand-new velvet-red Mustang, which he bought on credit, cost him $500 per month alone. That did not cover gasoline and routine care. He used one of his credit cards to purchase a top-of-the-line personal computer, another card for a brand-new leather sofa ensemble, an Indian wool rug, a brass-and-glass-top coffee table, and, of course, a fancy headboard to go with his queen-size bed. These things, plus the expensive dinners out on his "hot" dates, maxed out the first two cards in no time. And, because he could not pay off his credit cards every month, the interest charges kept climbing. Hence, more debts. A total trap.

He would have to try to find a way to make more money and

then some. But it would have to be by honest, whistle-clean means, he vowed to himself. His grandfather had taught him that much.

Tom combed his hair with his fingers and looked at his watch. He had a tennis appointment at the indoor club tennis hall in forty minutes. But first things first. He would shop for a sandwich at the supermarket. Hobbling to the bedroom with his tennis shoes half on, he fetched his wallet and checked to see if he had any cash. There was none. But a credit card was in it, and that would do.

A roar from the television filled the room. The New York Mets scored two more runs in the second half of the ninth inning and won. "Dora is finished, the game is finished, but I'm not," Tom said aloud to himself. "Fortune and wife, here I come! Time to make a home run—somehow, somewhere." His self-worth depended on it. Or so he thought.

Chapter 3

Ani did not have to wait long at the campus gate. The fairy godmother did appear—not in a carriage, of course, but in a large, royal-blue Ford van. A window electronically lowered. A red-haired woman with large, dangling blue earrings leaned out the open window. Her broad, toothy smile between thick red lips instantly set Ani at ease.

"You must be Annie, right? Or do you pronounce your name Ah-nee like in honey?" she asked with a warm, musical voice.

"Ah-nee is correct," answered Ani with a smile. She stepped toward the car. "Are you Mrs. Out—no, Osterhouse?"

"I sure am!" the driver answered with a huge smile. "You can call me Grace." Several lines across her neck, forehead, and chin betrayed Grace's age to be around 60, Ani guessed. But what followed did not. As the car door opened, a tennis shoe, a white sock, a bare shin bone and knee, and a flabby, cellulite thigh in yellow shorts emerged. Then another of the same. *Maybe she's younger after all,* Ani thought.

The woman climbed out of the van and swung open her arms. "Welcome to America!" she cheered with a broad smile framed in bright red lipstick. She wrapped her arms around Ani's small frame so that Ani lost her breath for a few seconds. And when she did breathe, she smelled a strong perfume.

Ani was used to neither a hug nor the scent of perfume, but she rather liked both. "I hope I don't bother you," she said. "Do you have time to help me?"

Grace laughed. "I've *made* time, honey, don't you see?"

In my world, time is instant and infinite, Ani mused*; but here,* *they have to* make *it!* "You are very kind. How can I repay you?" she asked politely.

"No need to repay me, honey. I'm the one who owes a debt."

"I don't understand."

"Never mind that now. I'll explain another time."

Soon the Ford brought them into Grace's neighborhood. Huge front yards with continuing carpet-like green grass (except for a walkway in front of each entrance), a tree now and then, and budding chrysanthemums framed the long rows of two-story redbrick homes. The colors of the window shutters varied from house to house.

"Watch for the sprinkler. It should go off any second," warned Grace as they walked up the narrow path to the house. "We usually park in the back in the garage, but I like to bring my new guests to the front of the house."

A brown beagle barked at the door as they entered. Unaccustomed to pet dogs in the house, Ani cringed and stepped back.

"Don't worry, she won't bite," said Grace. "Just gently hold out your palm under her chin. When she wags her tail, it says she trusts you. Her name is Oriole, and she loves ladies!"

Leading the way into the foyer, Grace announced melodically, "Fred dear, where are you? We have a guest!" They came into a large room with bookshelves, a sofa, a comfortable chair, and a television. "That's my husband in that chair over there, watching a baseball game," she said. She bent over him, blocking his view of the TV. "Fred! Ani is here. Can you say hello?"

A gray-haired, middle-aged man swiveled his chair around and quickly got up. About half a meter taller than Grace, he walked toward Ani and extended his arms. "Welcome to our home. I'm Fred. And you are again—?"

"Ani," she answered, stretching out her right hand quickly and letting him shake it, hoping he would not hug her as Grace had done.

Fred did not hug her, but he did manage to touch her shoulder with the other hand. "Pleased to meet you, Ani, and welcome to our home," Fred said warmly, turned around again, and sat down in front of his game.

Grace led Ani toward a counter and three bar stools dividing the family room from the kitchen. Grace pulled out a bar stool for Ani. "Won't you have a seat? Sorry, it's a bit cluttered in this house." Ani looked around, not sure what she meant by the word *cluttered.* A lot of furniture, yes. A stack of newspapers and magazines in one corner, plants in every other, a cream sofa with a few magazines on top, two matching recliners, a desk filled with papers, and a dining table with six chairs extending out from the other side of the kitchen counter. She had never seen a house so full of things one could do without!

"How long has it been since you've eaten?" asked Grace.

"I ate two meals on the plane from Jakarta, but I slept on the way from California."

"Oh dear! You must be starving!" Grace took out several rolls from the refrigerator, warmed them in the microwave oven, and poured tea into a tall glass with ice. "You can add sugar, if you like. And please help yourself to some grapes and apples," she added, pointing toward a bowl of fruit on the counter. She took a bowl out of the refrigerator and placed it into the microwave. "Have you had lasagna before, Ani?"

"I don't think so. Does it have pig meat?" she asked cautiously.

"No. I made it with beef and cheese. You are Muslim, I presume?"

Ani nodded. She did not understand the word "beef" but she was too hungry to ask.

"Sorry, I do not have halal meat today. Is that okay?" Grace asked.

"You know about halal?" Ani asked in surprise.

Grace nodded. "I've had many Muslim students in my home. So, do you eat only halal?"

Ani hesitated. "At home I do. But I can also eat Kosher meats. If neither is available, I can eat any other meat, except pig meat."

Grace placed the warmed-up rolls onto a plate and offered them to Ani. "By the way," she said with a twinkle, "when we talk about pig meat, we say pork. Hope you don't mind me correcting your English."

"Oh, no, always correct me, please! What do you say for cow meat?"

"Beef."

"And chicken?"

"Just chicken," Grace answered, chuckling. "English is crazy, isn't it?"

The next morning, Grace drove Ani to a vast parking lot twice the size of the huge outdoor market in Bandung. Then they walked into a supermarket that was at least a hundred meters long and wide and offered everything under the sun. All the items were wrapped and packaged neatly, with price tags already printed. The best part about the supermarket? It was indoors with air-conditioning, and there were no flies to shoo away!

"Let's see," Grace said as Ani pushed the grocery cart behind her. "Ah! Here's the halal meat section. Let's see if they have some kosher or halal meat for hamburgers. Have you had hamburgers before, Ani?"

"No. Muslims do not eat ham," Ani answered.

"No worries. In America, we make hamburgers from chopped beefsteak. Probably named after Hamburg, the city in Germany."

"Oh, I see," laughed Ani. She had seen an American fast-food chain in Bandung but never eaten there.

"Ani, do you need anything here?" Grace asked as they passed a long row of shelving.

"I think I need soup."

"You mean soup or soap?"

"Ah, yes. Soap," Ani said, giggling.

"For the body or the face?"

"For washing clothes."

"Oh, sorry. You'll find that in aisle four."

Two long aisles later, Grace's plump arm pointed to the large boxes of detergent, some of which were as large as Ani's night table back home.

"Which one should I buy?" Ani asked.

"Compare what it says with the volume and the price. And look, some are for colored laundry, some are for white laundry. Do you want to wash your clothes by hand, or do you want to use a machine?"

"By hand."

"Here, this should do." Grace picked out a generic liquid detergent. "Just use a teaspoon in the sink," she advised. "It's very concentrated."

A short, blond young man with Asian features helped bag the groceries. "You are beautiful!" he chimed with a broad smile as he looked at Ani. She blushed, never having had such brash attention from a male before. When she noticed the young man's combination of slanted eyes, pudgy face, and down-sloped shoulders—marks of Down syndrome—she relaxed. "Thank you," she said, smiling back at him as she started pushing the shopping cart away.

"Watch out, Ani!" cried Grace. "That's the entrance, not the exit!"

Ani tried to veer her cart toward the other doors—but too late. The entrance sliding glass doors opened, and—wham!—her wagon banged into something semi-hard.

"Ouch!" cried a man's baritone voice.

Ani saw that her grocery cart had hit a pair of hairy legs in white tennis shorts, white socks, and white tennis shoes. When she looked up, she saw that the hairy legs belonged to a handsome blue-eyed, sandy-haired *hidung mancung* (literally translated as "sharp nose" or Caucasian). "Oh! So sorry!" she exclaimed, nervously jerking the cart to the side. "Did I hurt you?"

"Yeah, you sure did!" she heard him say as she watched him bend down and stroke his leg. When he straightened and looked up at her, she saw his grimace soften and break into a kind, warm smile. "But

I think I'll live," he said with a twinkle, not at all with the lust-filled eyes of some Sunda men she had known.

Grace came around from the other door and tapped the man on the shoulder. "Well, hello, Tom. It's been a long time since I've seen you!"

He turned around. "Oh, hi, Grace! Is this beautiful rookie grocery cart driver a friend of yours, by any chance?"

Grace nodded.

"Aren't you going to introduce her to me?"

"We're blocking everybody. Let's move over first, shall we?" suggested Grace. She helped Ani push the cart toward the exit door. "There, now, that's better. Ani, this is Tom. Tom, this is Ani. She just arrived from Indonesia."

"Hi, Tom," Ani said politely, remembering that adding his name was the appropriate way to greet someone in North America. She also remembered to hold out her hand and smile, even though her smile actually expressed nervousness. She watched his hand extend toward hers and felt its warm squeeze. Just before she let go of it, she noticed a nickel-size dark mark under the nail of his right thumb. "Please excuse my…my bad driving," she stammered. "Did I hurt your finger?"

"Oh no. That's just a birthmark," he replied. "Your shopping cart banged up my knees. But all is forgiven. And welcome to Maryland, Ani! Will you be coming to the International Friendship Hour at the University Community Church?"

Ani looked at Grace with a puzzled look.

"I haven't told Ani about it yet, but I will," said Grace. "But we must get going now. Will you excuse us, Tom?"

Tom turned to Ani, bowed slightly, and with a friendly gleam in his eyes said, "Good luck in America! I look forward to seeing you again."

Ani smiled, this time for real. Life in America had begun to be interesting.

Certainly not just another Asian girl, Tom mused as he rushed past the cashiers to the deli on the other side of the supermarket. *Coy, cute, sweet, and intelligent. She'd make me look good. And she's new in this country, which means she'd have to lean on me and look up to me. That would make me feel competent. She needs me, and I need someone to need me.*

But then the old self-doubt showed its ugly head. Would he ever be rich enough to impress her?

He ordered a submarine sandwich at the deli, one foot long, stuffed with everything imaginable—lettuce, ham, pastrami, salami, tomatoes, cheese, mayonnaise, chili sauce, mustard, and pickles. A perfect feast with which to celebrate his find. He paid for it with a debit card, getting an extra $30 in change. Before he even made it back to the car, he devoured his sandwich as if he hadn't eaten in three days. Then he drove over to the sports club to play tennis with his friends.

Still excited about having met Ani, he decided not to join them afterward for a round of beers. He needed time to think. But now that he had met the woman of his dreams, he decided it was high time to find a way to earn more money. But how?

On his way home, an idea popped into his head: Call his friend Solomon Elijah! How many times had Tom repaired his computer for free? Countless. Solomon had once said, "If you ever need advice about investments, don't hesitate to call me." Tom had ignored that offer; he had no extra money to invest! But then he remembered that Solomon had also mentioned his need for help with some of his "moonlighting missions"—whatever that meant. Perhaps it was time to ask.

Chapter 4

At the end of a seven-hour drive northeast from Baltimore to Rhode Island, The brown large hand of Solomon Elijah turned off the ignition to his shiny grey Jaguar. The sound of saxophone blues also came to a sudden halt.

Solomon gaped at a tall iron gate with a two-story English Tudor estate behind it and let out a whistle. He wondered if he could ever afford such a place. Not that he was doing so badly, materially speaking. As the great-great-grandson of a cotton slave from Alabama, Solomon had risen from the slums in southeastern Baltimore to a suburban penthouse with a swimming pool. "Being black is no excuse," his mother used to say. "Just keep your nose clean and work hard, and you'll get somewhere in life," which wasn't always easy, even in the post–civil rights era of the 1980s. Solomon proved her right. A football scholarship paid for his college education at Newton University. He worked his way through graduate school as an assistant football coach at Newton and eventually became the same institution's public relations director. A talker, a charmer, and a philanthropist of sorts, he also dabbled in what he called "whistle-clean moonlighting missions." These included investing in people's private business endeavors, soliciting funds for large charity organizations, and playing the saxophone at weddings and parties. Not attached to anyone other than his Siamese cat, he used his extra money to pay off his younger siblings' college debts and his mother's medical bills and occasionally help his less fortunate friends.

On this particular day, he was about to learn about a new possible moonlighting mission. He could not remember the connection, but a man with a thick foreign accent had called him a few weeks earlier and asked to meet with him in his home in Newport, Rhode Island.

The double name Rianto Rianto appeared underneath the call button on the intercom at the gate. A double name? It certainly intrigued Solomon. He pushed the call button. Ten long seconds later, he heard a male with a strong foreign accent ask, "Who is there?" To Solomon, it sounded like a Dutch accent, but not quite.

"I'm Solomon Elijah. I have an appointment with Mr. Rianto."

"Yes, he is expecting you," the voice said. "The gate will open now."

Solomon pulled through the gate and to the circular drive in front of the mansion. His long, slender legs climbed up a few stairs and rang the bell. A light-brown young Asian man wearing a plaid vest over a starched white shirt opened the door. He was about seventeen inches shorter than Solomon. Showing all his buck teeth as he greeted the guest, the young man ushered Solomon into an exquisite foyer with mirrors everywhere.

"I am Putu, Mr. Rianto's butler, cook, and chauffeur," he said. "Please have a seat. Mr. Rianto will be here shortly." He motioned toward a plush settee against the wall and left the foyer.

Too fascinated with his surroundings to sit down, Solomon wandered around the foyer. Delicate Chinese porcelain flowers decorated the French provincial wall table on the other side. A giant photograph of a curved dagger hung on the wall opposite the stairway's first five steps. Solomon could not help but notice the dagger's hilt; it resembled a snake's head but had long ears and two tongues sticking out of its mouth.

"That is a picture of a keris, my family heirloom," explained a high-pitched voice behind him, rolling the *r* in each word containing it. Solomon turned around. A stocky man of medium height, his skin a slight bit darker than Putu's, stood in the archway of the foyer. Framed by thick, black, knotted eyebrows, the man's dark, Bali eyes appeared stark and lifeless. At the end of his flat nose, a thick, black mustache crowned his thick lips. A receding dark hairline mixed with grey strands and a growing bald spot betrayed his age to be at least forty.

"Note that the keris is curved, not at all like a dagger," the host continued with an even tone. "There are several such daggers, and each one has a special design on the handle which identifies the family that owns it. If you look closely, this one distinctively has *two* tongues, not one."

"Interesting. Mr. Rianto, I presume?" Solomon asked.

The man nodded without any change of expression.

Solomon extended his hand. "So pleased to meet you, sir. I'm Solomon Elijah."

Rianto glided his hand over Solomon's before the latter could grip and shake it properly. "Please follow me," Rianto said in a flat voice and led the way into the living room. They sat down on a wine-red corner sofa. A fish-shaped glass coffee table separated them from a wall-length window with a view of the Narragansett Bay.

A few seconds later, Putu appeared. His bucktoothed smile penetrated like an infrared light into the gloom surrounding his boss. He said something in a language that Solomon could not place at all. It was not any Asian language he could recognize. Neither was it Hispanic, Slavic, or Germanic (although the accent was Dutch when he spoke in English). Both men had Asian, features, although, in Solomon's estimation, Putu could have passed for a dark Peruvian, and Rianto for part Mexican.

Rianto nodded. Putu's head retreated, and the door closed again.

"May I ask what language you spoke just now?" asked Solomon.

"Indonesian. Our language is different from many other Asian languages. We roll our *r.* That's probably why the generation before me had no trouble learning Dutch."

"Dutch? Why did they learn Dutch?"

"Indonesia was a Dutch colony for a long, long time. Then the Japanese took over for a few years."

Putu entered the room and placed a small tray with two glasses, a pitcher of mango juice, and a bowl filled with chips onto the coffee table.

"I am sorry I have no alcoholic drink to offer you. I am a Muslim, you see," Rianto said.

"No problem," replied Solomon. "I never drink alcohol while on the job." As soon as he said it, he wished he hadn't. It implied he drank at other times. "But when I do, it's not like I have to," he added quickly. He looked at Rianto, waiting for a sign of approval. But he only got a blank stare in response. He nervously drew a chip from the bowl. "Hmm. These chips are good. Real good. What are they?" he asked as he took two long swallows of the mango juice.

"Plantain chips," his host answered and refilled Solomon's glass. "Your name is Jewish, is it not?"

Solomon smiled. "It is both Christian and Jewish. Maybe even Muslim," he said. "Both my first and surnames are from the Old Testament of the Bible. Solomon was a great king, and Elijah a prophet."

"I know. But I am curious. Are you Christian, Jewish, or Muslim?"

"I prefer not to say," answered Solomon. "Religion is a private matter to me, and I'm not passionate about the one I grew up with. Do you have a problem with that, sir?"

"No. Just curious. You see, I called you here because my friend and landlord Jerome Singer of Singer and Singer highly recommended you. He said you are a man of integrity. He told me how he tried to get you to do a certain illegal thing you refused to do once, despite the alluring capital gain you could have made."

"Glad he remembers it," Solomon chuckled. "So you want to know if my religion had anything to do with my integrity."

Rianto nodded slightly.

"I think the fact that I'm a man of integrity has more to do with the example and discipline of those I bonded with," Solomon explained. "I had parents who practiced what they preached. They also made me feel valued and loved, so I respected and loved them back because of that. So I've always wanted to be like them. And when I'm honest, I like myself. It makes me happy."

The stone-faced Rianto said nothing in response. He got up and adjusted the blinds so that the sun would not glare into their eyes. Then he sat down again and looked straight at Solomon. "I need a man like you," he said. "Honest, smart, and reliable. I need someone like you to help me with a project that would help millions in the third world. It's about fairness. Relief from starvation. A fair distribution of wealth. A chance for the rich to get richer, the middle class to get bigger, and the poor to survive. You see, my project is needed, especially after what happened in Asian countries this past summer. I'm sure you've heard about the Asian financial crisis, have you not?" He paused again, watching Solomon take another plantain chip from the bowl. "Did you hear anything I said, Mr. Elijah?"

"Oh, sure I did, sir. You talked about poverty in the third world, and you said something about the poor surviving. And you asked me if I know anything about the Asian financial crisis. But no, I do not know much about the Asian financial crisis. Sorry about that, sir."

Rianto waited for a moment before he spoke again. "Before I continue, may I ask why you always say "sir" to me? I am not your boss, or teacher, or a military superior."

Solomon let out a short laugh. "It's my custom, or call it a habit. See, I'm originally from Alabama. From the time we're wee-wee little, we learn to say "sir" and "ma'am" to our elders, new acquaintances, employers, and clients. It's considered polite. That's all. It's like that in Baltimore, too, where I live now. You know, it's a sign of respect. Don't they do that here in New England? If it bothers you, I'll stop doing that."

"Stop showing respect?" Rianto asked with a wry smile.

Solomon gave out a rolling laugh. "Of course not, sir. I mean, I'll stop saying 'sir' if it bothers you."

"No need to. I was just curious. People don't usually talk like that here in the North, except in the military." Rianto shifted in his seat and clapped his hands. "Let's get back to business. Tell me, Mr.

Elijah, did you ever hear about the International Trade Bill that was signed a few years ago?"

"Vaguely. What about it?"

"Well, it's practically outdated now. And since the Asian financial crisis this summer, many countries in Asia are in big trouble. Right now, the president of the United States has little power to help those countries. He hopes to reinstate a fast track bill that would give him more power in collaborating with the senators and the House to change the Trade Bill's policies."

"What happens if the new changes don't pass?"

"There's another option. It's called the IMF, or International Monetary Fund, a part of the new OCESA law, which stands for Omnibus Consolidated and Emergency Supplemental Appropriations, which will be voted on next year. If passed, it will make a big difference for many poor people in Asia. You are aware, Mr. Elijah, that poor people in the third world are much poorer than the poor here in the United States of America, are you not?"

Solomon only let out a tentative "I see." He did not fully understand what Rianto had just said, but it sounded good.

"I am sure the House will pass either or both of these bills, but I am not sure about the Senate. Because you seem to share my soft heart for the poor," Rianto continued, "I hope that together we could make sure that the first bill, or both bills, will be passed by both the House and the Senate."

"How do you propose to do that, sir?"

"I want to hire you to influence a few senators to vote in favor of the OCESA law and to change the minds of those who want to vote against it. In other words, I would like to hire you to represent me as a lobbyist."

"A lobbyist?" Solomon responded with a long, rolling chuckle, leaning back and cracking his knuckles. "That's not exactly my thing at all, sir. You see, I never get mixed up in politics. Haven't ever yet and don't want to."

"I see." Rianto's glance shifted from Solomon toward the

window. He then refocused on Solomon. "Not even for about half a million dollars?" he asked slowly.

Solomon stopped chewing on the last piece of plantain and swallowed it. "Half a million, did you say?"

Rianto nodded. "Let me explain. The fast track bill needs a majority vote to pass, or at least 51 yes votes. So far, only 15 have said they favor the bill, and 43 senators are still undecided. So your task is to meet with each of the undecided senators and persuade them to vote yes. I will pay you $2325 for every undecided senator you meet personally to explain the bill's benefits."

Solomon took out his pocket calculator and punched in some numbers. "But if it doesn't pass, and I've presented the bill to 43 undecided senators, I am still guaranteed the $2325 times 43, which is 100,000. Right? But what did you mean by half a million dollars?"

"If the bill passes, instead of paying you only $100,000, I will pay you $10,811 for every one of the 37 recruited senators who vote for the bill, which would add up to $500,000 for the job, plus expense reimbursement, of course. But only if either the bill or the new law passes and gets signed by the president, you understand."

"And what if I persuade all 43 to vote yes?" asked Solomon.

"Sorry, my friend. My ceiling is 500 grand. I suggest you aim for 43 votes to increase your chances of getting the needed 37 votes." Rianto got up, turned to a large desk behind him, and handed Solomon a stapled stack of pages. "Here. This document explains all the potential benefits to the countries involved. Your job is to sell these facts to each of these senators. You see, many of these senators and representatives do not know or understand anything about this." He sat down again and waited for Solomon to examine the document.

Solomon took his time. Then he shook his head. "Man, this would mean a lot of work and trouble. Just finding and meeting all those senators in Washington, D.C., scares me. I'm a nobody. What if they don't even want to talk with me?"

"You are right. These senators are busy people with lots of

people trying to get their attention." Rianto leaned toward Solomon, and after a dramatic pause, said, "You will have to lure them into listening to you."

"How do you mean?" Solomon asked, handing the document back to Rianto. He did not want to seem too eager to get involved in a job he hated at this point, even if the pay was good.

Rianto drummed his hand on the coffee table for a few seconds, then stopped. "You know the saying, 'Money speaks louder than words'?"

Solomon rose from his seat. "Wait a minute. You're not thinking of bribing them, are you, sir? I will have nothing to do with anything illegal."

"Oh, no, no, no. Of course not," Rianto replied with a voice louder than it had been since Solomon arrived. "I never give bribes, just gifts. You see, my friend, we first send them a money gift to get their attention, to get them to listen to what you have to say. By then, we have them hooked. Believe me. These government officials will want to vote for the bill simply because they hope to get more gifts as a reward. We're doing them a favor, and they're doing us a favor. You will see. It works."

Maybe in your country, but I'm not sure about ours. "I'm curious, sir. How much will you give them as a gift—before they vote and afterward?"

Rianto managed a weak smile. "Enough to make them want to vote. Rest assured, this is all good. All kosher, as the German Jews say in New York."

Solomon shook his head. Something made him nervous about Rianto's "kosher" proposal. It sounded too neat, too easy. He swished around the remaining juice in his glass and let it settle. Then he remembered something. He slammed the glass down and rose to his feet with a bounce. "Sorry, sir. I wish I could help. But I can't do that," he said as he slipped his pocket calculator into his pocket.

Rianto got up, too. "But why? What is the problem?"

"You probably didn't know this, but American government

officials are not allowed to receive monetary donations from foreigners. You are not a US citizen, are you, sir?"

Rianto held up his hands. "You are right. I'm not a US citizen. And I know about that rule, Mr. Elijah. But please sit down again. I will explain something."

Solomon reluctantly complied.

After pouring more juice into Solomon's glass, Rianto also sat down again. "That is why I am hiring *you*," he said in a flat tone. "You see, I'm not the one who will deliver the money to these senators. *You* are the one who will do this. And I believe you are an American, are you not? Besides, I never like to broadcast my generosity. It produces greed in others and a long line of beggars. Didn't the prophet Isa, or Jesus, your Christian founder, teach you that you should not allow the left hand to know what the right hand is doing? Even if I were an American like you, I would want to remain anonymous."

"You have thought this through thoroughly, haven't you, sir?"

Rianto's lips curved into another weak smile. "Thank you for noticing, Mr. Elijah."

"How will I give these senators their gifts when you are the one who has the money in the bank?"

"This is where my trust in you comes in. I will transfer the money from my Swiss bank account into a business account in your name. You will then transfer the promised donations to the senators' accounts."

Solomon gave out a hearty laugh. "Why in my name? You're tempting me to take that money and run!"

Rianto remained emotionless. "Mr. Solomon, I know enough about you that you will not do such a thing. You are a man of integrity. That is why I chose you, remember? And don't forget. This operation is about the poor in the Third World. Remember how you and I can help them. Remember what we must do to help Congress do what is right. It is our duty."

Rianto's low, flat voice and repeated word *remember* almost hypnotized Solomon. But Solomon also felt what he had seldom felt before: Fear. To what length would this man go to get what he wanted?

"So, are you in?" Rianto asked.

"Okay, okay, but I still don't understand how all of this will work."

Just then, Putu appeared from the kitchen. An aroma of delicious-smelling spices unknown to Solomon followed him. "*Bebek betutu* is ready," he said.

"That's a Bali duck. You will like it," said Rianto, taking for granted that Solomon would eat with him. "Come, I will explain everything after dinner. But first, I have something to give you."

Rianto escorted Solomon through the hallway to the dining room. Stopping in front of a mahogany chest, he opened one of the drawers and pulled out an inch-long item. He held it in front of Solomon's face. "Does this look familiar to you?" he asked.

Solomon peered at it closely and nodded. "It looks like that ugly thing in the painting on the stairway."

"You observed correctly."

"What is that sword thing called again?"

"A keris. What you have in your hand is a mini replica of our unique family keris. There is no other keris like this one. Every family's keris has a different design. Look at it carefully. How many tongues does it have hanging out of its mouth?"

Solomon bent over it and counted. "Wow, they're tiny. I can barely see those tongues. One, two. Amazing. Just like the one in the painting on the wall up the stairs, am I right?"

"Exactly. I am lending you this pin so that you can wear it on the lapel of your coat whenever you interact with the senators. That's how they will identify you."

"Well, sir, I will make sure to guard it with my life."

"Good. And when you've completed all the assignments and the fast track bill gets the votes it deserves, you can give me back the keris pin in exchange for your bonus. Is that a deal?"

Chapter 5

Driving from the Jamestown Bridge to Hhighway I-95 several hours later, Solomon could not help but feel flattered by the honor of having been entrusted with so much. Like the scum in a pool after dozens of people swam in it all day, a few questions and fears rose in Solomon's mind. Would the job be safe? Would it be squeaky clean? Would he want to deal with politicians? Write letters and transfer money—yes. But meet with senators personally? Not really. What bothered him even more was the fine print, which stated that if Solomon reneged before he finished within the time frame required, he would owe Rianto $100,000. That was far more than he owned in stocks and savings. But what would Rianto do if Solomon failed to get the needed results? Fear gripped Solomon at the thought.

Suddenly, a deer jumped out of the woods from the right. Solomon swerved to the left, his Jaguar spinning around ninety degrees onto the highway median. The deer escaped without a scrape, but he was not sure about his car. He turned off the engine and tried to recover from the shock of a near-miss collision with an animal he loved. And from the scare of nearly losing his Jaguar, and perhaps his life. All in that order.

As he sat there for a few minutes, allowing his muscles and nerves to stabilize, visions of his long-deceased mother came to mind. One of her favorite sayings was, "You filled the bath with water, now bathe in it"—even if the water got cold, which it often did where he was growing up. To Solomon, that meant he needed to follow through on his commitment, as unpleasant or risky as it might turn out to be.

The flip side? The pay would undoubtedly be fantastic. Rianto had handed him a check of $1000.00 for expenses in transportation and other incidentals. That felt good because it was a sign that Rianto trusted him. If such a gesture inspired Solomon to take on a job that irked him, Rianto's donations might motivate the senators to vote as he hoped. And that would be good for both of them. Not only for the poor in Asia.

It began to rain. Solomon restarted his engine, turned on the windshield wipers, and rejoined the flowing traffic. Suddenly, an idea surfaced in his mind: Why not hire someone to do that job for him? Someone adventurous, extroverted, amiable, innocent-looking, businesslike, and energetic—someone preferably Caucasian who would look less conspicuous than he? Someone he could trust fully? Someone who could use the money?

Just then, his cell phone rang. He looked down at the seat next to him and noticed it was Tom Hanson, an old friend and computer tech he had known for a long, long time. He smiled. Tom had credit card debts and was always short on cash. But he was an honest fellow, generous to the core, creative, reliable, hardworking, and fun. Could he be that someone who could be the courier for this moonlighting mission? Solomon pulled over to a parking lot and returned the call.

"Hey, Tom, just the man I'm looking for! Yep. I do have a job for you. Can you come over tomorrow night and talk about it?"

The next evening, at about 10:00 p.m., Tom arrived at Solomon's apartment to learn all about his friend's moonlighting job offer. A few bottles of beer accompanied the occasion. At the end of Solomon's instructions, Solomon fished something small out of his pocket and kept it rolled up in his hand.

"So how much dough am I making on this?" asked Tom with trepidation.

Solomon leaned back and gave a wry smile. "Want to guess?"

Tom shrugged. "No idea. This is not an hourly-rate thing, is it?"

"No, it isn't. See, I get paid for every senator I contact on the phone for an appointment. Then you show up and get their deposit slips or account number. You get paid half of each reward I get if those senators vote yes."

Tom looked at Solomon with suspicion. "I can't guess how much you're getting for this, so I can't guess my share."

"Let's just say that you could, potentially speaking, get a good $250,000."

Tom's head spinned as he thought of what that amount could mean for him. "How do I identify myself when I meet the senators?"

"Hold out your hand, bro," Solomon requested. He opened his fist and dropped Rianto's keris pin onto Tom's palm.

"Oh, how funny," Tom said, peering at the small pin. "I just saw something like that on an Indonesian girl's necklace yesterday."

Solomon shrugged. "I wouldn't worry about it. This one is unique, and it's rare. So it doesn't matter. Anyway, guard it with your life! It's what you must wear on your lapel when you meet with the senators. Otherwise, don't show it to anybody. And when this is all over, you must give it back to me. D'you understand? Only then will you get my bonus."

"A bonus?"

"Right. Another grand maybe. But that depends on the outcome."

Tom held the pin closer to his eyes. "A gross looking thing. It has two tiny tongues sticking out of its mouth. Just curious. Where did you get this pin from?"

Solomon held up his hand. "I can't say more. The less you know—"

"—the better. I know. So I wear this on the lapel—the right one or the left?"

"Doesn't matter. You choose. But normally we wear a pin on the left."

Tom stuffed the keris pin into his zipper pocket on the inside of his jacket. "Hope I remember . . ." he mumbled to himself.

"Guard it with your life, pal, and try hard not to think of all the money you'll get. You don't want to get too nervous doing this."

"So when do I begin with this mission?" Tom asked.

"Soon. I'll let you know when. I first have to set it up. Be sure to keep a record of your expenses." Solomon handed him a bulky five-by-eight-inch manila envelope.

"What's this?"

"I've decided to pay you for your expenses in advance. I know you could use some now."

Peeking inside, Tom noticed cash. Lots of it. "Do you want a receipt?"

"Already made one out for you." Solomon handed him a piece of paper. "But first, count the cash, then sign it, please."

Tom counted ten one-hundred-dollar bills. "One thousand dollars before I do any work? Isn't that trusting me too much?"

"To be honest, Tom, I don't want too much cash floating around here or in my bank account. The same goes for you. There will be lots more coming afterward. Let me give you some advice. Get one of your credit card companies to transfer some of the balance to one of the other cards. Then pay off what's left with this money at the bank, and use that card for your moonlighting expenses only. Can you do that?"

"I'll try. And when do I start getting paid for the job?"

"That depends on the results, which we won't know until the two bills are approved and signed. The earliest would be sometime this summer. Maybe not until fall. I can't say more than that for now. The less you know, the better."

On his way home after midnight, his father's words, "Don't believe anything too good to be true," drummed annoyingly in the back of Tom's head. But the prospect of so much extra income ignited enough endorphins that Tom needed to take on the challenge. How else was he to win the affection of the woman of his dreams?

Chapter 6

Classes at the university's English language program for internationals had begun. Although the English program placed Ani in an advanced-level class, her English language skills still needed more work. That meant hours of looking up vocabulary words she did not understand.

Grace called Ani one evening to remind her about the International Friendship Hour (IFH) coming up. "Remember? Tom had mentioned it," she said. "It's a social event for international students and American friends, sort of as an exchange to discuss cultural issues, cultural life, and practices in America, and it's a good chance to practice English, learn about American culture, and make friends. It meets next Tuesday at 4:30. I'm sure you will like it, Ani, but I won't be offended if you don't want to come. Would you like me to arrange a ride for you?"

"Where is it?" asked Ani.

"At a church near the campus. But don't worry. It is not a religious event. A Christian organization whose members come from various churches sponsors it. I'm actually in charge of coordinating this event. International students from all over the world and all sorts of religions come, including Muslims. But don't worry, no one will try to convert you. Each volunteer has to pledge not to proselytize. They discuss religion only if the students bring it up, and the volunteers can say what they believe only when asked, and no more."

Ani relaxed. Her uncle had warned her about aggressive Christian sects in America who invited international students to a social event and then tricked them into listening to their religious teachings. "Make sure they clearly state what the program is all about, and don't go if they start being pushy in their invitation," he had warned.

"Can I try it and see if I like it?" Ani asked.

"Sure! I'll ask Sarah to pick you up. She's a graduate student and one of my best volunteers. Oh, and by the way, Tom will be there. He's one of the discussion leaders. But Ani—I'm going to say this only once—be careful about Tom."

"Careful? Why?"

"Well—Tom likes to flirt. He has the reputation of dropping a woman like a hot potato."

"Dropping a woman? From where?"

Grace laughed. "It's an expression that means dumping someone quickly and unexpectedly. You know—breaking hearts. Got that?"

Ani nodded. "Thanks for warning me!"

Sarah turned out to be a Canadian graduate student who was also new to the area. Would she become a friend? So far, all the American peers in her dormitory had avoided Ani and walked past her with cold faces. Maybe, she thought, they disliked her accent and many questions. Even her roommate, Brenda, came across as cold and distant. She had a boyfriend in another dormitory building and hardly ever showed her face when Ani was there—not even at night.

Tuesday came. At 4:30 sharp, a sturdy young woman with a blond ponytail stood waiting in front of Ani's dormitory. She wore jeans and a tank top like so many other students. When Sarah spotted Ani, who was easy to identify as the only Asian coming out of the building, she greeted her warmly by name.

"It's such a treat to meet you, Ani," Sarah said as they started walking to her car. "Grace tells me you just arrived from Indonesia. I'm a sociology major, and I'm writing my graduate thesis about women in Muslim countries. Can you be one of my sources for what's going on in Indonesia?"

"I will try," Ani replied with a coy smile. Inwardly, she felt disappointed. Was Sarah interested only in using her for her thesis? Ani decided she would try to win Sarah's friendship regardless.

"If you don't mind me asking—are you pure native Indonesian or mixed with Chinese blood?" Sarah asked as they got into the car. "If you don't mind my asking," she repeated.

"It's okay," Ani replied politely, although that question from a perfect stranger rattled her a bit. "Why do you ask?"

"Oh, just curious. You look more Chinese than other Indonesians that I've met."

"You're right," Ani replied. "My mother's ancestors are Chinese. My father is a native Indonesian from Sunda in Java, the largest island in Indonesia. Do you know anything about Indonesia?"

"Not much. But I love learning about other countries and cultures—not just because I happen to be writing a thesis on one. It's the other way around. I chose this thesis because I thoroughly enjoy getting to know people from other countries." Sarah stopped at a red light and turned to Ani. "May I ask you another personal question?"

Ani nodded.

"How did your family fare during the big market crash in Indonesia in July? I hear it was pretty bad."

"My parents are poor, so it did not affect them. My uncle, who pays for me here, keeps a savings account in an American bank because he deals with an American computer export business. So I'm okay."

Sarah smiled. "That's good. But if you ever need more help, I hear there's financial aid available to students affected by the Asian market crash. Did you know that?"

"No, I did not. Good to know!"

By 4:45 p.m., only a handful of international students had found their way to the church basement where the International Friendship Hour took place. But by 5:15 p.m. many others had trickled in.

"This is an informal program," Sarah told Ani. "Many students think of it as a party, so they feel it's impolite to show up on time."

Sarah gave Ani a name tag to wear and put one on herself. "Watch me practice what I've learned as a graduate student in the field of international relations," she said, "and let me know if you see me doing anything wrong." Ani watched in fascination as Sarah greeted each of the incoming guests with a welcoming smile and a uniquely appropriate gesture. For example, Sarah avoided touching the head of Thai students, and she held the palms of her hands together when seeing an Asian Indian. Shaking hands with Africans and older Europeans, Sarah was careful to blow a kiss in the air next to her younger European friends' cheeks. She exchanged kisses with the Venezuelan young women on both cheeks while exchanging a kiss on only one cheek of Colombian young women. And offering a warm "hello" to each, Sarah discreetly refrained from shaking the hands of, or hugging, Persian, Afghan, or Arab *men*. But she did not touch *either* gender of the Chinese, Indonesians, or Japanese.

When a volunteer beckoned a Chinese woman to sit down at the table with the American gesture of the palm facing upward and the fingers waving toward herself, Ani gasped. "That's how we call a dog to come!" she whispered to Sarah.

Sarah laughed. "In Indonesia, what gesture do you use for asking a person to come?"

"Like this," Ani said, illustrating with her right palm face down and fingers waving downward.

A few minutes later, many more different accents, much laughter, and many enthusiastic conversations filled the hall. Ani hurried to the kitchen to get vases for the tables, as Sarah had requested. When she returned, she saw a brown-toned young man shadowing Sarah. He had a sharp Aryan nose, thin lips, round, dark brown eyes, and black eyebrows. One of his thick, wavy black locks draped over his forehead. His black mustache, trimmed to perfection, reminded Ani of an Indian movie star.

"May I be of some assistance?" Ani heard him ask Sarah with an accent she did not recognize.

Turning her head only slightly, Sarah simply answered, "No, thanks," and continued placing napkins and Styrofoam cups on a corner table. She turned around to go back to the kitchen. And as fate would have it, the tall man with the dark mustache almost collided with her.

"Beg your pardon," she said matter-of-factly, stepping backward. Sarah's "shadow" stepped aside, turned, and followed her again. This time, she stopped, turned around, and looked at him squarely in the eye. With a cheerful voice, she said, "Actually, I do need your help. Could you please carry the coffee urn to the table for me? It's rather heavy."

He bowed a little. "At your service, madam."

"Thanks." She turned to leave him, then faced him again. "I'm Sarah, by the way. And you?"

"Emmanuel is my name," he said with a broad smile and a quick bow of the head. "Nice to meet you, Sarah. Sorry, I forgot to put on a name tag."

"Glad to meet you, Emmanuel. Excuse me now," she said as she turned to walk toward the door where a group of new students had arrived. Ani quickly joined her on her way and whispered, "Do you think that man is stalking you?"

"I certainly hope not!" laughed Sarah. "He has nice dark, wavy hair, though."

"Do you think he's from Spain or South America?"

"No, from his accent, I gather he's most likely from India or Pakistan. But he could also be from one of the West Indies." Sarah's face suddenly lit up. "Ah, finally!" she said, looking in the direction of the entrance. "The gracious Grace Osterhouse has arrived!"

Gliding into the hallway like a queen, Grace smiled and waved at everyone, hugging some and greeting everyone around her. Her flowing purple blouse hung loosely over her rather round derriere and beige pants. Round red earrings dangled from her ears, matching her red handbag and shoes.

Just behind Grace came Tom, dressed in a light brown jersey jacket, tan jeans, and a royal- blue knitted shirt. Recognizing her supermarket victim, Ani immediately slid behind the large coffee urn that Emmanuel had brought in. She hoped the hairy-legged flirt would not see her right away.

"Welcome to the International Friendship Hour, everybody!" Grace announced via microphone moments later. The volume of the crowd's chatter diminished as she spoke. "So glad you could come. And a special welcome to the new students who just arrived. Please help yourself to some coffee, tea, and cookies. Everyone has a number on their name tag. Find the table that has your number on it, then sit down and wait for your discussion leader."

Ani peered from behind the urn and saw Tom approaching. "I see long black hair sticking out," she heard him say playfully. "Could it be—yes, it is—Ani, right?"

She pretended to pick up something from the floor behind the table and walked around it. "Hi, remember me, Ani?" he asked with a smile. "I'm Tom."

"I remember," she said politely, trying to smile. "Do you want some coffee?"

"No, thanks. I had some before I came." He bent down to see her name tag. "I see you're in group number six. That's my group. What luck!"

She joined seven other international students at a long table: a woman and a man from China, a couple from Venezuela, a man from Germany, a woman from Japan, a man from Haiti, and a woman from Kazakhstan.

"This is an advanced group," Tom began, "which means that you probably know English grammar better than I do!"

Everyone laughed.

"We're here to simply talk together so you can practice your spoken English and maybe learn more about our American way of life. If you have any questions at all, just pipe up and ask. And if it's okay with you, I will correct your English some of the time."

Several nodded.

"Today, we're supposed to talk about money matters, my least favorite topic," Tom continued with a smirk on his face. He looked down at a piece of paper. "Let's see. The first question I'm supposed to ask is, how do you save your money?"

"What money?" the student from Kazakhstan asked. The group laughed. "In my country, we live from mouth to hand. Or do you say 'hand to mouth'?"

Tom nodded. "Hand to mouth, meaning you have only enough money to eat and whatever is absolutely necessary, but never enough to save it for a later time."

"But here in the USA, I have no money at all!" added the Kazakhstani. "Tuition in this country is way over the sky."

"Okay, imagine your uncle dies and leaves you with more money than you need right now. What would you do with that money?" Tom asked the group.

"Hide it under the mattress," joked the German.

"Travel to Europe," said one of the Japanese.

"Send it to my family. They need it more than I do," added the Haitian. "What would you do with all that extra money, Tom?"

Tom scratched his head. "I would first celebrate with a nice dinner in a fancy restaurant, with a girl of my choice, of course. Then I would pay off my debts. If I had something left, I would put some of it in a CD account, which is safer and sometimes pays a little more interest than a regular savings account. Or I would invest it. What do you all think?"

"I have a question," asked the woman from Japan. "How can I get a credit card in the USA?"

"Usually, you have to start with a savings account and a regular income," said Tom. "I'm not sure if you can get one without either."

Some students nodded. "Ani, maybe you could enlighten us

on that subject," Tom suggested. "Grace tells me you're a finance major."

Ani smiled. "I think credit cards are more dangerous than cash under the mattress if you use it for more than you have in the bank. I use it only if I know I have enough to pay the whole balance at the end of the billing circle—cycle," she replied. "I would rather clean bathroom floors than have credit card debts, because the interest is at least 18%."

Tom stared at Ani as if in a trance.

"Did I say something strange?" she asked, laughing nervously.

"Does that mean," he stammered, blinking and straightening up again, "that you would not approve of a man who had credit card debt?"

Everyone laughed, even Ani, whose cheeks now reddened. "Yes," she said.

"Yes, meaning you would approve or not approve of that man?"

"Not approve," she said, cocking her head sideways, still smiling the incongruent smile she hoped would soften the blow.

Tom leaned back, scratched his head, and sighed dramatically. "I guess I'm in trouble," he said.

They all laughed—all except Ani, who said, "All you have to do is pay off more each month than you spend. Soon you will be free from your debt. You can do it."

Chapter 7

In an old high-rise office building in Providence, Rhode Island, a silver-haired man in a brown suit and loosened tie leaned back on his executive swivel chair. He propped up his shoeless feet on the windowsill. Gray socks with maroon polka dots stared back at him—a gift from a favorite female friend. He wiggled his toes and smiled at them. They seemed to return his smile.

His cell phone rang, a welcome sign that there was life besides him on planet earth. "Senator Johnson speaking," he said and paused. "Well, if it isn't Solomon Elijah, my basketball teammate from the distant past!"

"Yep, it's me. I might also be a man that will shape your success in the not-so-distant future!"

"Sounds inviting. Not another plug for an investment, I hope. I'll need every penny for the reelection campaign, so you know not to waste your time."

"Blunt to the bone as always," chuckled Solomon. "I'm not asking for money this time, bro. On the contrary."

"What do you mean? Are you thinking of making a donation?"

"Something like that."

"Something like that? It'd better be something. I could use anything I can get for my campaign. You know, it always costs money to make more."

"You're right about that. So tell me—what do you need for your next hot fundraiser?"

"Oh, I'd like to rent a fifty-foot yacht and invite all my former and potential financial supporters for the biggest swing party yet.

Charge them each a sizable fee, of course, and then raise more for my campaign. Great idea or what?"

"Sounds like a winner. Maybe I can help you with that if you'd let me."

"Let you?" The senator laughed. "You'd be invited on the yacht, too, of course. But in the meantime, how much would you like to invest in this endeavor?"

"I'll tell you in a minute. First, I have a friend who asked me to ask you a question. What do you know about the upcoming fast track bill to help support the countries recently affected by the Asian economic crisis? Or what do you know about the Omnibus Appropriations Bill, which includes the International Monetary Fund agreement?"

The senator mumbled an "excuse me" and sniffled to clear his nasal tract. "Blast these allergies," he muttered. Then he took out a nasal spray from his desk drawer and sprayed it twice into his nostrils, sniffling at the same time. He closed the drawer. "Fast track, you asked? The Omnipresent what bill? You know me, Solomon. I am terrible about international affairs and the economy. I'm into internal affairs, like raising rich people's state taxes to help the less fortunate."

"Wouldn't that mean you will have to pay more taxes?"

"Well, sure. I have nothing to worry about. Besides, lots of my fundraising expenses will give me a huge tax deduction."

"Look. I know you're not interested in international affairs, but since you care about the poor in this country, wouldn't you lend a corner of your heart for the starving in the Third World? I'm not asking for a donation, just for your vote on these two upcoming bills that would help them a lot. I'll fax you some pages of information in the next few minutes, and you can read all about it."

"Okay, if it's not too complicated. But what does that have to do with my campaign?"

"Well, I happen to have access to a fund that could help your campaign, sort of as a gesture of gratitude."

"Gratitude? For what?"

"For helping the poor in Asia. You know. Like voting for these bills that would help them."

"Do I know the source of this fund?"

"No. He prefers to remain anonymous."

"I see," said the senator, rubbing his chin.

"And exactly who is going to donate toward my campaign. He or you? If he is, then he better be an American, right? Because you know senators aren't allowed to receive gifts from foreigners, don't you?"

"Of course I know that!" he found himself saying with all the false confidence he could muster. "I'm the one in charge of the fund. I have the authority to donate toward your campaign, and I am very much an American!" *After all, Rianto isn't* personally *giving the senators gifts but is hiring me to do it!* (It wouldn't be until many, many months later that Solomon wondered if the sugar in the fruit juice had made his judgment so foggy. Or perhaps it was the slimy, sleek devil himself?)

"So how can I get money anonymously?" asked Johnson. "Surely you don't carry cash around, do you?"

"Of course not. And I know you don't. So this is how. I would set up a meeting between you and the courier in person. This guy works during the day and is free most evenings and weekends. He is Caucasian, in his late twenties, brown hair, blue eyes, nice-looking, and most important—he will be wearing a special pin on the left lapel of his coat so that you can identify him. I will fax you a picture of it. Then, when you meet him, you give him a deposit slip for the bank account or a slip of paper with your name, address, and bank number on it. We will then deposit the gift into your account."

"That's very generous. Anything I can do for you?"

"Glad you asked . . . Vote for that Omnibus Appropriations Bill. Promise?"

"Sure will. By the way, does your currier like to watch the Orioles play?"

"He sure does. They're playing the Yankees on Saturday, September thirteenth. Why do you ask?"

"Perfect. Could you ask him to meet me while watching the game?"

A case of beer was waiting for Tom when he arrived at Solomon's house the following night. Before he realized it, Tom had downed two cans. "Not so fast, Tom," Solomon warned. "You gotta stay sober so you can remember the details about your next moonlighting run."

Tom set down his can and burped. "I'm all ears."

"This is a job that won't take much time, but it's complicated. You'll need to do some driving. You'll need to be on your toes, wear your best suit, and put on your most charming self. And, of course, don't forget to wear that pin I gave you."

"Got it. By the way, Sol, that pin has a name. It's a mini keris, did you know that?"

"Never heard of that word. Does it mean something in English?"

"It's like a sword. I've seen it before somewhere," Tom said, vaguely remembering that Ani wore a pin like that.

"You will be meeting with one of the senators of Rhode Island at the Catacombs next Saturday at 4:00 p.m. He'll be watching a game at the bar, which I'm sure won't be over until about five. You know where that is, don't you?"

Tom nodded. He had never been there himself; it was too upscale and too expensive. "When you meet with him, don't talk much. Just wait for him to notice your pin and say, 'The pin you're wearing—is it Chinese or Japanese?' And you say, 'I don't know. It might be Thai or Indonesian.' Then he is supposed to drop a piece of paper onto the floor—inconspicuously. He picks it up and asks you if it's yours. You look at it. If it looks like a deposit slip, say, 'Oh yeah, thanks,' and keep it. You must remain anonymous. Don't ask or answer any questions. The less you know, the better," he repeated. "You must swear to me that you will not utter a word about any of this to anyone, you hear?"

"I swear I won't say a word. But why does it have to be so secretive? Is this operation illegal? 'Cause if it is, I wouldn't want anything to do with it."

"Now, you know me better than that, Tom! Would I get you involved in something shady? But I'm glad you said that, my friend. Because that's why I hired you. You're honest, and I trust you."

Tom was both nervous and excited. It was to be his first rendezvous with a senator. As he stepped out of his car and approached the bar called the Catacombs in Bethesda, Maryland, he checked the left lapel of his coat. Yes, the keris pin was still there.

As Tom opened the entrance door, the song "Toy Soldiers" blasted at him. Looking around at the customers, he realized he was way overdressed for this kind of place. He took off his tie but not the coat so that the senator could see the keris pin on his lapel. The name of the nightclub described it well. It was so dark. Tom had to be careful not to trip over people's feet as he worked his way to the bar. A small group of men hovered around a pool table at the far end of the room, laughing loudly. Tom strode toward the bar, where a soundless television high up on the wall beamed an Orioles baseball game. It soon claimed Tom's full attention.

A tall, stately, silver-haired man in a jogging outfit entered the building and meandered toward the bar. He sat down next to Tom. "Are the Orioles any good tonight?" the man's bass voice bellowed. It was the question Tom had expected.

Tom turned to him and smiled. "Not the best of games today, I don't think," he said, noticing the man's eyes glance briefly at Tom's shirt pocket.

"Nice pin you got there on your lapel. Isn't that from some Asian country?"

"Not sure about that."

The man pulled out a small piece of paper from the right pocket of his jogging pants. It fell to the floor.

Tom bent down and picked it up. "Did you drop this?" he asked.

The senator looked at it. "Nope. Not mine. Sure it isn't yours?"

Tom looked at it. It was a bank deposit slip with Senator Johnson's name on it. "Oh yeah!" he said and casually stuffed it into his pocket.

"Blast! Another out," the senator remarked, looking at the television screen on the wall.

The less I know, the better, Tom reminded himself while he stared at the TV, but secrecy never made him feel comfortable. To his relief, he saw out of the corner of his eye that the senator paid his bill, excused himself, and throwing Tom a brief smile, left the bar.

Chapter 8

The following Saturday, Grace dropped by Ani's dorm room. "Do you need anything at the supermarket, Ani? I can take you shopping," she asked.

"I don't need anything, but can I come with you anyway?" Ani asked. She was lonely, and her mouth felt dry from lack of use. Her roommate had not said more than "nice to meet you" since arriving, and Ani seldom saw her. None of the other American students had begun a conversation with her, and she still felt too unsure of herself to start one. As for the other international students, she avoided them as much as she could. She did not want their accents and bad English to influence the way she spoke.

As they returned from the supermarket, Ani asked Grace, "Do you go to church tomorrow?"

"Why—yes. Would you like to come with us?"

"Only to visit and watch. Is that okay?"

"Absolutely. I suppose if I lived in Indonesia, I would want to visit a mosque. Church starts at 10:00 a.m. We can pick you up at 9:15, so we have enough time to park the car, get a cup of coffee and see friends on the way in, and get a good seat."

"Do I need to dress nice?"

"You can dress any way you like, Ani. Will you have time to join us for lunch afterward? I can bring you home any time you want."

"Oh, thank you, Grace. But I can't stay long. I have to study," she replied, smiling to herself. She had not forgotten her father's warning, "Don't let those Christians in America influence you!"

But she decided to apply her uncle Lim's advice, "Face the danger before it gets *you*."

The next morning, Grace and Fred picked up Ani from her dorm as planned. As they drove through Towson, Ani noticed several churches within a block of each other.

"Why are there so many different kinds of churches in one area?" she asked.

"America is a country made up of people from many countries and cultures," Grace replied. "Some churches were started in Great Britain, others in France, or Germany, or Italy, or Greece, and so on. They differ in their music, rituals, and traditions. Others start new ones. Some are very ritualistic and formal; others are not. They don't all agree on their beliefs and rules, but here they tolerate each other. The best part about that is that we have many churches to choose from, and no one can stop you from your choice."

"Are there some churches you do not like or agree with?"

"I avoid any church or group of churches that add to or change the teachings of what you call the *Injil*."

"You mean, the book about the Prophet Isa?"

"Yes. We call it the New Testament. I also don't like churches or groups that regard their own original, extra doctrines as equally or more valuable than those in the Bible. And I don't like churches that say they're the only true church or the only way to Heaven."

"But as a good American, you have to tolerate them, don't you?" Ani asked with a smirk on her face.

"You bet!" Grace answered with a chuckle. "How is it in Indonesia? Do you have religious tolerance?"

Ani blushed. She had hoped no one would ask her that question. "Yes and no," she answered. "The law forbids religious intolerance and religious persecution. But some radical Muslims still persecute Christians anyway and burn down churches. I just got a letter from a friend whose family comes from an island which is mostly Christian. Some Muslims came from Java and did horrible things to them. I don't know why. The government is trying to stop them from doing those things."

"That's good," said Grace. "Sadly, persecution also used to happen between Christian factions in so-called Christian countries. And that's one reason why the United States was started. Separation of church and government, tolerance, and freedom for all, regardless of religious conviction or practices are the rule of thumb here. Intolerance should never be tolerated, should it?" The car pulled into a huge parking lot full of cars. "Well, here we are!" announced Grace.

"This is a church?" Ani asked, surprised to see a structure that looked more like an office building than a church with a steeple.

"Yes, it is. Our church just started two years ago. We're renting a former business," Grace explained. "You see, a church is not a building but a group of people who meet and worship God together and who care for each other in many ways. And that could happen anywhere."

Ani shyly stayed close to Grace as they entered the building. A swarm of women and men greeted them as they entered the foyer. "And who do you have with you, Grace?" asked a woman much younger than Grace, but she was not the only one who asked. Polite smiles, handshakes, and friendly "welcome" greetings were almost too overwhelming for Ani. She nevertheless kept smiling until it was time to enter a large auditorium.

The worship service began at 10:00 a.m. sharp and lasted an hour and twenty minutes. A music team of five young adults played the flute, a trumpet, a violin, the drums, and a guitar. The rest of the people sang along, reading the words from a large screen hanging behind the musicians. It sounded more like pop music—not at all like the organ music which Ani once heard on a television broadcast. The songs were mostly about "*Gee-zus*"—a name Ani did not recognize. But when she saw the name *Jesus* on the screen, she finally realized it must mean *Isa*, the Muslim name for Jesus.

A man in a semi casual suit, who Ani judged to be about 40

years old, talked about the teaching of Jesus to love one's enemy and forgive. He used the example of a woman named Corrie ten Boom, who had been in a Nazi concentration camp in Germany during World War II. She and her family had hidden Jews in her home. But despite her sufferings at the hands of one particular Nazi officer, she was later able to forgive him.

"So, how did you like it in our church?" asked Fred on the way back to the house.

"It is nice," answered Ani politely. "I liked the story about the woman who forgave the Nazis. Is it a true story?"

"Oh, yes! I heard this woman tell her story in person, and I read her biography. Her sister died in that concentration camp. A very sad, horrible, but moving story."

"Mohammed also said we should forgive. But it is hard. How can this woman forgive her enemies that killed her sister?"

Grace and Fred looked at each other and smiled knowingly. "Someday, we will have to tell you our story. Then you'll understand, Ani," said Grace.

They talked about food, world events, and Grace's grandchildren during lunch. "How about a quick walk around the neighborhood before I drop you off at the dorm?" Grace asked after they had cleared the table and placed the dishes into the dishwasher.

"Grace, can you explain why there were religious wars in Europe if Isa—I mean Jesus—taught his followers to forgive?"

"Good question, Ani. It's so sad, isn't it? I don't think those people who fought each other were real followers of Jesus," Grace replied. "They used different beliefs as an excuse to fight. The real reasons were hate, or prejudice, or hunger for power. And you're right. Jesus taught the opposite."

Chapter 9

Leaves in yellow, orange, and brown blew across the field outside the library's picture window. Occasionally, Ani looked out at the colorful trees to rest and feast her eyes. She longed to be out there, walking in the sunshine! But no, she had to study for her midterm exams. For her, that meant taking the time to look up words in a dictionary and repeatedly read the text.

One more page. There, now. Ani rewarded her focus and discipline by stretching out her arms, wiggling her shoulders, and bending her torso left and right. She rose from her chair and walked around the library room, stopping by a window to take in some sunlight. As she wandered back to her table, she saw a person in blue turn a corner at the end of a book stack. It registered excitement in her brain, but she could not identify why. Sitting down again, she picked up her textbook and resumed her study.

Moments later, she heard a man clearing his throat behind her. "If it isn't our expert on credit cards!" he said in a stage whisper.

She turned around. There stood Tom, wearing the same blue knit shirt he wore at the International Friendship Hour. "Oh, hi," she whispered back, smiling in surprise. "What are you doing in our library?"

Tom bent down toward her and whispered, "I will tell you all about it if you'll go outside and take a walk with me. Will you?"

"I would love to, but I have to study for an exam in business ethics."

He shook his head and smiled. "Wow. You're not only disciplined with credit cards but also with your time. You blow me away, Ani!"

Ani's smile turned into a worried frown. "I am sorry. I don't mean to do that."

"No need to apologize, Ani," Tom said, laughing. "'You blow me away' means you impress me so much I feel small!"

"Oh, I'm sorry; I don't mean to make you feel small."

"That's okay, Ani. I need some humbling now and then. You sure you don't want to take a break and catch some fresh air with me outside?"

His warm eyes and smile were hard to resist. Not to look too eager, Ani waited a few seconds before replying. "Okay, only for 30 minutes," she finally replied. "I will be out in ten minutes. I just need to finish up something."

Tom paced the entranceway of the library. He had every intention of borrowing a book about reducing debt, but he decided to wait. Ani's winsome smile and long, shiny black hair again awakened a longing in him—a hunger for more of her, despite her stance on credit cards. She was so unlike any other Asians he had ever known. Feminine and gentle, yet firm and resolute. And this special woman was willing to spend time with him today—alone!

"What are you doing here at this university?" Ani asked as soon as they began to walk down a path toward the pond.

"Well, first of all, I'm an alumnus of this university. Secondly, I have a contract with the university to install, repair, and upgrade some computers here. That's what I do for a living."

A couple approached from the other direction, arm in arm, giggling and then stopping now and again for a kiss. Tom noticed that Ani was staring at them as if she had never seen couples kiss before. "Guess you don't see that so much in Indonesia, do you?" he asked.

She shook her head and laughed. "Not even married couples do that in public in my country," she said.

"Hey, let's jog around the lake!" Tom said as he took hold of Ani's hand and playfully pulled her along. He felt Ani's arm stiffen for a moment, then relax. They jogged around the pond until her lungs burned. When they finally reached a bench, he released her hand and said, "You're a good runner, Ani, but listen to you! Huffing and puffing? You need to do this more often."

"You're right!" she said, puffing still. "I will, every day from now on. Without you, of course."

"Without *moi*? Why?"

"If any Indonesian students see me holding a man's hand in public, I would feel ashamed."

"Really? I bet all your life you've always dreamed of running hand in hand with a man," he said. "Besides, I don't see many Indonesians on this campus. Are there others?"

She nodded. "I heard there are some, but I haven't met them yet."

"Okay. I'll try to behave myself in the future." He paused. "Hey, Ani, how would you like to go to a Newton football game with me next Saturday? American football, not soccer," he explained. It's an American experience you've just gotta have at least once in your life!"

Ten days later, on a cold October day, a gunshot into the air and a loud shout from Newton's fans started up the Newton versus Brown football game. American football seemed to draw bigger crowds than soccer in this country, Ani noted. She guessed the number of spectators to be at least 5000. The game made no sense at all; it seemed so violent, so brutal. But she didn't care. Huddled together with Tom under one large blanket, Ani did not even feel the cold wind blowing across her face.

"American football is even more complex than a chess game," Tom said, raising his voice above the cheers of the spectators. "Not at all like what you call football in your country. Watch what happens to the man with the ball. Oh, there he goes!"

"What ball?" Ani queried, but he didn't hear her question. *Oh, yes, there.* Someone threw something that looked like a large brown egg. Someone else caught it and began to run with it. But soon five, and then eight heavyset players pulled him down, all piling on top of him. The spectators' electrifying cheers, shouts, and jeering amused Ani far more than the game itself.

"How can he breathe under there?" Ani asked, but the noises around her drowned out her question. "And what happens to the ball?" Tom ignored her questions. *No use asking anymore,* she decided. Even if Tom could hear her, he was too engrossed in the game to answer her questions. *Somehow, the one on the bottom emerges alive!* she mentally wrote to her brother Rudi, hoping she would remember each scene.

"Touchdown! Touchdown!" Tom's shout drove him to his feet. Even Ani got up and tried to clap and cheer. A short man entered the field and kicked the egg-shaped ball high up between two tall poles for an extra point. *Guess that's why they call it football,* she mused.

A moment later, Tom's elbow knocked over Ani's popcorn box, the contents of which not only flew all over but also scattered across their feet. She began to shiver despite the blanket. She hoped that Tom would notice, but he didn't. With each yard gained by the offensive team, Ani felt more left behind.

A roar of ecstasy suddenly filled the stadium. Another touchdown for Newton! In celebration, Tom wrapped his arm around Ani's left shoulder and squeezed her tightly to himself. And when he did, that feeling of abandonment left as quickly as it came. The same magic she had felt when they ran around the campus pond grabbed hold of her again. It was a feeling she simply could not explain away.

But that moment did not last long. As Newton's defense players tackled the opposing team's quarterback and piled on top of him, Ani felt Tom's hand glide off her shoulders, grab her arm, and drag her up with him to a standing position. She heard his voice join the deafening cheers around her. But only engrossed with the electric sensation of Tom's touch, she remained indifferent toward Newton's momentary victory. Ignoring the crowd's jubilance, she turned around and brushed off the popcorn from her seat. And as she did so, her necklace swung upward in the wind. And with it, the keris pin, shimmering in the sunlight.

Two rows behind Tom and Ani stood a tall white-haired fan of the opposing Bears of Brown University, namely Senator Johnson, who was also cheering. But the senator's eyes were not fixed on the game. They were fixed on Ani.

While everyone around the senator was either cheering or jeering, he took out his cell phone and pushed the keys. "Hey, Chuck, can you hear me?" he asked as he formed a cup over the phone with his other hand. He was sure neither Tom nor Ani could hear him over the cheers and jeers of the crowds. "I'm at a football game, and there's this guy I met the other day who collected my account number so that an anonymous donor would donate toward my campaign. He's sitting four rows in front of me with his Asian girlfriend or maybe his wife, who happens to be wearing a pin that looks just like the one he wore so I could identify him. I just hope the donor isn't a foreigner. . . . What? . . . Look, I can't hear you with all this noise. I'll send you a fax with a picture of the pin tomorrow. Please look into it for me, will you?"

Chapter 10

"I have a huge headache, Sarah. Do you have a jar with you, one with a metal top? Like a cream or Vaseline jar?" Ani asked before she went to bed on Sarah's couch on the Wednesday evening before Thanksgiving. Because the dorms were empty and the cafeteria closed during the four-day holiday weekend, Sarah had invited her to sleep at her place.

"What does a headache have to do with a metal jar top?"

"You must scrape my back with it. Will you, please?"

"Scrape you? What do you mean, Ani?"

"Oh—like this: Take the lid of the jar and scrape my back with it. Don't you do that, too?" She demonstrated by scraping on her left arm with the inside of the lid's edge. Then she turned over on the couch, lifting her pajama top so her back was bare. "Please do it for me on my back. I need this badly."

Sarah began to scrape as Ani had requested.

"Harder, much harder! Ah, yes, that's it! Ah, does that feel good!"

"But Ani, your skin is turning red!"

"That's good, that's good. The more, the better. Right down under the skin."

"No way, I can't do that. It looks awful. I'd rather pray for you."

"Pray for me?" asked Ani. "If you wish, go ahead."

Sarah covered her guest with a blanket, knelt by the couch, and then closed her eyes. "Dear Lord Jesus," she began as if she were talking with someone sitting next to her, "please make Ani's headache go away completely. And please protect and bless Ani's parents and family, and help us have a good night's rest tonight. Amen."

That was not a prayer ritual, Ani noted. Instead, Sarah seemed to converse with Jesus as if he were present in the room. *And why did Sarah pray to him at all? Ani* asked herself but did not dare to ask aloud. *Wasn't Isa a mere prophet?*

She woke up the next morning without a headache. The scraping helped, she concluded, but she was not at all sure whether Jesus, who she called Isa, had anything to do with it as well.

It was Thanksgiving Day, the annual holiday observing the first settlers' survival in New England in 1621. Grace and Fred Osterhouse had invited Ani and Sarah for the traditional family feast. The aroma of wood burning in the fireplace and fowl and sweet potatoes baking in the oven greeted them as they entered the house. The sound of children's laughter and screeches rose from the basement.

"No need to take off your shoes, Ani," said Grace. But Ani was already taking them off. "Well, okay. At least put on some slippers," Grace insisted as she rummaged through the hall closet for a pair. "It's cold on the floor. Then come on in and meet the family."

Grace introduced Sarah and Ani to her sons and daughters-in-law, who, along with two older grandchildren, were watching Macy's Thanksgiving Day parade and eating roasted chestnuts in the family room.

"Can we help you with anything?" Sarah asked.

"Oh, thank you, dear. I believe we're all set, as you can see," said Grace. She pointed to an extended table already set with fine china, silverware, a beautiful flower arrangement, and a pumpkin in the middle of the table. "Oh, I see we have forgotten the napkins. Sarah and Ani, would you please fold these nicely? I believe we are fifteen altogether."

"I counted only 13 people," Sarah said.

"Two more are on their way," Grace said.

When the parade ended, the doorbell rang. Sarah looked up from folding the napkins and peered through the archway to the hall as Grace opened the door. Emmanuel "The Mustache," whom the girls met at the International Friendship Hour, entered the hallway.

"Ahem, your charming shadow is here to follow you!" whispered Ani in Sarah's ears.

Sarah rolled her eyes. "Got a jar top to scrape me with?" Sarah whispered back.

The women watched Emmanuel as he followed Grace and helped her carry the food to the table. "He seems to be nice," Ani noted. "Why are you afraid of him?"

"I think he is a bit creepy."

"What does 'creepy' mean?" Ani asked.

"Strange. Different. Scary. This guy makes me feel uncomfortable, maybe because his mustache reminds me of someone I didn't like."

Soon, Grace jingled a hand-sized dinner bell, calling everyone to the table. The five Osterhouse grandchildren scrambled for seats around a separate table in the glassed-in veranda, while the adults sat down around the long oval dining room table with Fred and Grace on opposite ends. Fred gave a long prayer of thanks to the Father in Heaven for everything, from the turkey to the freedom and peace they enjoyed, and ended his prayer with the words, "in Jesus's name we pray, amen."

It was now turkey time. Fred Osterhouse set a huge 20-pound browned and roasted turkey on the table. Ani almost fainted at the sight, not because it was a dead animal, but because it was a dead turkey, and it looked just like a *maleo* bird which she had as a pet when she was a child. She used to take it for walks on a leash so it would not run or fly away. Her parents kindly let her keep it as a pet instead of killing and roasting it. They simply sold the offspring to neighbors or exchanged them for something else. Okay, this was not a *maleo*, but she still felt ill at its sight.

Fortunately, plenty of other food items filled her plate, so no one would notice if she passed on the turkey. Ani enjoyed the white rolls, cranberry sauce, bread stuffing made with nuts and apples, the chestnuts, lima beans, sweet potatoes, green salad, and corn. Not realizing that the gravy contained turkey innards, she poured it over the vegetables. She missed the rice, the *sambal* sauce, the *belinbing* (star fruit), and the hairy *ranbutan*. But the meal was made with love and devoured in the company of loving new friends.

The dinner discussion ranged from things they were thankful for to football, the economy, and politics—all without intense arguments. When everyone had eaten all they could, Grace said, "After we clear the table and get our dessert, let's play a game. Does anyone have a suggestion?"

"How about the game 'True and False'?" suggested Sarah.

"What's that?" asked one of the grandchildren from the other table.

"Sarah will explain after we stack up the plates. Randy, will you be our busboy and bring the dishes to the kitchen and wipe off the plates? And Jane, could you clear the children's table? Sarah, could you take some cups and saucers from the cupboard and put them around our table? Ani, could you help me cut the pies? Emmanuel, can you help me with the coffee and tea when it's ready?"

Pumpkin and pecan pies, a thermal carafe of coffee, and a teapot soon graced the dining room table. As soon as everyone sat down and began to eat the pie, Grace ironed out the tablecloth before her with her hands and said, "Okay, Sarah, we're all ears. What about this "True and False" game? You kids squeeze in with us if you want, or play your own game over there."

Sarah directed them to think of one fact or event in their personal history and fabricate another, not necessarily in that order. "After you tell your two stories in one sentence each, the rest of us have to ask ten yes or no questions, and then we all vote on which we think is true."

"Who wins?" asked one of the children.

"The person whose true story is the hardest to believe. We vote."

Grace offered to go first. She closed her eyes and a few seconds later drew a big breath. Then with a grave face, she said, "I once won a brand-new Cadillac in a sweepstake."

"What? Why didn't you keep it?" asked Fred, aghast. Everyone laughed.

"And the second story is, Fred and I almost divorced a year after we got married—in fact, at Thanksgiving!"

"We did?" Fred chuckled. Everyone laughed again.

Sarah cleared her throat loudly to get their attention. "We take turns asking yes or no questions now. Everyone gets one question, then we vote on which story is true. Do you want to begin, Ani?"

The round of questions went by quickly. Everyone voted for the Cadillac story to be true.

"Sorry, folks, but it wasn't the Cadillac. It was the 'almost' divorce."

"It was? You never told me about that before," said Fred. Everyone laughed.

"You can't remember that, dear? I wanted a turkey at Thanksgiving, and you wanted ham. We couldn't afford to buy both."

"It's slowly coming back," mumbled Fred. "We didn't speak to each other for two days and ate lots of tuna, didn't we?"

"That's right. But after we made up, we went to the mission downtown and helped dish out turkey and ham to the poor."

"I think they gave us some of both to take home afterward, didn't they?"

"Yes, they did."

Ani occasionally threw a glance at Sarah, who seemed quieter than usual and often left for the kitchen to fetch this or that. She also noticed that Emmanuel "The Mustache" eyed Sarah each time she entered the room and that Sarah avoided his glances.

"Okay now, who's next with their stories?" asked Grace.

"I am!" said Emmanuel. "When I—"

The doorbell interrupted him. "It must be Tom," said Fred. "Our football team captain is here!"

Ani almost spilled her glass of ice tea.

"No need to get up. The door is open; Tom knows to let himself in."

Sure enough, Tom dashed through the dining room into the family room where the television was. "Sorry I'm late, friends. Since I'm too late to join you anyway, can I please catch the last quarter of the Detroit Lions game? It's my home team, you know."

"No problem," Grace said. "Why don't you first go to the kitchen and help yourself to the food, then take your plate to the TV room? And if I remember correctly, I invited you to play football with the kids. I hope you're still planning on doing that."

"Yes, ma'am!" Tom answered and turned back toward the kitchen. That's when he spotted Ani. "Glad you're here, too, Ani! Are you going to play football with us after I eat?"

"Oh, Tom!" Fred chided. "Ani doesn't know how to play American football."

"I don't mind," said Ani with an eager smile. "I want to learn."

Playing American football proved to be much more fun than watching it, Ani decided. One of the younger boys faked having the ball, and she and Tom both chased after him together. All four collided in a heap, first Tom on top of the older boy, then Ani on top of Tom, and the younger one on top of Ani. Everyone began to laugh hysterically, and in between each roll of laughter, a moan and a groan.

"Hot chocolate and pumpkin pie are served! Come and get it!" Grace's voice resounded into the yard as the four-some footballers unscrambled from the pileup.

"Tom, what happened? Your cheek is all red," said Ani after they got up and faced each other.

"One of your elbows, I'm afraid," he said and laughed. "And look at your jeans!" They both noticed a dirty grass stain and a rip in her jeans just above her knee. "Now you're IN for sure."

"In where?"

"You're IN. It means you're in fashion."

Tom helped her hobble to the double swing in the corner of the yard and sat down next to her. They swung gently to and fro in silence. When he heard Ani sniffle, he asked, "Is your knee hurting that bad?"

She shook her head and covered her face with her hands. He pulled out a handkerchief from his pocket and handed it to her. "You know, it's not a bad thing for a lady to show her tears in America," he said gently.

"Really?" she asked with a sniffle. She bared her face and laughed a little as she wiped her eyes. "To be honest, Tom, I'm crying because this is the most fun day I have had since coming to the USA. I'm just so happy, I had to cry."

He let out a short whistle. "I'm so relieved," he said, putting his hand on Ani's shoulder and pulling her toward himself for a squeeze.

His tender words and touch stirred up something deep inside her. It caused her whole body to quiver. Was it romantic love? Merely sexual attraction? Whatever it was, it gave her a feeling she hoped she would feel again and again. Or that it would somehow last.

"Careful." The inner voice of her mother echoed inside her. "The warm, dancing flames of love do not last forever." If what Ani felt now were dancing flames of love, everything inside her yearned to let them stay alive. How could she feed them so that they would not die?

Chapter 11

"Ani, I need to buy some Christmas gifts today," said Sarah over the phone. "Want to join me? The mall is always fun at Christmas time."

"I don't know, Sarah. I'm studying for a reading skills test on Monday."

"That's too bad. Our mall is a fun place this time of the year. You get to meet Santa Claus. You know who he is, right?"

"No, I don't think so," Ani replied, still trying to read her textbook. The name *Santa Claus* sounded vaguely familiar. "Is he a friend of yours?"

Sarah laughed. "Maybe. Maybe not," she teased.

"Do you need me to protect you?" Ani asked.

"Not a bad idea, Ani. You could help me find good deals."

Ani decided she needed a little break. The environment with English-speaking people would do her good, she reasoned.

The mall buzzed with crowds of people. Ani tried to soak it all in—families with little children laughing together, groups of teenagers sipping sodas, older people sitting on benches, upbeat music blaring throughout the stores. An old, fat man with a long white beard, wearing a furry red hood, a white fluffy shirt, and red pants with black suspenders, sat on a stool with small children all around him and a photographer taking pictures.

"Come, Ani. You gotta meet Santa Claus," said Sarah. "You can sit on his lap and have a picture taken. Then you whisper your wish into his ear."

"Really?!" Ani asked, laughing. "That would be a photo to send home!" She almost followed Sarah's suggestion, but a long line of young children made her change her mind.

As the two women perused various items in a department store full of elegant household decor, a young teenage boy brushed by Sarah and tried to grab her purse. Ani saw it and stepped in, tripping the young man as he tried to run away. She quickly stooped down and yanked the purse away from him, stepped on his back with her boot, and threw the bag to Sarah.

"Ouch," the young man cried as he tried to wiggle himself free, but Ani's foot firmly kept him grounded. An alarm bell went off nearby, and soon a security guard came and accosted the young man.

"My, oh my, Ani, you are some bodyguard!" Sarah exclaimed. "Where did you learn all that?"

Ani smiled modestly. "I learned self-defense in high school. All the girls had to learn it. Aren't you glad?"

Sarah laughed. "You'll have to teach me. That was amazing! You deserve a reward. Come on. I'll treat you to some supper at the food court."

"Thanks, but ice cream will be fine," said Ani. "I want to eat as much of it as I can before Ramadan starts in January."

"Oh, it does? I almost forgot about that. You can't eat during the daylight hours for almost a whole month, right?"

"Right. Fortunately, this year it is in the winter, and here in the northern hemisphere the days are shorter than the night. So we have more time to eat."

"But you don't have a refrigerator in your room, do you? Is there a kitchen in the dorm where you can cook at night or heat some leftovers?"

"No. I just buy unperishable food and eat a lot of cold food."

"Oh, Ani. That's not good," said Sarah. "There's got to be a better way. Would you like to bunk up in my apartment for the month? I will ask my landlord if that's allowed."

"No, that is okay. Thank you. I will have to figure out a way to do this," Ani said with determination in her tone.

Sarah grew quiet. She wasn't sure whether or not she should insist. "I will ask the landlord anyway, and then you can decide," she said.

Sarah did ask the landlord a few days later, but he said Ani could stay with Sarah only for one week, which, they decided, would be better than nothing. Ramadan would begin on January 3 that year, and the campus cafeteria would still be closed until January 10. Ani would stay with her from December 24 to January 7. They would ask the Osterhouses if Ani could stay with them until the cafeteria opened on the 10th.

"What about your other friends from Indonesia and all the other Muslims on campus? Where do they get their special halal meat?" Sarah asked.

Ani shrugged her shoulders. "I do not know. They did not tell me. I think only some of them fast. They have cars and go out every night."

"Well," suggested Sarah, "could you ask if any of them need a host family or home during this time as well? I can ask Grace if she can round up some. She has a huge network of volunteers and friends."

Ani was surprised by the offer. "Some people would host total strangers who eat only during the night?"

Sarah laughed. "It's not very common in the USA, but some people do it for students when asked by a person they trust."

"It's December 24th, Christmas Eve," announced Sarah the day Ani came to stay with her. "In my family, we kids always went ice-skating during the day, and when we came back, we had to shower and dress nicely. My grandparents were German. They celebrated Christmas Eve by singing together and reading the Christmas story from the Bible—you know, the story of Isa's birth. I like that tradition. Would you mind if I do that with you?"

"No problem. We Muslims believe in that story, too—not the same way, but some of it."

"And would you believe," Sarah continued as she ripped open a bag of peanuts and poured them into a glass bowl, "my grandparents made me and my sister go with them to a midnight church service?"

"Will you go to church at midnight tonight?" Ani asked.

Sarah shook her head. "No. My church already had their service earlier today."

"Where does your family live?"

"They're all scattered. My parents got a divorce when I was eighteen. My father remarried and moved to Georgia, and my mother moved in with her sister's family in Ohio."

"Are your grandparents still alive?"

"Only my grandmother. She has severe dementia and lives in a nursing home. She doesn't remember anyone anymore. Can you believe she is 94 years old?"

"You have a brother in the Navy, right? Where is he now?"

"He's on a ship somewhere in the Pacific."

"Why did you not go home to your mother and her sister for the holidays? I thought everyone goes home and celebrates with their families at Christmas."

Sarah said nothing for a moment, then got up to turn on the water kettle. "I love them, but I don't care to spend Christmas with them. It's too depressing because of all the changes. They all celebrate Christmas without Christ, and that makes me sad." She wiped a tear or two from her eyes.

"I don't understand," Ani said. "How do they celebrate?"

"Oh, you know—with all the exterior trimmings, decorations, gift-giving, food, games, and so forth, but not remembering Jesus as my grandparents used to do. I miss that."

"So how about you? What do you do?"

"Well," Sarah said with a mysterious twinkle, "you mean—what are *we* going to do tonight?" We're going to make and string some popcorn, decorate my little tree together, bake some cookies, make eggnog—all while listening to my favorite Christmas music.

Then we'll order Chinese food and watch the classic movie "It's a Wonderful Life" like I do every year. Have you ever seen it before?"

Ani shook her head.

"It's sort of a spin-off from Dickens's *Christmas Carol.*"

Ani's blank stare told Sarah she hadn't heard of that, either.

Chapter 12

As Ani pulled up the blinds on her dorm window the following morning, she saw lots of small, white puffs flying down from the sky outside. Could it be—?

"Snow!" she yelled as she pulled up the lower window. Never having experienced the white, powdery version of rainwater before, she had always dreamed of this moment. It was thick and wet, the kind of snow that comes only when the air temperature has just turned to freezing. She held out her hand to catch some of it. Yes, it was cold, but she endured the thirty seconds it took for the soft, fluffy snowflakes to look like sugar frosting on her palm.

Popping her head out of the window once more, she took a deep, cold breath. The air had a smell that was different than she'd ever known, and for the first time, Ani did not mind the cold. She looked out in awe. As if painted, each branch of every tree had turned white, blending with the white puffs of clouds above. On the hills beyond the dormitory complex stood some tall, partly dark green, partly white fir trees—just like the ones she had seen on Christmas cards in stores. The world looked clean today, so pure and innocent. Nothing wrong could ever happen to her—neither here nor in Indonesia. The brightness of the snow confirmed it.

From the corner of her eye, she spotted Tom's red Mustang turning into a parking spot below. As she watched him leave the car and walk toward her dormitory, she could see snowflakes landing on his sandy brown hair and earmuffs. That was one sight she did not want to forget. She took her camera, adjusted the telescopic lens, and took a picture of him.

Then, with boots, jacket, and gloves, she ran down the stairs. Before Tom could see her, she crept into the bushes. She scooped up some of the white frosting on the ground and formed it into what now looked like a Chinese steamed roll.

"Here, catch," she yelled, throwing the snowball too quickly for Tom's hand to respond. It hit him smack in the face. When Tom fell backward into the snow and did not move, she ran to him and bent over his face. "Are you all right?" she asked.

Tom remained motionless. Twenty eternal seconds passed. "Tom, wake up!" she cried in a trembling voice. She rubbed some snow on his cheeks. His eyes opened. With a sudden movement, he swung Ani around and pushed a handful of snow into her face. She howled, then managed to wiggle her way from under him. But while she turned around and scooped up some more snow, he quickly shoved a handful of snow between her neck and her collar. More squeals, spits, and laughter followed until they both landed in the snow, exhausted.

"Truce?" he offered after they had caught their breaths.

"Truce," she said with a sigh and a smile. They shook hands.

Tom helped her up. "How about if I treat you to some hot chocolate at the café?"

She nodded. Accompanied by the rhythmic crunching of boots against the snow, they trudged silently toward the campus café. Tom grabbed her hand at one point when she began to slide and kept it longer. "Ahem," she said aloud. "Remember, there are other Indonesians on this campus."

He politely let go of her hand. "Ani, I respect your rules and regulations, but I wonder—what do you think of an East-West romance? Do you think it has a chance?"

"A chance at what?" She laughed nervously.

"Oh, you know. Of ending up in a happily-ever-after marriage with happy children, et cetera, et cetera."

Ani felt a tickle creep down her spine. She had been trying not to think about this question, hoping it would never come up—at least not for a long, long time. But there it was.

"Brown-eyed should never marry blue-eyed people," she offered with a twinkle and a cocked head in reply.

"And why not?"

"Because brown eyes see better than blue eyes, and the two will never agree on what they see!" she teased.

"You're a funny one," he snickered.

Crunch, crunch—the snow got thicker under the soles of their boots. They reached the café and sat down in a booth. "So, do you want to give me a more serious answer to my question about an East-West marriage?

"In most of Indonesia, people are Muslim," Ani began again, this time in a somber tone. "A Muslim is not allowed to marry a Christian."

"Really? That's lame." He bent down, packed a snowball in his hand, and threw it hard against a tree. "But supposing they lived in America? What do you think then?"

"I think it could work if two people treated each other with respect," she replied, "but I don't think it would work for me."

"Why not?"

"Because," she said and paused a few seconds, groping for the right answer, "I'm supposed to think what my parents think and do what my parents want me to do. And I know they would not like it."

Tom's mouth dropped open. "How simple," he said slowly. "That means you don't have to think or decide anything—just obey."

Ani nodded. "Yeah. My father said I would not be his daughter anymore if I married someone from another religion or culture."

Hoping he could appeal to her sympathy, he lowered his head and said in a sad voice, "Then I don't have a chance, do I?"

She laughed, showing no sympathy.

But Tom's raging testosterone did not allow him to give up. "Didn't your father marry a Chinese who is not a Muslim?" he asked.

"Yes, he did. Before my parents got married, my mother promised my father that she would become a Muslim. But she never did. What about your parents? What would they think if you married someone from another religion, race, or culture?" she asked.

He let out a single, caustic laugh. "My parents? They're generally against anything I'm for, so it doesn't matter what they think. I figure if I did something against their wishes, I would find out if they *really* love me." He threw a snowball toward a lamppost, missing it by ten inches.

"And why do you need to know that your parents love you? Don't you already know that?"

"I know they don't. They always find something to criticize me for. Nothing I do ever pleases them. So I usually go my own way, do my own thing. It makes no difference as far as I can tell."

"But they gave you your life, Tom. Don't you want to show them some thanks and respect?"

He threw another snowball at a lamppost. This time he didn't miss. "Now you're acting like my mother," he said, avoiding eye contact.

"I'm sorry."

"No. Maybe you're right. I just don't know how to show my gratitude in such a way that they believe me. As I said, I can never do anything right by them."

Ani touched his arm and squeezed it. "I hope that will change. Just do what we do in Indonesia."

"What's that?"

"Honor your elders. Show them respect and kindness. Regardless of what they do or say."

"Really?" Tom asked in disbelief. "And that works?"

"It does in my culture," Ani replied.

Tom wrapped his arms around Ani and kissed her forehead. "You're good for me, Ani Sunatu. I think you might just be smart and pretty enough to transform me into the man I've always wanted to be but never knew how."

Ani smiled. As irrational as those words might have sounded

to her only three months earlier, she believed them. They made her feel as powerful as the woman in the fairy tale *Beauty and the Beast*, except that the beast she was taming was much more handsome.

"Ani, I have a big favor to ask you. Could we go out on a real date tomorrow night—New Year's Eve? We have two reasons to celebrate: the end of your first semester in the United States, and the beginning of the year 1998. What do you say?"

Ani smiled. "That will be nice. I can think of a third reason to celebrate. I passed the TOEFL and the GRE," she said with glee. "Can we go to a fancy restaurant?"

Tom paused a moment. "Of course!" he said, his brain churning as to which of his credit cards might still allow him to charge such an expense.

"Then it will be my treat," she retorted.

"No way! I asked you on this date."

"If you can pay in cash, I might consider it."

Tom shook his head. "I never carry cash. It's safer that way."

Ani laughed. "Okay. You pay. But promise me something."

"What's that?"

"Pay off at least one of your credit cards before you pay for the next meal."

Chapter 13

Bought at a rummage sale with Grace, the newly purchased silver pumps, white wool slacks, and aqua-blue cashmere top suited Ani well. Tom was wearing a dark smoking jacket, a gray shirt, and a bright red tie.

A candle at their table in the restaurant called The 13th Floor of the Belvedere Hotel danced in the reflection of a large window overlooking the Baltimore skyline. Ani was shocked at the price of the dinner buffet. It cost more than a month's groceries for the whole family back home!

Soothing jazz music played by a pianist in the background mesmerized Ani. Tom ordered wine for both of them, but Ani gave hers to Tom. They told each other stories about their childhood. When they had finished eating the main meal, Tom invited her to dance with him. "Only a slow dance," she insisted, as she had never danced before. Tom was a gallant and patient teacher. She felt safe in Tom's arms as he led her slowly around the dance floor. When she stepped on his feet, he did not complain. Close to midnight, a few fireworks outside drew everyone's attention, and everyone cheered when the countdown reached zero.

Soon afterward, the waiter in a tux stopped at their table. "Pardon me, but we want you to be aware that our buffet is closed now and we would like to clear the tables in ten minutes. He discreetly placed a black leather folder on the table. Tom pulled out a credit card, tucked it inside the black folder, and handed it to the waiter.

The waiter left with the folder. A few minutes later, he returned and handed Tom the card. "I am sorry, sir, but your card—no good. You have another one?"

"No problem." Tom took out his wallet and opened it.

But Ani already had her wallet open and pulled out a hundred-dollar bill. "I think you are happier with cash, are you not?" she asked. "Just give me back forty dollars and keep the change." The waiter took the money, bowed a little with a polite "thank you," and retreated.

"You've got to let me pay you back," Tom said to Ani in a lowered tone.

"With a credit card?" Ani asked, laughing. "I invited *you* originally, remember? And then I said you can pay only if you pay off one of your credit cards first. Did you, or did you not?"

Tom squirmed and looked away. "I was going to, but forgot. But don't you realize you just burst my ego bubble?"

"Burst *what*? Oh, don't bother to explain."

"At least let me apologize. And say thanks for rescuing me. Look, Ani. We have only ten more minutes. I wanted to bring you here to celebrate with you, right? Well, I also wanted to give you something." He reached for his coat pocket and pulled out a small package wrapped in red satin paper and tied with a white ribbon and bow. He set it before her. "Open it."

"Oh?" she mumbled, smiling shyly. She slowly unwrapped the little package. Emerging from beneath the tissue paper was a box. She opened the box and pulled out a tiny thumb-sized, heart-shaped globe on a base.

"Oh, how sweet! Thank you, Tom, it's beautiful," she said as graciously as she could muster.

"This little globe describes us," he said. "See? We might be worlds apart, but love unites us more than our worlds divide us. Get the picture?"

"Yes, but I feel awful. I have nothing to give you in return. I'm sorry."

"Look at me," he replied gently, reaching over the table and lifting her chin.

Ani looked up into his gray-blue eyes.

"Now smile. Thanks. That was your gift to me," Tom said. His hand reached for her hands across the table.

Ani's smile lingered while her eyes glistened with oncoming tears. The memory of another world, a world she had loved and felt loyal to for twenty-one years, was growing dimmer. A new reality was luring her now—that of a new world, a world that included Tom. Resisting it was becoming as impossible as pulling a loaded two-wheel cart up Mount Pangkuban Perahu.

Half an hour later, Tom's car stopped in the dorm's empty parking lot. "Thank you for a wonderful last night in 1997," she said. She opened the car door and started walking briskly to the entrance of her dorm. She heard him get out behind her and soon felt his hand on her shoulder. "Wait, Ani. Please!" he pleaded gently. She complied and stopped.

"May I kiss you?" she heard him say. She froze. She could not say no, nor could she say yes. But before she could think or answer, she felt his lips pressing against hers, his gentle hands caressing her neck.

A fire ignited her whole being, and she wondered if she could—or even wanted to—put it out. The only way out was to flee from it. But how or where? A voice inside her urged, *just run*!

"Good night, Tom!" she said quickly, pulled away, and dashed toward the dorm without looking back.

An eerie quiet reigned in the building as she entered her dormitory. Almost out of breath, her heart pounding fast, she stopped in front of the mailboxes and unlocked hers. No mail. She badly longed for something from home—like a cover of protection, something that would restore her centeredness. A feeling of homesickness rolled over her like a chilly wind. She wearily climbed the stairs and used her keys to open the computer room. Perhaps an email from home would cheer her.

Only one personal email was waiting in her inbox. It was from her sister, Indri.

> *Hi, Ani,*
>
> *Happy New Year in America!*
>
> *Our parents told me not to tell you this, but I think you should know that Uncle Lee is in the hospital with cancer of the pancreas. The doctor gave him only a few months to a year to live. Cousin Budi took over the shop, but the business is not going as well as when Uncle ran it. I think you better think about coming back home soon and help Cousin Budi. That would be good for me because I miss you so much!*

Ani could read no further. This was not the news she had been hoping for. She turned off the computer, moved the keyboard to the side, and beat her head against the computer desk. Tears flowed. She even wailed out loud since there was no one else around to hear her. When she had no more tears left to shed, she prostrated herself and bowed her head to the ground to "recite" her Arabic prayers.

She then asked herself, would Allah the Almighty heed her prayers if she talked freely to him as Sarah and Grace always did? But if Allah prescribed her destiny, why should she bother asking him for anything? Would he even care enough, or was he too far away, or too busy to listen?

But just in case he would listen, and in case he would want to override her destiny, she left a message in her Sundanese dialect. "Have mercy, Allah! Please make Uncle Lee better! And please help my cousin do well in the business so I can stay and finish my degree."

She also wanted to mention Tom but wasn't sure what or how to ask.

Chapter 14

Ani decided not to mention her uncle's decline to Sarah or Grace just yet. She hated to bother other people with her needs, or even hint that she could use their help. Her mother had taught her to be modest, and her father had taught her to be self-sufficient. Only if someone offered financial support, as Uncle Lee Salim had done, would she welcome it. And if it was Allah's will that she stayed, she believed he would find a way.

She also did not want Tom to know anything was amiss. However, she did send him an email asking for a month of quiet and reflection during the month of Ramadan. "Please don't call or write or show up at my dorm. I need this," she wrote. She counted on his gentlemanlike manners to respect her wishes.

The clutter of books, magazines, photos, unopened junk mail in Sarah's apartment did not bother Ani. Neither did the narrow sofa. The only thing that annoyed her a little was that Sarah kept the radio on all day long! But Ani said nothing. She liked Sarah and did not want to hurt her feelings.

But by the third day of Ramadan, Ani decided she would try the American assertiveness approach. Well, sort of. "Sarah," she said, "I have to get up very early to recite my prayers, then cook and eat before sunrise. Does that bother you?"

"Not really. I sleep like a log. I hear nothing."

"That's good." Ani waited a few minutes, hoping Sarah would ask if she did anything that bothered Ani. But she didn't. "I'm amazed how you can study with the radio on, Sarah. I can't do that," she ventured to say.

"Oh, I'm sorry, Ani," Sarah said. "You should have said something about it earlier. Feel free to turn it off whenever you're home to study. I won't mind. Really."

"Thanks."

"Is there anything else that bothers you?" Sarah asked with a kind voice.

Ani smiled a little. "Not really. It's okay."

"No, come on. Please tell me," Sarah coaxed.

After a moment, Ani said, "You sometimes hand me an apple or a piece of bread with your left hand. In my culture, you never hand food to someone with the left hand because you clean yourself with your left hand when you're on the toilet, don't you?"

"Sorry, Ani. I'm a leftie and sometimes forget it's impolite in many cultures to hand food to someone with the left hand."

"But it's okay in America?"

Sarah nodded. "We use either hand to clean ourselves when using the toilet," she said with a giggle. "But with lots of toilet paper, and then we wash both our hands with soap and warm water afterward."

Ani chuckled. "Now tell me something that bothers you about me."

Sarah thought a moment. "Well, I wasn't going to say anything about it. But since you asked, here's one. After you shower, shampoo, and use the hair dryer, I wonder if you could pick up your long black hair from the tub, the sink, and the floor. I mean, bending down and getting up is a good exercise for me, but—"

Ani laughed. "No, you shouldn't have to do that! I'm sorry, Sarah. I didn't realize. You see, I take my contacts off before I shower every time, and I can't see the hair. But that is no excuse. I will pick up my hair from now on."

Ani vowed to observe the month-long Ramadan fast, despite the fact that in the USA, doing so was far more challenging than in her country. Here, she had no choice but to resume all her normal activities during the day while fasting at night. No one woke her up in the middle of the night to eat with them, and no one cooked a meal for her before dawn.

"Can I ask you something?" asked Sarah one day.

"Sure."

"I know that part of the goal of Ramadan is to give yourself time for reflection and spiritual recharging. But how can you do that when you have all that extra work at night and no rest during the day?"

Ani said nothing for a moment. "I don't know if my reflection and spiritual recharging are conscious. You're right. I don't have much time for that. Or maybe I don't take as much time as I should. But maybe subconsciously, I do. Or maybe it just makes me feel good about myself. You know, I'm doing what is right and what pleases Allah."

"Well, that makes sense. Do you feel Allah gives you more attention and hears you more during this month?"

"Maybe. I hope that the holy Allah does hear me more. Especially if I pray more than five times every day and give more to the poor."

"I bet you miss your family and friends back home more than ever, don't you?"

Ani felt tears coming to her eyes. "Yes, I do," she said quietly. "Getting up and eating all by myself at night is the hardest thing for me."

Sarah put her hand on Ani's shoulder. "I'm sorry," she said. "That must be hard." She turned to go to the kitchen and make a sandwich. Then she stopped and turned around. "You know what? I'm going to fast during the day, too. At least while you're here with me. I want to try this. I mean, why should you have to do this alone? I hate eating alone, too! It would be so much more fun for both of us if I joined you in your nighttime-only food binge, don't you think?"

Ani smiled as she wiped her tears. "You would do this for me?"

"The only thing is, you're going to have to wake me up before dawn and throw water on my face."

The permitted one week at Sarah's ended, and Ani had to return to her dorm. The Ramadan fast now became more of a challenge. All day long, students around her were munching on doughnuts, crackers, chips, sandwiches, or pizza—or drinking a soda. When she smelled the food, saliva would form in her mouth. And the late-night and early-morning mealtimes? They were lonely. For convenience's sake, she chose to eat by herself rather than meet with some of her Muslim acquaintances on campus. Grace had lent her a rice cooker, and Sarah had lent her a thermos container. So she thought she would do just fine.

But homesickness crept in once again, and it reached its peak during the last two weeks of Ramadan. Ani missed the food from home. She also missed *ngabuburit*—the custom when she and her sister and mother would go window shopping and buy sweets to eat when breaking the fast. When Ramadan ended, Ani missed the *buka bersama* get-together with her family back home. All she could do was email the traditional *Mohon maaf bathin* asking each family member for forgiveness for any wrongdoing she had done in the past year. At home, there would be a huge feast of *opor ayam (*chicken curry) and *ketupat* (steamed rice), and lots more delicious dishes. But here, no one brought Ani *cendol (*a special drink with coconut milk). And no one congratulated her with "*Selamat hari lebaran,*" as was customary back home on this special day.

The more she thought of her loved ones back home, the less she thought about Tom. The more she prayed to Allah for his will to be done, the less she longed for Tom. It would just have to stay this way, she resolved.

Chapter 15

On the second day after Ramadan ended, Ani heard a thud on her window. When she pulled up the shade, she saw Tom standing outside her dormitory door, bent over the white, snowy ground. She lifted the storm window and leaned out. Just then, a snowball swished by her face and landed on the floor of her room. A laugh and the words, "Oops! Sorry, Ani. I didn't mean to—" reached her ears.

"I'll meet you down there in ten minutes," she yelled back. She quickly shut the window and threw on her winter jacket and boots. It was time to face the music. *Stay strong! Stay strong!* she reminded herself as she descended the stairway and exited the building.

She saw Tom open his arms wide in greeting, but she pretended not to notice. "Can we talk somewhere where we can sit down?" she asked.

"Sure. I know just the place to go." He walked her to the car. They rode in silence to a small café in Reisterstown. "Want anything to eat or drink?" asked Tom. "They make fantastic hamburgers here."

"Just a soda and fries," she said quietly. How many more times would she be able to eat French fries with Tom?

Once at the café, Tom ordered a smoothie and double cheeseburger for himself and a soda and some fries for Ani.

"So, what's up, Ani? What do you have to tell me?" he asked, drumming his fingers on the table. "You look pretty glum. What was the bad news you got from home?"

She shook her head. Holding back tears, she lined up the salt and pepper shakers beside the ketchup on the side of the table. Then she said, "My uncle who is supporting me has cancer. That means I have to go home to Indonesia by the end of this semester."

"You *what?!*" Tom exclaimed loudly so that others around them turned their heads. "Oh! That's terrible, Ani!" Tom said in a lower voice. He reached across the table and took her hand. "I'm so sorry about that. But Ani, isn't there another way you can stay, or come back?"

Lowering her head, she stared at the table, aching more for him than for herself.

"No, this can't be," Tom pressed. "There's gotta be another way for you to stay. I know you are not allowed to work off-campus, but have you checked with Ms. Daniels to see if you can get a campus job?"

"I already asked. They don't have any openings for the next term. And there's a long waiting list." Ani took a deep breath and wiped her eyes, reminding herself to stay calm and collected, especially now that Tom did not show much strength or poise.

"I—I just can't believe this is happening to you—and us," he whined.

For the first time in her life, Ani saw tears welling in a man's eyes. They were Tom's tears, and they were for her! She leaned forward. "Destiny doesn't always allow us to do what we want, does it?" she said quietly. "That's what my father always taught me," she added, not fully believing in destiny herself. Didn't Uncle Lee teach her a different way of seeing things? Didn't he always say the world is bigger than it seems and that all you have to do is explore it until you find what you're looking for?

"Destiny?" Tom repeated the word with a tinge of sarcasm. "In America, we think of that word as a bad excuse. We try to think of options and possibilities. Reach for the stars and try to find a solution to our problems. That's what we believe. We don't give in to what you call "inshallah." We keep on searching." He leaned back and looked out the window, deep in thought as he watched the falling snow.

The waitress came and brought them what they had ordered. “Could you also bring me some coffee, please?” Tom asked. “With cream. Do you want anything else, Ani? A grilled cheese sandwich, maybe? Or an apple pie? Another soda?”

“No, thanks. I’ve had enough,” Ani replied. Her stomach was still adjusting to eating during the day after a month of eating only at night.

Tom leaned forward again and gently touched Ani’s hand. “Listen, Ani. While you were on your Ramadan fast, I was doing a lot of thinking about things, especially about you. I’ve known a lot of women, but none like you. You’re smart, beautiful, and you’re not afraid to tell me what you think. I respect that in a woman. I just can’t imagine losing you. You’re the first woman I’ve fallen in love with, and—well, I don’t want to lose you. Do you—don’t you feel the same way about me? Just a little? Maybe it’s just wishful thinking, but I see the love in your eyes when you look at me.”

She laughed, shaking her head. “Even if there is love in my eyes, love is not enough. I’m a Muslim, and you’re not. We’re too different in our cultures and ways of doing things. And besides, I am going back to Indonesia soon to help make it a better country. It’s just an impossible situation. I’m sorry, Tom. There isn’t time to make it work. Can’t we just be casual friends?”

Tom squeezed both her hands now. “We’re already more than friends. And we’ve already begun to learn from each other. I’m slowly paying off my credit cards. And you are using a fork instead of a spoon or chopsticks. We can figure something out together so you can stay longer. You can’t just throw this all away because your uncle can’t finance your education anymore. That’s simply not a good enough reason. There’s gotta be another way. Like . . . maybe we could get married so you can stay, and then we’ll slowly work it all out, including our cultural differences, as you say.”

Ani pulled her hands away, threw her head back, and laughed. Shaking her head, she then said, “Thanks for the thought, Tom. But I don’t think it’s honest to marry for a visa. That’s definitely too risky and complicated. Look. I have made the decision to leave at the end of this semester. And this semester is going to be very hard. I must study. I think it is better if we don't see each other anymore."

"You want to give up that easily?"

She nodded. "We don't have time on our side now, do we?"

Tom stared at her for a while, in total shock. *Play it cool, be a gentleman*, his adult ego urged him as he forced himself up from the chair and helped her put on her coat. *Be the gallant loser, not a sore one. Circumstances change; politics and policies change*, he told himself. *Even one's cultural rules can change.* Mustering every grain of hope he could find in himself, he asked, "Can we at least be friends for now, Ani? I mean, still see each other? Like maybe let me give you a tennis lesson during spring break?"

"Spring break? I'm sorry, Tom. I won't be here then," Ani replied, her voice trembling. I promised to go to Florida with Grace, Fred, and Sarah. But yes, we can still be friends. Can you please take me back to the dorm now?"

Tom relaxed. *At least we're still friends!* On the way to the dorm, Tom asked, "I'm just curious. What cultural difference would still be a problem between us?"

"Too many!"Ani blurted.

"Just name one."

Ani tried to think of something quickly. But for the moment, only one thing came to mind. "In my country, when you receive a gift, you give something in return. So people always give to get something back. But here, the receiver just has to say 'thank you.'"

"You mean—you give gifts to receive something in return?"

She laughed in embarrassment. "Maybe some people do."

Fine, Tom told himself. *That means if I make enough money with Solomon's moonlighting mission to pay for Ani's college expenses and fees, perhaps then she'd be open to marrying me—out of gratitude. Wouldn't that be the Indonesian way?*

Chapter 16

The trip to Florida was about to begin. Fred placed Ani's duffel bag into the bin on top of the van. As soon as Ani climbed in, she told them the news about her uncle's prognosis and her decision to return home at the end of the spring semester.

"I don't think you should think about going back to Indonesia so soon, Ani," said Grace. "There must be an alternate solution. You just try to relax with us this week and try not to think about it. Promise?"

But Ani could not imagine relaxing. The pain of aborting a lifelong dream, the embarrassment of leaving behind something unfinished, the thought of abandoning her newfound friends—especially Tom—all these paralyzed her.

Sarah was the next passenger pick-up. When she climbed into the second row of the van next to Ani, the grandchildren in the back urged her to sit with them.

"Sorry, guys," Grace protested. "Emmanuel will be sitting with you back there."

"Emmanuel is coming, too?" Sarah asked with an expression of disappointment. She turned toward Ani and whispered, "I thought I could relax during the Christmas break and wear my bikini."

Ani nodded. She knew why Sarah said that. Emmanuel was from conservative India. She would not feel comfortable wearing a bikini around him, either.

"Maybe he's been here long enough not to mind seeing women in bikinis," Ani said.

"Or he might like it too much and cause a problem for us,"

suggested Sarah. "Haven't you noticed that he looks at me funny? I can't make him out."

"Maybe because he likes you."

"Likes me? Oh, no!" Sarah moaned. "I wanted to relax, not deal with a—"

"—a romance?" Ani teased.

"Right. I wanted so much to relax in the sun, listen to and watch the rolling waves, and feel the warm breeze again. Bummer. Now I have to wish for cold weather."

"Again? You've been to Florida before?"

"Lots of times, with my parents when I was younger. I haven't been there since they both died."

Grace turned around. "Why wish for cold weather?"

"Because you invited Emmanuel to join us. I can't let him see me in a bikini."

"Oh, no problem. Fred will take Emmanuel and the boys fishing while we girls go swimming."

Emmanuel squeezed in with the boys in the back of the van and played card games with them. Fred stopped the van every two hours for a rest and a stretch. A cooler between Sarah and Ani was filled with drinks, snacks, sandwiches, and cookies for refreshment. When the van crossed the North Carolina border, a markedly warmer, soothing air greeted the travelers, and off came the winter wear.

"Sarah, do you want to drive?" called Fred from behind the steering wheel just as he entered a rest-stop area.

"Sure."

"And who wants to keep her company up front while we two old folks take a snooze for an hour or so?

"I will," shot Emmanuel from the back. "I'd like to see some of the scenery, and besides, I'm getting a bit carsick in the back."

"You mean, 'card sick'?" Fred joked as he drove the van into the rest-stop. After they all used the restrooms and had a bite to eat, Emmanuel moved to the front next to Sarah at the wheel, Fred and Grace moved to the middle seat to sleep, and Ani asked to play with the boys in the back. "But please keep the sound down, kids," Grace begged. We old folks need a nap before we cross into South Carolina."

A good twenty minutes later, Emmanuel and Sarah heard snores from behind. "Would a conversation help you stay awake?" Emmanuel asked Sarah in a low tone so as not to disturb the ones asleep.

"It might," she said guardedly with a polite smile, but couldn't think of anything else to say. So she waited for him to begin. Ten minutes of awkward silence went by.

"You know, I just remembered," he finally said. "You never had your turn in the True–False game on Thanksgiving Day."

She smiled. "And neither did you."

"Right. Want to do it now?"

"All right. Let me think. The first statement is—I never use rouge on my cheeks. The second is, I used to chain-smoke."

A long silence followed—a long, long silence.

Emmanuel finally cleared his throat. "I think you are a real person, an honest person. So I would guess your cheeks are naturally pink."

Sarah laughed. "True. I don't apply rouge on my cheeks. But I never thought that wearing rouge would make me a dishonest person any more than wearing clothes would."

"You mean, you used to smoke?"

"A lot."

"How did you stop?"

"When I learned that my body belongs to God, I asked him to help me smoke a few less each week until I stopped altogether."

"That's amazing."

"How about you?" Sarah asked. "I mean—your true or false story?"

"Let's see . . . okay. First story: I once worked part-time as a personal escort to Princess Diana," he began. "And my second one is: My parents arranged a bride for me in India."

Sarah relaxed a little, hoping the latter was true. "Is she beautiful?"

"You mean, Princess Diana or the bride?" he asked.

"We already know about the princess. Of course, I mean the bride."

"Indescribably beautiful, more beautiful than the princess. Or else my parents wouldn't have picked her for me."

Silence followed. *Why would he flirt with me so much if he had a bride waiting for him back home?* "I think the princess story is true," she finally said. "Not that I don't believe your second story could be true also."

"You're right. But it's not exactly how it sounds. Princess Diana was the name of a dog I had to take for a walk when I was house-sitting for a Communist last year."

She chuckled, careful not to awaken the others. "And what about a bride? Haven't your parents ever tried to arrange one for you?"

"They have." Emmanuel took a deep breath. "I was engaged to a girl by proxy. I had met her years ago when we were still in grammar school, and we used to play together with the other cousins during family festivities."

"You mean she is a relative?"

"She was the daughter of my uncle's wife's brother."

"Was? What happened to her?"

A moment's silence followed. "She died of typhoid fever last year."

"Oh, how sad. I'm sorry."

They rode in silence for a while. "What do you like to read, Sarah? Romance novels?" he asked.

"No," she laughed. "I'm currently reading a commentary on the book of Genesis, the first book in the Bible." She hoped he would be turned off and have nothing further to do with her.

"Really?" he said, laughing. "You are reading the first book in the Bible, and I'm reading the last book in the Bible."

She looked at him with surprise. Was he serious, or was he just trying to impress her? "You are not a Hindu or a Muslim?" Sarah asked.

"Neither. My parents were originally Hindu. They converted to Christianity as adults."

"Why? How did that happen?"

"A man named Bakht Singh traveled through their village and told them about Jesus. He was originally a Sikh. So when I was born, my parents named me Emmanuel and taught me about Jesus, too."

"And what did you do with what you learned? Did you also become a follower?"

Emmanuel smiled. "When I was a child, yes. But before I came to the States, I decided to give up my faith. I was pretty much an atheist by the time I came here."

"So, why are you reading the Bible now?"

"About two years ago, some friends invited me to hear a lecture by Josh McDowell on campus. He was a lawyer who set out to disprove the validity of the Bible. During his research, he discovered that the Bible is historically reliable, and he became a Christian. He ended up writing the book *Evidence that Demands a Verdict*. Have you read it?"

"No, but I've heard about it," answered Sarah. "And then what happened?"

"Well," he said with some hesitation, "it brought me back to the point that I had to swallow my pride and confess I was wrong. I was looking for an excuse to live my own life the way I wanted to. Now I had no excuse. It was hard, but once I got through that, I could begin a personal relationship with God again. And it's been—well, amazing, and I have no regrets. It's still a relatively new journey for me, so I can't describe it more than that."

Sarah smiled in the dark. *Finally, a man who believes as I do!* But she would be very, very careful, she resolved. She knew that their cultural differences alone would present a challenge—not to mention the question of geography. Wasn't he returning to India after his graduation?

The morning after they arrived, Ani slipped into her shorts and walked alone to the beach. The warm breeze, the morning sun, and the gentle waves of a low tide stirred in her a longing for Tom. She knew it was a longing based on a painfully impossible dream that would end soon. Politics and economics simply demanded it. For a moment, she allowed that longing and ensuing pain to smolder inside her. She did not want to squelch her pain like a Chinese male stoic. Instead, she envisioned the Gulf breeze blowing it all away. She could now set aside her thoughts and feelings about Tom and enjoy the beach, the sun, the wind, and the fun with dear friends.

And enjoy she did. The Osterhouse family rented two apartments on the beach. Sarah, Ani, and the two grandchildren shared one, while Fred, Grace, and Emmanuel shared the other. Except for one day of rain, the weather was almost always perfect. Fred, Emmanuel, and the boys rented a fishing boat and gear and went out on the bay while the women went to the beach. Careful not to get too brown, Ani sat in the shade under a beach umbrella. Grace and Sarah sunned themselves in their bathing suits to get a tan.

At sundown, when the beaches were cleared of most swimmers, Sarah did not have to worry about Emmanuel seeing her in a bathing suit. They took walks together in their T-shirt and jeans.

On their last evening, they all watched the sunset together. The family and Sarah sang old folk songs, Negro spirituals, hymns, and what they called "camp songs." When they sang religious songs about God, or to God, it gave Ani goose bumps. The Christian God seemed different from the Allah she knew. Christians viewed him as personal, as though his presence intertwined with all they did and said—any time and in any place. *Was he the same Allah?* she wondered.

The six days of sun, recreation, and exercise were soon history, but for Ani, they stayed forever in her memory. Crossing over the Virginia-Maryland border on the way home, Ani's new reality set in. Unless a mysterious alternative came to pass, her American dream might soon have to end.

The dormitory that evening felt more ominous to Ani than on the day she arrived. Doom rolled over her like a heavy fog in the dark. Returning to her room, she found her cell phone lying on the bed. It was dead. She quickly set it in the charger, unpacked her bag, and went to the computer room on the first floor.

Several advertisers and "spam" mail appeared in bold. One email from Tom begged her to call as soon as she got back.

Early the next morning, Ani checked her phone messages. There were only three, and all of them were from Tom. The words "Please call me as soon as you get back, Ani. I miss you" were the gist of them. She decided to wait a day or two before returning his calls. She needed more time of quiet, more time to think, and more time to muster the courage to combat feelings that surged like wind-driven rain.

Luckily, Tom could not surprise her. All the dorm buildings were still locked due to the break. But he left several email and phone messages. Finally, Ani gave in and called him. All he had wanted, he said, was to see if she would allow him to give her a tennis lesson. He had bought an extra racket at a garage sale.

She laughed. "I'm not athletic, Tom," she protested.

"That's all right. I want you to give it a try. If you don't like it, I won't ever ask again. How about Saturday?

"I can't promise, Tom."

Chapter 17

"It's Easter on Sunday," Grace said over the phone on a Tuesday morning. "Can you join us this coming Sunday afternoon, Ani? I could use your help to hide some Easter eggs in the backyard while Fred takes the grandkids on a hike."

"What fun! I'd love to!" replied Ani. She longed for an outside activity during the spring. The trees had partially turned green, and the soothing temperature felt just like it was after sunset at home in Indonesia.

"By the way, Tom is coming over, too," Grace announced while driving Ani to the house the following Sunday. "He's been begging me to invite him over. Do you think he's trying to find an excuse to see you again?" Grace's voice betrayed a trace of concern. "If that makes you feel uncomfortable, I'm sorry. I didn't know how to put him off."

Ani smiled, hiding her secret excitement. "Don't worry. We're just friends." She wished it could be more, but she also knew it could not be. *It simply should not be,* she told herself.

Tom was already waiting for them when they arrived and opened the car door where Ani sat. With a flushed face, Ani fleetingly looked at him, then hurried past him toward the front door.

"Hey, Ani, wait up! It's been so long since I've seen you," Tom said as he darted after her.

"Sorry, I'm in need of the ladies' room," she said over her shoulder as she disappeared behind the bathroom door.

As soon as Ani joined them again, Grace handed each a big basket of colored eggs. "Hide them anywhere in the backyard within the fence. But not in the trees! I don't want the kids to climb them. Count them first so we're sure to find them all again. And don't bury any of the eggs underground! I don't want the kids to get too messy."

Tom and Ani set to task. When they finished hiding all the eggs, Ani sat down on the swing. "You make a pretty Easter bunny," Tom teased as he gave her a gentle push.

"Really?"

"Not really. You're much cuter, of course. But I wish you wouldn't hop away from me."

Ani ignored his complaint. "What are you doing these days?" she asked.

"I am working extra hours for my friend Solomon so that you can finish your degree."

"What do you mean?"

"My friend Solomon and I are doing this project that earns me lots of extra money. By June, I will be able to pay for your expenses at least for another semester. Would you let me do that for you?"

"Really? But what about paying off your credit cards?"

"I'm working on that, too."

"The kids are back from their ride with Grandpa," shouted Grace from the porch. "Are we done? Good. Remember, each gets only five eggs. The first one who finds five gets a prize."

It did not take long for the first two to find their five eggs. "Don't eat them yet, kids," Grace announced. "We'll first go inside and have our Easter dinner. Save the eggs for later."

When they were all seated at the table, Grace nodded to Fred to say grace. But before he started, he looked at the grandchildren and asked, Which one of you would like to tell Ani what two events we're celebrating today?"

"The Easter bunny," piped the youngest.

"True. You know why?"

"Because bunnies have lots of babies this time of the year."

"Right. What else do we celebrate?"

"Jesus dying on the cross for us and rising from the dead," said the oldest.

"Fred smiled. "The two just happen to fall around the same time in the northern and western European tradition. That's why we celebrate them together."

Ani had just finished sweeping the kitchen floor. "It's still sunny out," said Tom as he rinsed the last knife and fork and placed them into the dishwasher. "How about if I show you Baltimore at its finest in the spring? There's this private garden I used to visit when I was a kid. It's open to the public during the day. You would love it. Are you game?"

Ani gave an enthusiastic yes. She had been studying inside since January and felt eager to be out in nature again.

Tom drove into the Guilford area, off York Road. The smell of wet grass and azaleas filled the air as they entered Sherwood Gardens. A sea of red, white, yellow, and pink tulips spread before them.

"Tulips!" Ani screeched excitedly. "I saw them in pictures before, but never for real. They are lovely!" She pulled out her small camera and took pictures of the flowers. "This would make a great card," she said.

Tom struggled to ignore his senses as he watched Ani's graceful body glide between the tulips and azaleas. He smiled each time she smiled at him. But inside he wept. How could he lose her? Did she really have to go back to Indonesia so soon? If he could only prove to her that he loved her, and if he could only make himself worthy of her love!

"Look, Tom," she said with glee, as she broke off a twig from an azalea bush. "Smell this. Isn't it heavenly?"

He couldn't help himself. He gently took hold of her arm and pulled her close. But she wiggled away playfully, running onto a narrow path around a few dogwood trees.

When they sat down on the grass to rest, Ani asked him, "Do you believe in reincarnation?"

"No. Where did you get that idea?"

"That's what Jesus did. Didn't he?"

"No. You mean *resurrection*, not reincarnation. When Jesus rose from the dead, he came back to life on earth as the same person. Is that what you mean?"

"Yes, that is what I mean," replied Ani. She broke off a small twig from an azalea bush and stuck it in her hair. "We Muslims believe Isa did not die. He was too good to be killed in such a horrible way. Allah would never have allowed it," she said matter-of-factly, venturing to express what she had been taught all her life in the Muslim religion. It says in the Koran 'they did not kill him.'"

Tom shook his head. "Yeah, but the word 'they' was probably referring to the Jews. And that is technically correct. It was the Romans who actually killed Jesus, not the Jews." Tom couldn't help but feel a bit snug for remembering what he had heard at a formal Muslim-Christian dialogue a year earlier.

Ani said nothing for a moment. "I had not heard that argument before. Another difference between our religions is that the Koran teaches that Jesus was a prophet, not God. It teaches that God is One. Not three."

Tom scratched his head. "That's strange. The New Testament of the Bible, which you call what again?"

"Ingil."

"Oh yeah. Ingil. It clearly teaches that Jesus was God in human form. How do you explain that?"

"That's probably because the scribes who copied the original writings made a mistake, or simply changed it."

Tom guffawed. "Look. I'm not a sincere, professing, or practicing Christian, so it's not like I'm trying to defend the Christian faith. But I do know one thing: If the scribes who copied the Bible manuscripts made mistakes or changed any teaching by or about Jesus, they would have had to make the same change or mistake hundreds of times! There are hundreds of manuscripts or copies of the New Testament, and those copies are all alike, and the copies found are much older than the original Koran. They all clearly teach the divinity of Jesus, his death, his resurrection—not just once, but many times throughout these writings."

Ani said nothing in reply and looked away.

Tom did not notice that Ani felt increasingly uncomfortable. "Mohammed could not read or write," he said, slowing his pace as he spoke. "His followers only wrote down what they heard him say. And he said whatever he remembered hearing what Isa's followers said they believed. It's also possible that those followers could not read and didn't know everything in the Ngil. So when some of Mohammed's followers years later realized his teachings were different from the teachings of the Ingil, I think they simply concluded that the Ingil had been changed." By the time he was finished talking, he noticed that Ani had walked ahead of him and did not appear to be listening to him anymore.

"Ani, wait!" he said, running to catch up with her. "I'm sorry. I don't really like to argue about religion."

"Oh, it's okay," Ani exclaimed in polite protest. "I think this is an exciting discussion, not an argument. That's how we learn from each other. You can't do that everywhere in the world. But here, you have freedom of speech. So why not?"

"Yes, but I don't want religion be a dividing issue between you and me."

"It doesn't have to be. My parents come from two different religions, and they never argue about it. They each state their opinion and listen to each other with respect."

"Wow. That's cool."

"May I ask you another question?" Ani asked after they got back into the car and rode toward the university. "If Americans believe that Isa is God and that he died for them and came back to life, why do they live as though it didn't happen? Why are there more crimes and immorality here than anywhere else?"

He shrugged and scratched his head. "You got me there. But most Americans are not really Christian. Many people who call themselves Christians don't actually believe or follow Jesus's teachings. They just pretend to. They're probably not true followers. Like me, for example. I'm not a true follower."

"You're not?"

He laughed nervously. "It's hard to follow Jesus's teachings. That's why you don't see many so-called Christians do what Jesus taught them to do."

"Not even you? You mean—you might be one of those criminals?" she said, laughing.

Tom noticed a speed limit sign and slowed down. "I try to be kind, generous, honest, non-violent, and follow the laws. I have a standard of sorts. But do I forgive those who harm me? Or give everything that I have to the poor? Nope. And I don't pray or go to church anymore. Too many hypocrites there—you know, pretenders. I don't want to be one of them. It's dishonest."

"So you throw the baby out with the garbage, right?"

Tom laughed. "You mean, I throw the baby out with the bathwater. Yeah, you could say that. But don't get me wrong, Ani. I'm not like what you see at campus parties or on the TV news. At least I'm not *that* bad, am I?"

She laughed and slapped his arm. "Only a little bad, I hope."

"You hope? Does that mean I can be a little bad right now?" he asked seductively as he stopped the car in the parking lot across from Ani's dorm. He reached over toward her, pulled her to himself and kissed her gently, gliding his hand down her back.

Her spine began to tingle. *Think! Think of something!* But with each second of his touch, she found herself less and less able to think. She squirmed away, gasping for breath. "Please stop, Tom. You know we can't do this," she said as she reached for the handle on her side of the car and opened it.

The gentleman he was, he quickly got out of the car and helped her out of the car. "I'm sorry, Ani. I promise I won't do it again." He hoped his apology would be more effective in winning her over than another attempt at a kiss would.

"Thanks for showing me the garden," she said as she let him walk her to the dorm. "I need to go back. I have a test tomorrow!"

Ani allowed Tom to meet with her every week after that, sometimes for a fast-food lunch or just ice cream, other times at a tennis lesson or two, or for a walk. Ani could not help but notice that Tom had grown quieter, more serene, less flamboyant, and more responsible. He seemed to accept their "mere friendship" relationship—no more kisses, no hugs, no innuendoes. Ani gradually felt safe and relieved in his presence and looked forward to each rendezvous with increased eagerness.

But sometimes, a part of her wished that Tom would bring up the subject of marriage again. The memories of his fleeting suggestion of marriage to extend her visa, his soft kiss, his warm hands in hers, his sparkling blue eyes that made her want to dive into them—those memories would surface again and again—sometimes at will, sometimes not. And each time she allowed them into her consciousness, she tried to pray to Allah to show his will all over again.

Part II

Thousands of miles from Baltimore, in the Sunda region of Java Island of Indonesia, Ani's younger sister, Indri, trudged up a steep incline, carrying a basket full of rice on her head. "Indri, hurry up, come home!" the adolescent voice of her younger brother Rudi shouted from the top of the hill. Indri's heart began to pound like Sunda drums. The word "hurry" rarely reached the lips of anyone in her part of the world unless something grave had happened.

Just then, something irritated her throat. The smell of smoke reached her nostrils. She turned around and saw a dark gray monster of smoke loom upward into the horizon of the southwestern sky. She had heard of riots and fires in Jakarta a few days ago, but could they have begun in Bandung now? Why else was there smoke?

The swishing sound of her sarong increased with her nervous speed. She followed the dry, parallel tracks down the hill and up again—tracks that reminded her of what she aspired to be—faithful, steady, and predictable. She felt safer that way. After all, she was only eighteen.

A mosquito landed on her right arm. Instinctively, she slapped it away with her left hand. The sudden movement caused her basket to sway so that her left foot began to slide. "*Sunda women never drop their baskets,*" her mother had always warned. She fell on one knee while holding on to the basket with both hands. A sharp stone caused her left knee to burn like fire, but that didn't matter. It was more important that the rice was safe.

"Where is your Allah today? Is this his will, too?" Indri heard her mother say to her father as she entered the courtyard of their house. Of Chinese descent and not religious, her mother, Lan, always questioned her Muslim husband's fatalistic attitude.

He rarely argued with her. But this time, he did. "Does it matter whether I think it's his will or not?" Sunatu asked with a tone of sarcasm. Sitting on the bench by a wooden table along the wall of the house, he took a long puff on his cigarette and slowly blew it out.

Indri carefully lowered the basket of rice onto the floor. "I saw smoke from a big fire in Bandung. Have you heard anything about it?"

"Yes, Indri. We know from the radio report," her mother answered.

"What about Uncle Lee and his family? Are they okay?"

"The family is fine, and so is their home. But your uncle's former store burned down. He is lucky that he had sold it a few months ago and that your cousin runs the business from his home."

Just then, a teenage boy ran into the courtyard from the house and faced his father. "The radio says the fires are spreading. Bapak, do you think someone did this on purpose?"

"Possibly, Rudi," Sunatu replied.

"Who is burning whose buildings, Bapak? And why?"

Sunatu lit up another cigarette. "Some of the poor are angry and blame the rich Chinese for the bad economy in this country," he replied.

"Is the bad economy their fault?"

"Not really. They are just the scapegoats."

"Then it's a good thing for us that we're not rich anymore, right?"

Sunatu's lips curved to a wry smile. "You have a point there, Rudi."

"It isn't just the rich Chinese that are targets for violence," Lan added. "So are the Christians and the not-so-rich Chinese."

Her husband nodded.

She sat down across from him and poured him a cup of coffee from a ceramic pot. "Our nephew's business is going to suffer. No one will have enough money to buy computers. We will all suffer now. Surely my cousin Lee's money will run out soon, and Ani will have to come home, don't you think?"

Sunatu hit the table with his fist, sweat trickling down his forehead. "Never!" he said. "Ani is our only hope for a good future—not just for her, but for all of us. She must finish her studies in America."

"But how? How is she going to do that if there's no money?" Lan asked in an agitated, high-pitched voice. She waited patiently for an answer. She could tell an idea was brewing in his head by the way he stared into the swaying bamboo trees as he sipped his coffee. She knew if she waited long enough, he would eventually answer.

"We will find some way. Somehow," he finally answered in a low tone. He drank his coffee in, then rolled himself another cigarette. "Do you remember my second cousin Rianto, the son of my mother's cousin in Jakarta?"

"You mean the one who wanted nothing to do with you after you married me because I am Chinese? The one whose wife killed herself by drowning? I bet he probably drove her to it if he didn't murder her."

He pounded the table again. "All we know is that she drowned. Why do you believe these lies?"

"I have my reasons," she said, pouring her husband another cup of coffee. "So why are you mentioning him?"

"He is very wealthy," Sunatu said, puffing on his cigarette. "And he travels to the United States very often. He has a house somewhere not far from where Ani is. We could invite him here and ask if he would bring Ani some of our spices and gifts."

"Why should they meet? Can't you just ask him to transfer some money to her if he's so rich?"

He looked at her for a moment. Then he looked away into the bamboo trees again. "That is not how it works in my family. There are other ways."

Lan stared at him in disbelief and gasped. "You don't mean—! No way! When did you become so money hungry that you would marry off your daughter to an ugly man who might murder her? Besides, he's too old for her. What if he died the day after they were married?"

Sunatu's lips formed a slight curve upward. "She would be rich, no doubt."

"But never as sad as I if you should die."

Chapter 18

It was the warmest Saturday so far in May, 1998. The Osterhouse clan had invited Ani, Sarah, Emmanuel, and Tom to join them for a picnic on their large backyard deck. Everyone had arrived on time except Tom, who called with the excuse that his extra weekend job delayed him an hour or two. Fred and his sons grilled steaks and burgers. Ani added her chicken sticks dipped in peanut sauce, Sarah had made coleslaw, and Emmanuel brought a curried potato stew. Grilled corn, green peppers, and tomatoes were also on the menu. The daughters-in-law had contributed salads and pies.

Tom finally appeared, but with a solemn expression on his face. “Sorry I’m so late, everybody. Grace, I put the ice cream in your freezer just now.

“You don’t look your usual happy-go-lucky self, Tom. Are you okay?” Grace asked. He nodded, but then moved next to Grace and quietly said, “I just heard some bad news on the radio on my way here. I think I should wait to tell everyone once we’ve all finished eating.” He threw a side glance at Ani, who was pushing one of the younger grandchildren’s swing.

“Last call for hamburgers, hot dogs, and steaks!” Grace chimed loudly. “Please throw your paper plates, etcetera into the garbage bin once you’re finished. After we’re finished, all the adults please come into the porch for ice cream. I will serve it to the kids outside.”

“On my way here, I heard an important and very sad news flash on the radio,” began Tom when everyone had consumed their dinner and ice cream. He looked at Ani. "They said something about riots and fires in Indonesia."

Ani gasped, tears coming to her eyes. "What? Really? Where in Indonesia?"

Tom shook his head. "I don't know, Ani. I think they mentioned Jakarta, but I didn't recognize the names of the other cities."

Fred shot up from his seat. "Well, let's have a look at the PBS news, shall we? It should be starting about now," he said, and led everyone inside. He turned on the television and searched for the right channel. Sure enough, fires in Jakarta and Bandung filled the television screen before them. They saw people running frantically from burning buildings and shootings, children bleeding on the streets, mothers screaming, young men looting stores, soldiers beating with sticks. Ani frantically looked closely at each face, fearing she might recognize someone.

A commercial came on. Tom muted the sound and asked, "Is this anywhere near where your family lives, Ani?"

Ani nodded slowly, her eyes still fixed on the television. "Bandung is about two hours from our home," she replied with tears. "My uncle and cousin own a business there," she said with a cracking voice.

"You should call home, Ani. From our landline," offered Grace. "Never mind the long-distance charges."

"Thank you, but I will wait until later," Ani answered. "It's the middle of the night there right now."

"Okay. Fred, honey, can you please offer a prayer for Ani's family in Indonesia right now, and for the whole country?"

"Good idea," Fred said. With only the formality of closing his eyes, Fred prayed, "Father, we don't know how Ani's family is. But you do. You see all things, and you grieve at the horrors and injustices of this fallen humanity. Please protect Ani's family and friends. May you fulfill your ultimate purpose and plan. Comfort Ani right now and give her peace. We ask in Jesus' name, amen." The *amen* was echoed by the other adults present.

Grace placed her hand on Ani's shoulder. "We're here for you, Ani. No matter what."

"Thank you," Ani replied with a weak smile and tears in her eyes.

"Want to go outside and play softball with the kids and me?" Tom asked cheerfully. He hated long, drawn-out sadness.

Grace gave him a glare of disapproval. "Tom, I don't think Ani is in the mood for that right now."

"Oh, it's okay," Ani said, getting up and turning toward Tom. "I need the destruction."

Fred's rolling belly laugh filled the room. "Distraction, you mean, or did you mean instruction?" he corrected.

"Distraction and instruction," she corrected, managing a small smile. "Is this game really played with a soft ball? It can't hurt me, right?" Ani asked. She did not notice the suppressed smiles and giggles from the others as she followed Tom outside.

At twilight, Ani sat in the Grace's den upstairs, talking with her mother on the phone. She did not want to talk long because a long-distance call to Indonesia was very expensive.

"Don't worry," her mother said. "The fires are far away from us."

"How is Uncle Lee and his family?"

"Their house is safe. It's a good thing he had already sold his store."

"How is he? Is he still very sick?"

"Yes. There is nothing they can do for him now."

Ani choked up, not able to speak for a minute. "Shall I come home?" she finally asked.

"No, Ani. There is no need for you to do that. For now, use the money you have from Uncle Lee as long as it lasts. As for the future, I think your father has a plan. We will let you know about it later. Don't worry. Just do well in your studies. Promise?"

Ani hung up and sank to her knees, weeping. What plan would Father have? He had no money, no job. All they had were a rooster, ten hens, and a small tea plantation. Not noticing that Grace had entered the room, Ani prostrated herself and muttered a recital of prayers in Arabic. When finished, she felt Grace's hand on her back. "Do you want to talk about it?" she heard Grace ask. Ani straightened back up and faced her friend. "I will have to go home in June. My uncle is dying," Ani stammered, new tears rolling down her cheeks. "His business was paying for my expenses in the U.S. I don't know what will happen now."

Grace stooped down on one knee and wrapped her arms around Ani. "I'm so sorry, dear. I'm so sorry."

Chapter 19

The latest riots in Indonesia had ended. Rianto, the billionaire banker, returned to Indonesia to check on the condition of his home and bank. Descending from the steps of his aircraft at the Jakarta airport, his whole body smiled. The warm, moist Java air caressed his face and knees like that of a sauna. What a welcome change to the unstable climate of New England! But within minutes of riding in a taxi to Jakarta, he felt a surge of shock. He barely recognized the city he so loved. Blackened buildings with broken storefront windows, garbage scattered on the sidewalks, burned-out cars without wheels parked in every direction, yet people everywhere walking about as if nothing had changed. On the news back in the United States, the riots had seemed far away. But now, their consequences felt like a splash of lemonade onto his eyes.

A smile crossed his face. He calculated the millions it would take to rebuild the stores and businesses destroyed. That meant that people would have to borrow from the money stored in his Swiss bank account. He would benefit big from the interest. If those who borrowed could not pay back or keep up with payments, Rianto would repossess their properties. And he was sure there would be plenty to repossess.

Another fringe benefit: The revenues gained would more than replenish his generous gifts to the US senators and representatives, even if the hoped-for fast track bill failed to pass. Once Indonesia's economy bounced back, there would be less cause for hatred, strife, or riots! The wealthy would no longer be the scapegoats, and there would be peace in the streets. Best of all, he would become more prosperous than he had ever been.

But there was another reason why he had decided to return to Indonesia this time—namely to find himself a new wife. It had been two years since the body of his much younger and pregnant wife was found dead off the shore of the Sound of Narragansett Bay. The child would have been their first. Ever since then, his whole inner and outer being longed for a woman to keep him warm. He also wanted heirs badly.

As a semi-devout Muslim, he resisted the temptation of hiring a call girl to still that scream, and dating in the Western fashion did not fit his image, either. He was sure he would find the right woman again, even if she would marry him only for his wealth.

Arriving in his home, Rianto surveyed it carefully for any damage. His faithful servants had guarded the place well. The house and its contents seemed to be in order. As he leafed through the stack of bills and solicitation letters lying on a dark mahogany table, a small square envelope caught his attention. The letter was hand-addressed and stamped in Preander, the next biggest city near Bandung. He guessed it was from his less fortunate distant cousin Sunatu asking for financial aid. The billionaire banker loathed such requests. He believed that generosity encouraged the poor to become dependent and lazy, but others judged him to be stingy. Either way—he just longed for acceptance for who he was rather than for what he gave.

He decided to open the letter after his Jacuzzi bath and laid it on the bed so he would not forget. And when he did open it and read the letter from Sunatu, he was surprised. There was no hint of a request for financial help! Instead, it merely contained an invitation to visit the family!

As Rianto began to tuck the letter back into the envelope, he noticed a photograph inside and pulled it out. Two lovely young women sat in the foreground, a younger boy next to them, and the parents in the back, all wearing festive Sunda attire. The older daughter looked fair like a Chinese and the younger more bronze, like a Sunda. He wondered if they could be marrying age, and which of the two would be the better mother and manager of domestic affairs. Because he was a Sunda himself, he hoped it would be the woman with the more native Sunda look.

The letter from his cousin Sunatu reminded him of the loneliness he had suffered far too long. Even if the Sunatu family were beggars, he had to admit that any connection with a relative might be better than none. How long had it been since he'd seen any? He decided he would visit Sunatu and his family the following week. Better yet, maybe the day after tomorrow. And in case Sunatu had an ulterior motive for inviting Rianto, such as asking for money, why not attempt to turn his cousin's needs into a solution for his own needs?

Chapter 20

"Cousin Rianto is coming!" shouted Rudi from the top of the wall outside the Sunatu family compound.

"Where did you see him?" Lan asked her son.

"At the corner below our hill. He is getting out of a taxi. Now he's walking up the hill. But very slowly." Rudi paused, then added, "He looks old, Mother. Very old!"

The word "*old*" stung Lan Sunatu to the core of her being. She bristled at the thought of her daughter marrying an older man—especially *this* older man. And when she suddenly envisioned a city bus running over him, she did not feel guilty. Not because he was old. She hoped that Ani would be smart enough to see so for herself.

A few minutes later, Lan saw a short, stocky figure with grey sideburns, a bald top, and a mustache stop at the gate and shoo a chicken out of the way. True, he looked old. Her husband looked younger, though he was about fifteen years older than his nephew.

With short, quick steps, she rushed to the gate to greet Rianto. She bowed to him slightly, a compromise version of a custom passed down from the occupying Japanese a few decades earlier. Chills went down her spine as she got up and dared to look at him. His second-long smile revealed a golden tooth. The crease between his thick, graying eyebrows dug deep into his bronze Indonesian skin. Wrinkles around his expressionless eyes and a scar on his left forehead reminded Lan of an Indonesian version of Frankenstein. She couldn't help wondering if he seemed so cold because his wife had died or whether his wife had died because of his chilling coldness.

Lan pointed to the slippers at the threshold. "Please help yourself to them."

"It is so quiet in this house," commented the guest as he followed Lan through the hallway. They entered a small room with a comfortable easy chair, a small sofa, and a bookcase against the wall. "Where are your servants today?"

"They are on holiday, sir," she replied. It was a lie. They could afford only one servant since her husband had retired, and that one servant was home sick.

"And your children?"

"You will see two of them shortly," she replied as she ushered him into the living room. But before Rianto could ask where the third might be, she bowed and left the room.

Rianto walked around, taking note of the various artifacts, pictures, and photos. He picked up the family photo framed in bronze and studied it. It was the same photo his cousin Sunatu had sent, only enlarged.

"Ah, there you are, cousin!" Sunatu said as he entered the room. "Good to see you again. I am sorry I did not greet you when you arrived. I had a problem with the electric circuits. But I think it's fixed now. Do sit down, please. My wife should be bringing some water and fresh coffee at any moment."

As soon as his guest sat down, Sunatu offered him a cigarette, which Rianto gladly took.

"Beautiful children," Rianto said, pointing at the photo that he had placed back on the shelf. "Lan said I would soon see only two of them. Which ones are here?"

"Only the younger ones. Ani, the eldest, is studying business administration near Baltimore, Maryland. Do you know the area?"

"Yes, I do. Baltimore is about seven hours from my home in Rhode Island." He paused, studying the photo again. "Your elder daughter is very fair, very Chinese looking. The younger ones look more like our side of the family. Do they not?"

"Yes, true," Sunatu replied with a chuckle.

"May I ask—how do you, or can you, afford Ani's education? I hear you retired early because of some health problems."

Sunatu nodded. "Ani has a scholarship that pays for her tuition. My wife's brother is—or rather, *was* paying for all her dormitory and living expenses and books, but he recently lost his business during the riots. Ani will have to work illegally or find another sponsor."

A long silence followed. Rianto cleared his throat. "She could always abandon her studies and get married instead, couldn't she?"

Sunatu smiled. "I brought up my daughters to decide for themselves what they want to do with their lives. As long as they remain moral and upright, and as long as they marry Muslims, they can choose whatever they want to do."

"That is very modern of you, cousin," said Rianto. He puffed on his cigarette long and hard. "So now, where are the remaining two children? I would like to meet them."

"Our son, Rudi, is around here somewhere. Indri is in town purchasing seafood from the market. She will be back any minute now."

"Ah! Fresh seafood! Do you mean that this young woman is strong enough to carry a bucket of water with sea urchins from town? That's very impressive. Is she also the academic type? Does she also want to attend university in the United States?"

Sunatu did not answer right away. Instead, he let out a puff of smoke, wishing it could blow his cousin back to Jakarta. "You have to ask her. I think she prefers to draw pictures and design batik."

The string curtain in the doorway parted. Lan entered with a tray of cups, spoons, a coffee jug, sugar, and cream and set the tray on the coffee table. "I hear you go to the United States very often. Are you planning to go there again soon?" she asked.

"Yes, in a couple of weeks. I have a business visa with multiple-entry privileges, and I am renting a house an hour away from Boston year-round, which is my American headquarters. From there, I travel all over the world, and of course, back to Jakarta whenever I am needed here."

Lan's face could not hide her amazement. She bowed slightly and left the room again.

The gate outside squeaked, then slammed shut. The light *pat-pat* of sandals through the courtyard outside followed. "Do I hear the arrival of your younger daughter?" Rianto asked, staring with anticipation at the vertical red strings hanging from the top of the archway

Before Sunatu could answer, the strings parted, and Indri burst in, her bronze skin glazed with sweat. Her batik skirt reeked of seafood, and her straggled hair fell unevenly on her shoulders. She almost tripped over a wrinkle in the carpet but caught herself. Noticing a stranger in the living room, she smiled shyly and looked quizzically at her father.

"This is our daughter Indri," he said. "Indri, this is your Uncle Rianto from Jakarta."

Just then, Lan came in. "Excuse us," she said as she took Indri's arm. "We must go to the kitchen and prepare supper now." The firmness of her mother's voice convinced Indri to follow her without question.

As Rianto's eyes followed Indri, they softened, and his mouth slightly widened—the first evidence of any emotion since he arrived. "Charming young woman," he murmured, still glancing at the swinging strings in the doorway. "Very charming."

What a hungry boa, thought Sunatu. At that moment, he regretted having written that letter. He rose from his chair and opened a cabinet drawer to look for something. "Where are my cigarettes?" he mumbled.

"I believe they are here on the table," said Rianto calmly.

"Ah, yes." Sunatu laughed nervously. He offered a new one to Rianto and took one himself.

Rianto began to smoke in silence, staring at the picture on the desk again. "I will gladly finance your children's education. But on one condition. Would you allow me to marry one of your daughters if she accept my proposal?"

Sunatu coughed loudly, half laughing. "You are welcome to ask them, but on one condition. You must ask Ani first. If she refuses, you may ask Indri."

"I take that as a challenge, cousin," Rianto replied. "If neither of them accepts my offer of marriage, then *takdir*, so be it. But you have my word of honor: I will finance their education regardless. My bank accounts and bank were somewhat affected by the riots recently, but I secured most of my money in Swiss accounts. It was safer that way."

And they shook hands.

Chapter 21

Ani's spring semester at Newton University had ended. She still had not heard from her parents and was wondering if Tom's plan was just a pipe dream. She thought she had better start to pack her suitcases in case there was no alternative plan after all. And that meant she had better start saying goodbye to her friends.

A part of her could not help but be excited about the prospect of seeing her family again. She even purchased a few US souvenirs and products to bring home, like M&Ms, chewing gum, and Washington, DC magnets and T-shirts. But she would wait until the last minute to ship whatever she could not fit into her suitcase and carry-on bags. It would take two months to get there anyway, so there was no hurry.

Late in the evening of June 14, Ani checked her emails. Deleting a barrage of spam and advertisements, she noticed one other personal but unread email. The subject line read *Visit from your cousin.* What cousin was that? She did not recognize the sending email address. Was this another spam mail that might damage her computer? She decided to take the risk and open it.

> *Cousin Ani,*
>
> *Remember me? I am Rianto, the eldest son of Awang, your father's cousin, and I live in Jakarta. You may not remember me because you were very young when you saw me last. Your parents asked me to contact you. I live in Newport, Rhode Island (near*

Boston) for part of the year, but I return to Indonesia for at least six months every year.

Your parents gave me sauces and spices to bring you. I would like to see you and to talk with you about your future now that your mother's brother can no longer pay for your education. I am in the Baltimore area on business in early June. Can you meet with me in the Towson Diner on June 15, at 1:00 p.m. for lunch? I will pay for your taxi and lunch. Please reply and confirm.

I look forward to seeing you.
Your cousin, Rianto

Ani's heart almost stopped as she read the name *Rianto.* Wasn't he the wealthy banker who lost his wife to some kind of drowning about two years ago? And didn't her mother say she thought his wife drowned herself because she was unhappy in her marriage?

Ani looked at her calendar. June 15 was tomorrow! Gifts from home? YES! And if her cousin Rianto was as wealthy as she had heard he was, perhaps he had in mind to help pay for her expenses. Then she could stay in America after all.

She wrote back as politely as possible, confirming that she would meet Rianto at the Towson Diner by noon the next day. Seconds later, she received his reply saying he would meet her as planned.

Tom felt some panic as he drove to Solomon's on June fifteenth. Two more weeks and Ani would have to return to Indonesia! He had asked Solomon for an advance on the next few moonlighting assignments, but so far, Solomon had not said yes. Tom had paid off two credit cards and needed the extra cash to pay for Ani's tuition next semester. How else was he going to secure her stay in America?

Just as Tom was making a turn from a busy intersection onto Route 45, his cell phone rang. By the time he could answer, it was too late. The caller ID said Solomon. He pulled over into the next commercial parking lot, turned off the ignition, and dialed Solomon's number.

"There you are," said Solomon with an upbeat tone. "Are we still on for today?"

"On my way. I'll be there in about twenty minutes," Tom answered.

Thick raindrops began to fall on the windshield. When Tom turned the ignition key again, the engine would not start. He waited a minute. Again no response. Was the battery dead? He looked at the gas gauge and noticed it was empty. "Oh, blast it!" he yelled as he beat his head on the steering wheel in self-punishment.

He tried to call Solomon again, but no answer. It was pouring rain by now, and he had no umbrella. Pulling his jacket over his head, he climbed out of the car. There was no gasoline station in sight. Cars whizzed by him at top speed, including a taxicab with the silhouette of a pretty Asian woman with long black hair sitting in the back. *Just like Ani,* he thought.

Sinking back into the car, he looked up his automobile club on the phone. "I think I ran out of gas," he told the woman who answered. "I'm somewhere between Towson and Timonium on Highway 45, going north. Probably just five minutes outside of Towson. Can someone come to the rescue?"

He heard no reply from the woman. His phone had died. Desperate, he locked his car and began to walk in the rain. No umbrella, no hood on his raincoat. It was at least a two-hour walk to Solomon's, he figured. He wasn't even sure hitchhiking was allowed anymore, but as he walked and heard a car approach from behind, he would pull out his arm and thumb. But no one stopped.

Finally, about thirty minutes later, he arrived at a small no-name gasoline station. A young man filled a bucket with a gallon of gasoline and drove him to his car.

"That was the nicest thing anyone has ever done for me," Tom lied politely. "I'll follow you back to the station so I can fill it up."

"You got cash? I only take cash," said the attendant.

"No, I don't have any now, but I will later after I get back from my job."

"I won't be there then. Guess you need to drive to another station further down the road. Not sure if your gallon will get you there, but you can try."

Deep in thought, Ani was looking straight ahead inside her taxicab, noticing nothing but windshield wipers swishing aside the thick drops of icy rain. A man without an umbrella was walking along the highway, getting soaking wet while holding out his thumb. He looked a lot like Tom, she noted. *But it couldn't be . . .*

Twenty minutes later, the taxi pulled up in front of the Towson Diner. The stocky form of Rianto stood on the curb, wearing a long black woolen coat and a purple scarf. *Undeniably a Sunda*, Ani recognized as she watched him blow out a puff of smoke and walk in her direction. She noted his worn face. his grey sideburns, and the moon-shaped bald spot on the top of his head and concluded he must be by far her senior. Her heart began to race. Was it fear? No, it was aversion, she decided. His sinister expression resembled that of the beast in the cartoon version of the Western fairy tale *Beauty and the Beast*. It made her shudder. She could not imagine turning him into a gallant gentleman, even if she tried.

She got out of the taxi and greeted Rianto cordially. But he looked her over like a piece of baggage, and then he handed her a package. "Some *sambal* sauce and spices from home," he said. "Let's go inside and have something to eat."

He asked the waiter to return the water with ice cubes and bring him just water. Then he ordered steak for them both without asking Ani if she wanted anything different. While waiting, he sat looking at her without any expression on his face. No smile, no questions, no small talk. His fingers played piano on the table. At one point, he pulled out a small notebook from his coat pocket and scribbled something in it. After a few moments of silence, he asked in a mechanical tone, "How do you like America?"

She had heard the same question asked so many times that she was ready with a rehearsed answer. "It's fine," she replied in an equally mechanical tone. "How is my family?" Ani shifted to their Sunda dialect. Her tongue had been starving for her regional dialect, and she could not help but smile while using it. Not that she needed to know from him how the family was. She had communicated with them by email not too long ago.

"I'm sure you know all that already," he replied coldly. "Don't you talk with your parents on the phone?"

Ani laughed. "Calling home is too expensive. I email them, and occasionally, they email me back. You saw them recently, didn't you? You might know more than they tell me."

"Your parents are fine, but they are sick worrying about you, of course. And that is one reason why I'm here. To check up on you, to make sure you are all right, and to see what I can do to help you."

Ani smiled, blushing a little. She did not expect such words from a man whose face seemed frozen in a block of ice. The waitress brought the salad and a basket of Italian bread. Ani had not had breakfast, and her mouth began to water. But before she took a bite, she asked, "Cousin, how are the conditions in Indonesia now—especially Jakarta and Bandung?"

Rianto pushed the salad aside and took a piece of the bread, chewing it slowly before answering. He took a sip of the water the waiter had just brought him. "Everyone is a bit shaken. Jakarta and Bandung are a mess. You don't want to go back there."

"Unfortunately, I must," said Ani.

"Well, that is why I am here. I promised your father that I would help you with your education now that your mother's brother is not able to help anymore."

"Really?" she said cautiously. Somehow, she perceived danger. *What ulterior motive does this man have?* she wondered. *Dependence and neediness make people vulnerable to predators.* That is what her mother had always warned her.

The waiter placed two plates of steak with a baked potato and green garnish before them. Ani stared at her plate while Rianto began to cut the meat with eagerness and eat it. The aroma stimulated Ani's saliva. She assumed the meat was not halal. How could Rianto even eat it? Was he not also a Muslim?

"Why are you not eating?" Rianto said. "Because it is not halal? It's okay to eat the meat here. We are not in Indonesia, and there are no halal restaurants around here. I've already checked."

Ani looked at him, shocked at first. But Rianto had eaten several bites already, and Allah had not struck him dead! And since he was older than her, she decided to follow suit. She slowly picked up the steak knife and fork and began to cut the steak. It was cooked rare, and the blood gushing out almost made her sick. Too hungry not to eat it, she poured red pepper sauce all over her steak and baked potato, making the meal more tolerable.

They ate in silence, too busy chewing the steak. Ani smiled at Rianto at one point, saying, "You know, I'm going home in two weeks. My uncle's money is—"

"Yes, I know," interrupted Rianto stone-faced. "We will talk more about that after we eat."

Solomon's face never looked so anxious as he did when Tom finally arrived. "No gasoline, no phone. You must be in love!"

"I sure am! You know that's why I'm here, don't you?" Tom said.

"Well, lucky for me, you're here. I'm not sure what I would do if something bad happened to you, man. You're my number one guy. You know that, don't you? Wait here in the foyer. I'm going to lend you some dry clothes to change into."

"Your clothes? Will they fit me?"

"Better too large than too small!" the six-foot-two Solomon said, chuckling.

Two hours of further instructions breezed by as the men ate a pizza and drank several beers. "So you paid off two credit cards? How many more do you have, Tom?" asked Solomon.

"A couple more. What I need now is enough money for the

woman of my dreams to stay in the USA. Any ideas how I can get some?"

"Well, you can always borrow some from the bank and stuff some cash into her purse when she's not looking."

"No, no, no. I want her to know who it's from. Why else would she want to marry me? See, she'd have to marry me out of gratitude, whether she loves me or not."

Solomon stared at Tom in disbelief. "Is that right? And you want to marry her on that basis?"

"Why not? She'll eventually fall in love with me because I've been so generous, don't you think?"

Chapter 22

Ani looked up at Rianto in the restaurant and noted no sign of expression. "You wanted to ask me something?" she asked politely.

"Yes," he said. "Will you marry me?" Rianto asked as dryly as if asking for the salt and pepper shakers.

She burst out laughing. "Excuse me?" she said in English.

He nodded, stone-faced as usual. "You heard correctly. I want you to marry me."

He raised his arm to get the waiter's attention. "Dessert menu, please," he shouted to the waiter across the room as if the conversation topic between him and his guest were no more significant than the weather outside.

The waiter brought the menu. "Their chiffon pie looks good," said Rianto. "Would you like one?" Ani nodded.

After ordering slices of pie for her and himself, Rianto turned to face Ani. "Marrying me would give you security," he explained in a businesslike manner. "Your parents would not have to worry about you anymore. And you would not have to study or have a career anymore. I am rich. You will have everything you need. Well? What do you say?" He asked the question in an even less convincing tone.

Ani smiled nervously. There was no sign of life or feeling in the eyes of the man who had proposed to her. So, in an equally cold businesslike manner, she said, "Maybe I do not need any degrees or a career if I marry you. But I want to have them anyway."

Rianto looked out the window. "Sorry that you feel that way. I believe a wife's duty is only to her husband and children and the household. That is enough responsibility. Besides, women are weak. They might be led astray by the other gender in the work world."

"And men are not as weak?" Ani retorted with a sardonic smile. "Or you do not want women in the work world because men cannot handle the temptation of being led astray?"

Rianto coughed as if he were choking on his saliva. "Excuse me," he mumbled. "My condition stands. No further education, no career, but you will have all the money and security in the world. And children, of course. So, what is your answer, Ani? Yes, or no?" Again, the voice he spoke with was mechanical, as if he didn't care how she would answer. Ani saw his eyes follow a pretty waitress on the other side of the room and waited until his eyes focused on her again. Even if she were willing to give up her education, she would not want to marry him, she decided. But how could she say no to this man without being disrespectful?

"I am not sure, cousin," she finally answered, mustering diplomacy. "My mother's brother, Lee Salim, sacrificed so much to get me here. I do not want to disappoint him. And besides, I think you would be happier with someone else," she added. "I do wish to finish my education and have a career, besides getting married and having children."

Rianto shifted in his seat and cleared his throat. "I see that your education is important to you. But I want you to think about it some more. I won't be cross if you say no. You see," continued Rianto, "if you say no to my proposal, I have an alternative plan."

"An alternative plan?" Ani asked.

"Yes. If you turn down my marriage proposal, I will ask your younger sister Indri to marry me. In that case, would you put in a good word for me—to both your sister and your parents?"

Ani gulped. *Indri is so young, and he is so old! She is like a tender leaf in the wind*, Ani thought. *She might just be naïve and pliable enough to say yes.* On the positive side, if married to Rianto, her sister's life would be defined and uncomplicated. Both Indri and Rianto came from the same culture, held to the same religion, and shared the same broader family clan. But wouldn't Indri, like countless other women in Indonesia, be a mere side figure at his bidding, a glorified slave? Then again, Indri might not mind that.

"Well, what do you say?" pressed Rianto.

"Indri is not as ambitious as I am," Ani finally said. "I don't think she would mind being your household manager and the mother of your children. But there is a problem."

"What is that?"

"She wants to study art! She has her heart set on it."

Rianto scowled. "Art? Yes, your father mentioned that. Does she have to attend school for that? And can't she do the work of an artist at home?"

"To answer your first question, yes. I don't think Indri will be happy doing art at home until she has first had some kind of art education for at least a year. After that, she could probably do the work of an artist at home."

Rianto drummed his fingers on the table without changing his stern expression. "I might consider it once the children are in school."

Ani flushed with anger. "I hate to be disrespectful, Cousin, but if you want me to influence Indri to marry you, I suggest you pay for one year of art school *before* you marry her. Sort of as a dowry."

Rianto shook his head. "I am over 40. I have no children. I can't wait that long. If your sister married me, she could study both English and art here in the USA."

"Before she gets pregnant?"

"While she is pregnant."

Ani tried hard to suppress a laugh. "And what about the men she might meet at the school?" she asked.

"That's why I want her to study art while she's pregnant or already has a child. Less danger then. So if you refuse to marry me, I hope you can persuade her to be my wife. Perhaps as a thank you for my generosity in paying for your education?"

Ah, there it was—the favor he was expecting in return for his generosity! Inwardly she immediately vowed *not* to comply with his request but instead, warn Indri *not* to marry him. She took a bite of chiffon pie, drank two sips of water. "I will think about it. And if I refuse your marriage proposal, I will try to convince Indri to marry you," she said weakly. And as soon as she said that, she felt sick to her stomach. "Would you excuse me for a minute, please?" she asked, pushing back her chair as she shot up.

Rianto also rose, reached for her arm, and held it tightly. "Not before you explain where you are going," he said sternly.

Ani froze. His grip hurt. No man had ever touched her forcefully like that—not even her father, and indeed not Tom. She took a deep breath, her mind groping for the right words. "To the restroom," she said calmly. "My stomach..."

Rianto let go of his grip without apology.

With a flushed face, Ani hurried to the ladies' room and vomited into the toilet. As she washed her face and hands afterward, an image of Tom flashed into her mind. What a contrast between her cousin Rianto's harsh, frozen demeanor and Tom's playful grin, between Rianto's conditional marriage proposal and Tom's unconditional, gallant offer to help! What bothered her even more now was that if she refused to marry Rianto, he would propose to Indri, her pliable sister, who would take anything that would come her way as Allah's will. Would Ani be able to convince her not to marry this man? She was not sure.

When she returned to the table, she noticed a hundred-dollar bill, an envelope, and a small velvet box. "The money is for your taxi," he said. "The envelope contains a check for your educational and living expenses for the next six months. I promised your parents I will continue supporting you even if you did not marry me. But you understand, if you do marry me, your education will have to stop."

Ani nodded. "I understand."

"Now open the velvet box."

She obeyed. It contained a small keris pin, similar to hers.

"This pin is a replica of my family keris," Rianto said. "Note that *your* keris has only one tongue, but mine has two tongues. Just think—if our families merge through marriage, we'll have three!" He then handed her his card. "This is my Rhode Island address. Give yourself a a week to think about my proposal. If you say yes, you can keep the keris pin. If no, please return it to me. I will need it to give to your sister when I ask her to marry me."

Ani nodded in acknowledgment and put the velvet box into her purse. Taking his keris was not her first choice, but it was the polite thing to do for now. Besides, she owed him some show of gratitude for the money that would support her another six months. She would mail the keris back to him in less than a week, she was sure. After all, he really wanted to marry the more compliant and less ambitious Indri, did he not? And if Indri refused him, too, that would not be Ani's problem.

As she watched Rianto's short, stocky figure close the door of her taxicab and get into his, a mixture of loathing and gratitude toward her cousin churned inside her. Benefactor or not, he was one person she hoped she would never have to see again.

Chapter 23

Ani's concentration on studying hit a low after her luncheon with Rianto. She wished she could tell Sarah about his proposal. But would Sarah understand Ani's refusal? Or would she try to talk her into marrying him for his money? Ani also wondered how Tom would react if she told him about it.

"What are you doing right now, Ani?" she heard Tom ask when she answered her cell phone that Saturday afternoon.

"I'm trying to study. Why?"

"Have you had dinner yet?"

"No, but I had a huge lunch today, and I'm not hungry."

"Look. I've got to see you. It's rather urgent. How about dessert at Buffy's Buffet?"

"I'm trying not to eat any more desserts, Tom," she said, playing hard to get. "I have gained several pounds in America!" she added with a laugh.

"How about Buffy's Buffet for dinner tomorrow? It's not a fancy place, but you can pick and choose what and how much you want from the buffet. Given your high level of self-control and discipline, you won't add many calories there. I'll pick you up at 5:30. My treat this time—promise?"

At Buffy's the next day Ani ate as little as intended, confirming Tom's assessment of her self-control. After Tom had paid the waiter in cash, he ceremoniously placed an unwrapped black velvet box, two inches square, in front of Ani.

"What's this?" she asked. She slowly opened the box and peeked inside. She gasped when she saw a white gold ring with a small, glistening diamond nestled inside. A moment of stunned silence followed. "Tom," she finally stammered. "Where did you get this? Did you rob a jewelry store?"

"Of course not," he said, laughing. Then he grew serious, looking intently into Ani's face. "Do you know what this is and why I'm giving it to you, Ani?"

She stared blankly at him, faking oblivion. "As a farewell gift?"

"No," he said with a chuckle. "Go ahead. Try it on."

She did. It fit perfectly. "But why, Tom? This is too beautiful and expensive. Why are you giving this to me?"

"This is not just a gift, Ani. It has a special meaning." He waited a moment, hoping she would show signs of understanding. But she showed none. He swallowed hard, groping for the right words. "It means that you can finish your degree. You don't have to leave. You can even get a PhD here. And it means you can stay here in the USA indefinitely."

"This ring is worth *that* much if I trade it in?"

Tom shook his head in exasperation. "No, it's not. I mean, yes. But it's much more valuable than that. I'm not giving it to you so you can exchange it for money."

By then, Ani knew precisely what he had meant by this gift, but she decided to make it a bit hard for him. "Then why—?" she asked.

He leaned forward and took her hand. "This is an engagement ring, Ani. It's for you to wear for the rest of your life if you want to marry me."

"But why do you think I want to marry you?"

"Why would you *not*?"

"I asked you first."

"Okay. Well, I—" he stammered, "I think marrying me would make life easier for you! First, you wouldn't have to live in the dorm anymore. You could cook your favorite Indonesian food. I would pay for those extra expenses you can't pay now because your uncle got sick. I would offer you a home and teach you to drive."

Ani lowered her head. Her brows formed a slight frown, her lips tightened. *The whole thing sounds like a gesture of charity, not true love,* she thought. *What would he really think of me if I said yes? And what would he want in return?* She looked down at the ring on her finger and took it off, placing it back into the box. "It's a beautiful ring, Tom. But do you mean this to be a temporary arrangement? You wish to marry me so I can stay and get my degree? Is that all?"

"Of course not! You can also get a good job and stay in the USA forever!"

Ani shook her head. "I don't want to marry an American just so that I can get a degree and stay in the USA forever."

Tom hung his head. "Not even if it means being with me?"

"I didn't say that. Tom. I said I don't want to marry you for a visa or your financial support. It's unethical. Maybe even illegal if Immigration finds out." She wanted to add that she would marry him even if she did not need a visa or green card. But that would be too forward. She wanted him to be the first to express feelings of romance. And so far he had not done so. She looked into his eyes, waiting for the magical words *I love you. Will you marry me?* But he did not say them. And because he didn't, she asked, "May I ask you a few more questions?"

"Sure, ask all you want."

"I'm the eldest child in my family," she began. "In Indonesia, the eldest child has to care for her parents when they get old and then also for her younger siblings. Could you imagine having your parents-in-law live in your home so that you and I can take care of them?"

He nodded slowly. "Maybe."

"And can you see me financing my younger sister and my brother's education after we're married? Because that's my responsibility, too."

"It is? I guess that's okay."

"And I would maybe want my parents to live with us when we have a baby so that they can help take care of the baby when I'm working."

Tom gulped. But with a steady look into her dark almond eyes, he heard himself say, "Sounds like something we'll have to figure out when the time comes." *By then, we'll be rich anyway*, he thought. *We'll have a big house, a separate apartment in the house for your family, and we could even hire servants to help clean and cook.*

"Another question, Tom. What if I *never* learn to like American football?"

"Why would you *not*?" he asked, surprised.

"What if I try to like it just to please you, but later on, we both realize that I don't enjoy it as much as you do?"

Tom said nothing for a moment, scratching his head. "That's impossible. But if you really won't learn to like it, you could at least be sitting next to me or bring me beer and popcorn, right?"

"Maybe," Ani said, smiling as she shook her head. "The last few questions are the hardest: Would you be able to pay off all your credit cards at the end of each month and live without going into debt?"

His ears reddened. "I—I'm working hard on that," he stammered. "I will certainly try. You're good at managing money, so you can help me, right?"

Ani ignored his suggestion. "Could you survive without pepperoni pizza and beer when you come to my country?"

He sneered. "Why would I want to come to your country?"

"To meet my parents, of course. And who knows what the future will bring? I might get a better job in Indonesia and live there again. Don't you want to be with me forever, no matter where?"

His forehead wrinkled. "You aren't serious, are you?"

"I am very serious," as calmly as she could.

"Look," he said with a sigh. "Can we cross that bridge when we come to it? I mean, some things we can't know ahead of time. I just can't imagine why you would ever get homesick and want to go back there anyway. Isn't the USA almost like Heaven for most people? That's why we have so many immigrants!"

She laughed outwardly, but not inwardly, then shook her head. "Tom, I like America. But I also like my home country. My goal is to go back to Indonesia and make it a better place."

He scratched his head and let her words sink in. "Okay," he said slowly, "I'd be willing to consider all that, I guess! For you, I would try to do anything, Ani," he said. A promise to consider fulfilling a request is not the same as a promise to fulfill it, he reasoned. And, if necessary, even a verbal promise could be broken. That was an American value he knew would give him an out, just in case.

Ani shifted in her seat. "One last question. Would you consider becoming a Muslim?"

Tom gave out a loud laugh. "Now you are kidding, aren't you?"

With a serious face, she let him sweat it out for twenty seconds. Then she broke into a broad smile. "Yes, I'm kidding. And I don't expect you to turn me into a Christian."

"No worries. I'm not much of one, anyway. If I were, I probably wouldn't marry you."

"You wouldn't?"

"Well, a true follower of Jesus shouldn't marry someone who isn't one. It says that somewhere in the Bible." He paused a moment. "Well? Have I passed the test?" he asked, studying Ani's face. Her eyes were glowing, and her lips were formed into a Madonna smile.

Not waiting for an answer, he leaned forward and reached across the table to take both her hands into his. "Look, Ani. I think we're good for each other. We will enrich each other's lives. We can learn about each other's religion and tolerate our differences. We can decide to adapt to each other, negotiate, and renegotiate so that we'll both be happy. And your parents will come around to love me, too. You'll see." And with a slightly hoarse voice, he added, "You said earlier you *might* marry me if I were not your rescuer. What I want to know is, would you *want* to marry me even if I were not your rescuer?" It was a question he did not really want to ask for fear the answer would be a clear NO.

She smiled at him weakly. *Would I* want *to marry him?* She never dared to utter the word "want" as a child. No one ever asked her what she wanted except Uncle Lee. She wasn't even sure whether she knew what she wanted at all. Yes, she felt a flutter each time Tom called her on the phone. And yes, she felt flattered by his gallantry. He had proven to be humble and teachable. As for her parents, they would eventually forgive her if she married a non-Muslim American. The more Ani thought, the more she had to admit that her objections held as little water as fog under a warm sun.

But still, would she *want* to share her life, meals, bed, children, and future with him? As soon as she asked this question, the feeling of *wanting Tom* became more real than the ring in the velvet-lined case lying on the table.

"Ani, please answer me. Don't you *want* to marry me?" she heard him ask again. But something was still missing. The word *love,* for one. And a more romantic proposal, like the one in the movies. She stared at the ring in silence and waited.

Then, the magic moment happened. She saw Tom rise from his chair and, lowering one knee to the floor, kneel next to her. "Ani," she heard him say. "You are the smartest, most beautiful, nicest woman I have ever known. I want to spend the rest of my life with you. I'll do anything for you, even go to the opposite end of the globe. I love you, Ani. So, will you marry me?"

Those words produced just enough magic to result in an affirmative response, but her mouth was too dry to give it. She took a sip of water from the glass still on the table and looked down into Tom's face. "Yes," she whispered with a tear in her eye.

"What did you say?" she heard Tom ask timidly.

"Yes!" she repeated with a shout of glee. And when she said it, she felt like a seagull being carried away by a gusty breeze, and she didn't care where, or how far, that wind would take her.

Chapter 24

Ani could not sleep for a long time that night. Tossing and turning, she wondered whether her family should know or not. She realized she could not tell them for a very long time. Had not her father made her vow never to marry a foreigner? A small part of her wanted to tell Indri about Tom, but she knew Indri could not keep a secret for long. She finally decided to relay to her family only two facts for now: first, that Rianto would pay for her college expenses only if she did *not* marry him, and secondly, that she therefore declined Rianto's marriage proposal. She would send back Rianto's keris in the morning and thank him for his financial support. Then, she vowed, she would write and warn Indri not to marry Rianto.

The following weekend, Ani asked Sarah if she would bring her to the Osterhouses' house. She said she had some news to share with them in person.

A bear hug from Grace awaited her as usual. "Come to the family room, where I have some hot chocolate and peanut butter cookies waiting," Grace said.

Ani cringed. She liked peanut butter only when mixed with soy sauce on a chicken barbecue stick, not in sweet cookies. But she knew she had to try appreciating more American cuisine if she was going to marry Tom.

"Is it okay if we have a little farewell party for you the Sunday before you leave? You can invite anyone you like," said Grace as she pulled up a stool opposite the young women at the kitchen bar.

"That's very kind, Grace. But I came to tell you something you need to know," said Ani.

"Is it bad news? Don't tell me you're leaving sooner than expected."

Ani shook her head. "I'm not leaving at all!" she said, grinning impishly.

"You're not?" Sarah asked excitedly. "Why? What happened?"

"Another relative of mine, a very wealthy cousin, has agreed to pay for all my living expenses, academic fees, and books as long as I study here."

"Why, that's simply wonderful, Ani! We're so glad we're not losing you so soon," Grace exclaimed, giving Ani another big hug. Sarah chimed in with a cheer as well.

Fred stirred from the corner sofa in the family room. "What are all the hallelujahs about?" he shouted, turning down the volume of the television news.

"Ani can stay and finish her studies!" Grace answered.

"Well, that's real dandy," Fred said, getting up from his chair. He walked to the bar and grabbed a few cookies. "How did that happen?"

"Her cousin is paying for her expenses," said Grace. She clapped her hands. "We can have a party to celebrate, can't we?"

"I have one other news to share with you," said Ani with a nervous smile. "I'm engaged to be married. And we are planning a simple court wedding in two weeks."

In unison, her three friends cried, "What?!" and "Who?"

"To Tom Hanson," she replied in a soft voice and a telling sparkle in her eyes.

Silence fell into the room like a flannel-covered bomb. "Wow, Ani, that's sure a surprise," Grace finally said in a somber voice. "We had no idea that you two got to know each other well enough to get this serious."

"And why did you keep your relationship such a secret?" asked Sarah, visibly hurt.

"How long have you been engaged?" asked Grace.

"Are you pregnant?" shot Fred as he walked back toward his chair.

"No!" protested Ani with a laugh, blushing. "I don't believe in sex before marriage."

"Ah, so that explains the rush!" laughed Fred.

Grace sent Fred a reproving look. "Maybe we understand Tom's rush, but what is yours, Ani?" Grace asked with a concerned look. "You don't need to marry an American for a visa, now that your uncle is paying your way. And you always said you wanted to return to your country after you graduate."

"That's right. I want to marry him because I love him, and he loves me. And he said he would go to Indonesia with me."

"But Ani, do you know him well enough? I mean, how and when did you two see each other all this time without us knowing about it?"

"Yes," Ani replied. "We saw each other a lot. I didn't tell you about it because you warned me about him once, Grace, and I felt ashamed. But I was careful, and I believe he has changed a lot since I first met him."

Again, the response was silence. Grace got up and walked around the kitchen counter, pretending to get something from a drawer. Then she sat down again and faced Ani. "Honey, may I give you a bit of motherly advice?" She waited for a nod from Ani before she continued. "Marriage is a big step. You're entering a lifetime relationship with someone from another culture and different religion. That alone is a huge challenge." Grace touched Ani's hand across the counter. "But you need more time to prepare for such an important step, Ani. Can't you two wait until December? You should take a marriage preparation class together. I think the campus chaplain offers one."

"Yeah, Ani," chimed in Sarah. "We could have a real wedding then. You know, with a ceremony and a reception."

"It's your decision, of course," added Grace, touching Ani's arm.

Ani nodded in tears. She agreed with their advice, but how

would she convince Tom? She would tell him that her cousin gave her money to live on until then—which is the truth, anyway. But would Tom respect her wish to remain a virgin for another four months? What if he lost control and seduced—or worse, raped her? Or what if she gave in to him sexually, and she became pregnant, and he decided not to marry her in the end?

That night, Ani called Tom and asked to meet him in the student lounge.

"Fred, Grace, and Sarah want to help us have a real wedding," she began when they sat down on a sofa. "You know, a ceremony and a reception. And they think we need more time to prepare."

"So, they're worried about us rushing things?" Tom asked. "Don't they know we can always divorce later if it doesn't work out?"

Ani hit him in the forearm. "What?! No way!"

"Just kidding, my dear!" Tom said, laughing. He instantly realized this was not a joking matter to Ani. Marriage seemed to be sacred to her; he had better be careful not to say or do anything that would threaten her trust in or regard for him.

She snuggled close to Tom. "You know, honey, this next semester will be very stressful for me. I need to study for the GREs so I can be sure to get into graduate school by next January. I think I would rather spend the first month of marriage with you when I'm relaxed. So can we move the wedding to early December?"

"December?! But Ani!—"

"If you love me, you can wait, right?"

Tom gulped. "Of course. But I just don't want anything to come between us, Ani. That's all."

"Like what?"

"Like—" He paused for a moment. "Like I'm worried that the more time we spend arguing about our differences, the harder it will be to stay together."

Ani snickered and shook her head. "I think the opposite is true. The more we think and talk about our differences before we marry, the better chance for a happy relationship later on! No surprises, no shock."

"Yeah, okay. But we've talked so much already! I prefer celebrating what we have in common, for heaven's sakes, and getting on with the show!"

"Show? Marriage is only a show to you?"

"That's not what I meant. It's an expression that means 'let's get started.' Let me be honest, Ani. I'm a man. It will be hard to be around you that long without touching you."

"I also promised Grace and Fred that we would attend a marriage preparation class first."

Tom hit his forehead. "That, too? Oh, brother."

"Maybe you don't need it, but I do," she said in a childlike tone as she laid her head on his shoulder. "This is a big step, and I'm scared."

Tom put his arm around her and caressed her neck. "You bewitch me, you know," he cooed. "How can I refuse any of your wishes?"

Ani closed her eyes and smiled. She had appealed to his chauvinistic, rescuing nature once again, and it had worked.

"Wait a minute," Tom suddenly said, gently moving his hand away from her neck and facing her. "What about the money you need for your dormitory housing and student fees? You could save that money if you moved in with me."

"Oh, that's right," she said with an embarrassed smile. She did not know for a moment what to say next. She did not she want to tell him about Rianto, her long-term benefactor. If she did, she might lose Tom. "Oh, I just remembered something! My family has an emergency fund with a little savings set aside for me. I will ask if enough of it is available."

"Well, that's a relief. But Ani, please let me know if that doesn't work out. I can find another way, I'm sure."

Tom tried hard to hide his disappointment. He wanted to be her one-hundred-percent hero. And now it turned out that Ani might not need him as imminently as he thought she did. At least it was only an "emergency savings" she could fall back on. For her long-term need, he would still be her hero.

He felt a tight squeeze on the hand. "And you will have more time to pay off your credit cards and pay for our honeymoon," he heard Ani say. "You promised that, remember?"

Tom groaned a little. "Guess so," he mumbled.

The first semester had begun. In search of a chaplain who could perform their wedding ceremony in the university chapel, Ani made an appointment with Ms. Shirley Daniels, the international student advisor on campus.

"Do you know of a priest or mullah or someone who would perform a marriage ceremony between a Muslim and a non-Muslim?" Ani asked.

"Oh dear, not one of those again!" said Ms. Daniels, rolling her eyes. "It's you that's getting married, isn't it?"

Ani nodded and smiled.

"When are you planning on getting married?"

"The first weekend in December, right after my exams."

Ms. Daniels leaned forward in her chair. "And your fiancé is an American, and he doesn't know anyone who could perform such a ceremony?"

"Yes."

"He *does* know someone? Or do you mean no, he doesn't?"

"No, he does not," Ani corrected with a smile of embarrassment.

"Glad I asked," said the advisor as she typed something into the computer. "I assume you are just interested in a marriage certificate so you can get a permanent visa, isn't that so?"

"Oh, no, Ms. Daniels. I would never do that. We're in love!"

"That's what they all say," mumbled Shirley Daniels as she pulled out a brochure.

"My uncle pays for my education here, and my fiancé plans to go back to my country with me some day."

"I've heard that before, too," said Shirley. "Well, that's none of my business now, is it? Back to your question. I'm sure one of the chaplains at the university would perform a ceremony for you if available in early August or early December." She pulled out a business card and handed it to Ani. "Try this one—the Reverend Nanette Underwood. She also conducts premarital counseling sessions, which I highly recommend before you get married." She scribbled the name on a piece of scrap paper and handed it to Ani. "You'll like her. She's real nice."

A wedding ceremony with a woman presiding? Why not? Truly very American, Ani thought.

"One more thing, Ani. Did you know that you have to wait two months after your official wedding is registered with the county court before your husband can file a petition with the US Immigration and Naturalization Services for a permanent visa for you?"

"No problem," Ani replied. "No hurry for that."

"Well, just in case… You should know, once you apply, you will have to wait for an interview and some more months before being granted permanent resident status. If, for some reason, you separate or get a divorce before then, the petition will be counted null and void. It's also wise to collect pictures of your relationship with dates printed on them, to show them you've been married and living together for at least six months. Also, bring a list of witnesses who can vouch that you are married and not just fake married. Do you understand me so far, Ani?"

"Yes, I understand," Ani said politely. "But—"

"One more thing, Ani." Ms. Daniels interrupted. "I have to ask you this. Has your family in Indonesia been struck hard by the Asian market crash?"

"Yes, some of them have."

"So, how are you going to finance your stay here?"

"I have a cousin who said he could pay for everything."

"That's good. But if anything changes with your finances, don't be afraid to let me know," Shirley Daniels said in a softer tone. "I hear you are a good student. We can get you some aid or try to help you get a campus job if you need one by fall."

"Thank you," Ani said.

Ms. Daniels rose from her chair. "Glad you're not marrying for a visa or money. But I'm going to be very blunt with you, Ani. Love is often blind, even between people of the same culture. And from my observation, cross-cultural marriages seldom last long. *So* may I give you a piece of advice? Make sure you and your fiancé take that marriage preparation class with Ms. Underwood."

Chapter 25

"Call me Nanette," said Rev. Dr. Nanette Underwood when Ani and Tom sat down in her office. Ani guessed Nanette to be in her late thirties.

Nanette's warm welcome toward Ani and Tom put them at ease. She wore a long, flowing chiffon skirt with purple flowers, and her blouse matched a hip-length jacket of the same color. A long string of black beads hung loosely over her chest.

"So you two want to get married," she began. "Can you tell me how you met each other?" Bent slightly toward them as she sat on her secretarial chair, she listened to them tell their story in a ping-pong fashion. Her gray eyes moved from one speaker to the other, her head nodding occasionally, her lips partially opened for an instant smile.

"You certainly look and sound like you're in love," Nanette remarked. "But I marry couples only after they've had at least five hour-long sessions of premarital counseling and two group sessions. Are you willing to do that?"

They nodded.

"And since you are an intercultural couple, I recommend you talk a lot about your cultural differences."

"I think it would be safer if we don't talk about our differences," Tom retorted.

"Safer?" Nanette asked, smiling wryly. "Nothing is 100 percent safe in this world. But I think it's safer if you know what might eat away at your relationship and deal with it, and the sooner, the better. Those underlying differences will come up, whether you like it or not. Of course, how well you deal with these differences depends on how well you resolve conflict."

"Here is a question I want you to think about and discuss before I see you next week." She handed them each a piece of paper with the following questions:

1. *Which of your partner's cultural tastes, beliefs, customs, and hobbies are you willing to take on as your own?*
2. *Which ones will you at least tolerate (without trying to change them)?*
3. *Which ones do you feel you must try to change in your partner so that you can live with him or her?*

"Well, I know about some of our differences, and we're okay with them, aren't we?" asked Tom. He looked at Ani. "Like—you're a Muslim, and I'm not. You eat lots of fried rice and chicken, and well—I'd rather have a pork chop and a baked potato. You're learning to like baseball and American football, and I'm trying to keep a budget and spend within our means."

Ani hung her head and waited a moment before speaking. "I do miss many things about my Indonesian culture. I am starting to forget them. I am afraid I must give them up."

"That's very noble of you, Ani, but if you squash them now, they might pop up—you know, surface—when you're under stress. They are part of who you are, whether they're always evident or not. And when they do pop up now and then, they might cause trouble between you both. Want to give question one a try?"

Tom piped up first. "You don't have to give up any of your culture or religion for me," he asserted. "Same way you don't expect *me* to give up football for *you*, do you?"

She laughed. "I will let you watch all the football you want, but on one condition."

"What's that?"

"That you don't expect me to like it as much as you."

Tom hung his head, suppressing his disappointment with a weak smile. "Okay," he finally said. "But what can we do together on a Sunday afternoon?"

"I suggest you write down your answers on the back of the sheet. Then plan a time when you can exchange your answers and talk about them."

The next session with Nanette had to do with power in the relationship. "Let me venture to guess something here," Nanette began. "Tom, I bet you think you're really worth a lot in this relationship because you think you hold the key to Ani getting her education. Am I right?"

Ani was about to protest when Nanette added, "That gives Tom full power in the relationship. And that makes me wonder—once Ani gets her degree, what would be Tom's role—or power—in the relationship?"

Silence hung in the room for a few seconds. Tom finally spoke with an impish sort of smile. "I hope she will be eternally grateful and love me forever."

"But—but that is not why I want to marry you, Tom," Ani protested, careful not to reveal the whole truth about her financial status. "I do not need your money to love you forever."

"Not even a visa?" Nanette asked.

Ani shook her head. "Not even a visa."

"I like that, Ani. What do you think about that, Tom?"

Tom squirmed in his chair. He had not thought of that. He had to admit that his version of power meant providing his woman with a pretty house, nice furniture, and a new car. But if at some point she did not need his money anymore, would she still stay at his side? He wasn't sure. He shook his head and combed his hair with his fingers. "I'm not sure if she would love me once she's got it all," he said slowly.

Ani hit him on the arm. "Tom! What makes you say such a thing? I love *you* for who you are, not for anything you would give to me." Her eyes watered as she said it.

Tom just stared at her. Her words hit the top of his head, but not his understanding. He could not imagine them to be true.

"Never mind about that now, Tom," said Nanette. "Let me ask this: How would you feel about *yourself* if Ani became more self-sufficient and independent—and even more successful than you?"

Tom's ears reddened, his every muscle in his body tensed. "I'd have to think about that," he muttered. He knew right then he would have to be more successful in material gain than Ani. He would simply have to be.

In one session with other couples, Nanette asked Ani to tell the group about a typical wedding in Indonesia's Sunda region. Ani's eyes lit up as she remembered her cousin's wedding the year before. "The wedding lasts for days, but I will try to give you a summary. Is that okay?"

"The day before a Sunda wedding," she began, "the couple has an hour of Islamic prayers and Koran scripture reading. Then a respected person advises the couple. In a ceremony after that, the bride uses holy water from Mecca in a pitcher full of flowers to wash her father's feet while he strokes and kisses her head. It's a very emotional ceremony. While she does that, she asks forgiveness of her father for anything she might have done or said that displeased him. And then she repeats the same thing with her mother."

"That's unreal!" piped up a young African-American woman in the class. "On the Oprah Winfrey show, I saw the *parents* kneel before *the children* and ask their forgiveness for their wrongs. That's the American way."

The group participants laughed. "What happens after that, Ani?" queried Nanette.

"They all go to the garden, where the bride sits on a stool under a ceremonial yellow umbrella. There's a carpet of long pieces of batik sarong material on the ground, sprinkled with jasmine blossoms, all the way from inside the house to the place where she sits."

"Cool. Like for a king and queen," interjected a Caucasian American woman.

"Exactly," Ani continued. "And that's how they're treated the next day—like a king and queen. After that, a respected elder takes a vessel of water filled with flowers and—"

A loud snore next to Ani caused a ripple of laughter from the others. It had been Tom's snore. He sat up, bewildered. "What do they do on the Oprah Winfrey show?" he asked. Everyone laughed but Ani. She knew he was tired because of another late-night moonlighting expedition, but she felt embarrassed for him.

"One by one," she continued, "the guests dip a ladle two or three times into the large brass container of flower water and shower the bride with it while saying a short prayer of blessing over the bride."

"Not the groom?" asked Tom.

"No, sorry, not the groom," laughed Ani.

"This is fascinating, Ani," Nanette said, getting up from her chair. "But we're running out of time today to hear the rest. I'm wondering, Ani, could you somehow integrate some of these traditions into your wedding ceremony here?"

"I don't think so," Ani replied, shrugging her shoulders. "I have no batik sarong. No holy water. No jasmine flowers. And my parents won't be here. And none of this is done here in the United States." She fought back the tears. The reality of that last sentence pounded at her brain like the pecking of a woodpecker.

But she had chosen it to be that way—for Tom.

When she returned to her dorm room that evening, she checked her email. She found one from Indri.

Dear Sister,

I hope you are well and happy. I have some exciting news: Father's cousin Rianto came to our house yesterday and proposed to me! Of course, I accepted! I know you warned me about him, but I think he is a

> *good man. He brought us many gifts from America, and he gave me a beautiful gold necklace.*
>
> *We will have the wedding in early May. Then we will fly to his home in a small city near Providence. How far away is that from Baltimore? He promised to let me go to an art school. Can you imagine me, a bride? I will try not to run up the hill anymore.*
>
> *Please write soon!*
>
> *Your sister, Indri*

Ani stared at the email for a long time. Yet the news came as no surprise. She knew Indri would welcome anything that came her way, even if Ani had warned her not to. Indri believed that everything was Allah's will and would therefore end well. And sometimes it did! But how could Indri ever learn to love a man like him? He was so cold and unromantic, not to mention much too old.

It did surprise Ani that Rianto would allow Indri to study art. The thought of Rianto marrying her sweet, innocent sister made Ani shudder. And when she realized she would be missing her sister's wedding and all the festivities and traditions along with it, her eyes welled with tears.

"Life is unfair," she said aloud as she bit her lip. For the first time, she was not proud of her own choices.

A pang of fear followed: What if Indri somehow found out that Ani had married an American? Indri could never keep secrets.

Chapter 26

"Emmanuel, could you be the best man just in case Solomon doesn't make it on time?" asked Tom nervously as they waited in a side room just outside the front of the chapel. "He's already nineteen minutes late."

"Sure, but I'm not wearing a tux, and I don't have the rings."

"Forget the tux. And I have the rings," said Tom, pulling two rings from his pocket and handing them to Emmanuel. "I think we better go in." The soft tones of an electric organ accompanied them as they entered the chapel. They saw that a small group of people had already taken their seats when the two men entered. A green wreath with a white bow hung over each window in the college chapel. An enormous arrangement of chrysanthemums, also known as Chinese snowballs, in lilac and soft blue graced the podium. On a high table in the corner stood two unlit white candles in bronze candleholders with an even taller one between them.

Just then, the side door opened, and Solomon entered, tall and stately in a black tuxedo. He filed between Tom and Emmanuel. "You must be Solomon," Emmanuel whispered, handing him the rings. "I'm Emmanuel, the almost–best man."

Moments later, a rich alto voice sang the Celine Dion song "Because You Loved Me."

As Tom's eyes perused the group of twenty guests seated in the pews, he felt a tinge of regret. His parents were not there! His father had pneumonia, and so neither came. Tom consoled himself with the thought that they might have complained about the cost of such an event. Not that the wedding cost him a fortune; the Osterhouse family were to thank for that. They paid for Ani's bridal gown and arranged for friends from the church to provide the flowers and the reception dinner. Solomon's advance covered the tuxedo rentals for Tom and himself—also the use of the chapel and the honorarium for the chaplain. But still, it would have been nice to have his parents there.

Bill, the youngest of the Osterhouse sons, stood to the side, waiting to take pictures. He said he would produce a photo album for the couple as a wedding present. Bill's wife, stationed at the far right, covered both the audience and the wedding party with her video camera.

Sounding out from Tom's old boom box, which hid behind the corner flower arrangement, the majestic overture of the third act of Wagner's opera *Lohengrin* now filled the chapel. Tom's German grandfather used to listen to that opera many times. Sarah slowly walked down the aisle wearing a yellow floor-length chiffon dress and a bouquet of blue and lilac snowballs while the music played. She lit two of the three candles, one on each side of the one in the middle, then stood to the left side of the altar.

When the operatic chorale began to sing the famous wedding tune, "Here Comes the Bride," in German, the small group of wedding guests rose to their feet and watched Ani glide slowly and gracefully toward the altar. Tom's eyes shone, and so did hers.

Dr. Nanette Underwood stepped forward in her long black robe. "Today, we celebrate a new beginning," she began in a formal, high-pitched tone. "The beginning of a confirmed and hopefully long-lasting union between Ani Su Li Sunatu and Thomas Jay Hanson. We are all here to witness this timeless ceremony of leaving and cleaving, a ceremony that in the sacred writings of Christendom symbolizes an even greater union—the union between Christ and his followers, or the church."

A slight frown formed on Tom's forehead as he inwardly apologized to Ani. He had not expected Nanette to use Christian theological lingo. Didn't she remember that Ani was a Muslim? But

Ani's face showed no disturbance. Hers was that of an angel, looking as if she focused on nothing but happiness itself.

Nanette continued in a more conversational tone. "Today's ceremony is like a send-off into orbit!" she said. "Imagine Tom and Ani in a space capsule together—for life!"

Everyone laughed, except Tom. He almost froze at the thought, but when he saw Ani's laughing eyes, he relaxed. If she was willing, he would be, too, he told himself.

"Fortunately, marriage isn't quite like that," Nanette continued. "But there's a point to this analogy, which you will see in a minute. When we're born," Nanette continued, "we humans are naked, alone, and vulnerable. We survive only by connection with others. When we grow up to be adults, we're still in need of being intimately connected with someone other than ourselves. There's proof that adults who have such a connection are healthier than those who do not. Marriage should be such a connection. But it is so much more than a formality between sexual partners. It should be a couple's deep, continuous commitment to being there for each other until death separates them.

"Before all of us, Ani Sunatu and Thomas Hanson declare their intention of such a lifelong connection and commitment to each other." She turned toward Tom and Ani and asked, "Am I right?"

"I'm sorry," said Tom. "I wasn't listening. Can you repeat that, please?"

Everyone laughed, even Ani.

"You're declaring before everyone here your intention of a lifelong connection and commitment to each other. Right?" repeated Nanette.

The couple nodded.

"As I said before, you two are about to embark on a journey in a space capsule together. Your hormonal and emotional attraction to each other gave you just enough fuel to get the rocket into orbit. But I have bad news for you both. Your space capsule may run out of fuel sooner than expected. And in case it does, I'm now going to give you five tips, which, if you follow them, will turn this romantic send-off into a beautiful ride in orbit. Here we go.

"First, resolve to make it work, no matter what. That's what astronauts do when they climb into that space shuttle and take off. Once that shuttle takes off, there's no turning around.

"Second, watch out for your health and safety. For the two of you to function well together, you will each need to be a strong, able, and high-functioning partner. To become that and stay that way, you first need to stay connected to the One who created you, who knows how you function as individuals, and who can show you how you can click together as partners.

"Third, don't wander off in space by yourself without staying connected. That means, keep in close and open communication with each other, affirm and express regard for each other, and honestly tell each other what's troubling you. It also means don't allow anyone else to get as much devotion and romantic attention from you as your spouse.

"Fourth, celebrate your differences! Accept and value the fact that you are two different individuals. If you can't do that now, most likely, you never will. *To accept* does not necessarily mean to *agree with* or to *like.* It means to *respect* each other's individuality without pressuring the other to change. And to *value* the other person's uniqueness means allowing that person's culture, beliefs, thought, and habits to supplement and enrich yours. And when new differences pop up, don't panic. Resolve to focus on what unites you, then accept, tolerate, adapt, and adjust when it comes to the new. It's hard work! But it's worth it.

"And fifth, if possible, keep the morale in the capsule as high as your orbit in space. How? Speak and do what's best for each other's whole person, body, mind, and emotions, no matter how you feel. It means affirming, encouraging, and comforting each other, telling each other the truth in a loving way, forgiving each other, and sticking together through thick and thin.

"And now," Nanette continued, "are you ready to state your marriage vows?"

The couple nodded and turned to face each other.

"I, Thomas Jay Hanson," began Tom as he read from an index card he pulled out from his pocket, "pledge to commit myself to you, Ani, as my exclusive lover and marriage partner."

"I, Ani Su Li Sunatu, pledge to commit myself to you, Tom, as my exclusive lover and marriage partner," she echoed from memory. Then, they each repeated the rest of the vows that Grace and Sarah had helped Ani write with Tom's quick approval:

"I promise to love, value, and honor you as you are, to support you in your goals, dreams, and endeavors as long as they are healthy for the both of us, and to pursue peace and truth in resolving conflicts as long as we both shall live."

Then, Nanette asked the question, "Tom and Ani, do you promise to care for your physical, emotional, and spiritual well-being so that you can serve each other well as long as you live?" They both said, "Yes."

"What token do you give each other, symbolizing your commitment to each other?"

Solomon handed them the rings. Tom placed one on Ani's finger, and Ani placed Tom's on his. Then the couple walked over to the three candles in the corner. They each picked up a lit candle and held it to the wick of the third until it lit up. Then they blew out the other two and laid them down.

"This lit candle symbolizes that Tom and Ani are now one," exclaimed Nanette as they faced her again. "Tom and Ani, by the authority given to me by the State of Maryland, I now pronounce you man and wife. You may now kiss each other."

They kissed ten seconds too long for Nanette, who finally tapped Tom on the shoulder. Laughter filled the room.

About twenty adults and four children filed into the adjoining room for tea and hors d'oeuvres. Indonesian *gamelan* music blasted through Sarah's boom box. Sitting at the head table, Ani stared into the dancing candlelight on the lavishly laid buffet table in front of her, trying to capture this happy moment and freeze it into her memory.

But a nagging funnel of pain twirled its way into her consciousness—the realization that her family and friends were far, far away. They didn't even know about this most significant event in her life! She felt disconnected; her past and present seemed too far removed from each other. Not even her Indonesian friends—both in Indonesia and in Maryland—knew about this joyous event. Her marriage had to remain a secret.

Ani felt Tom's hand rubbing her back gently. "Are you all right?" She nodded as she wiped her eyes.

"Ladies and gentlemen," Fred Osterhouse called out, "we now have a surprise. The bride will sing us an Indonesian wedding song."

Tom's mouth fell open. "I didn't know Ani sings," he muttered to Solomon as Ani stood up and walked over to the microphone. Everyone quieted down their chatter and looked at Ani.

"This is a love song to you, my groom," she said. "It says I am your only love forever." Sarah's boom box accompanied Ani as her silky voice began to sing a melody with words in the Sundanese Indonesian dialect. She guessed that most people present might not appreciate this style of music. But she hoped Tom's smiles meant that at least he was touched by it. And as she sang, her eyes filled with tears. Tom had been willing to wait and to marry later than he had wanted. And he did so for her.

"More, more!" Solomon urged as everyone clapped at the end of her song. But Ani coyly shook her head and allowed Tom to hug her.

"Could you translate the whole song, please?" someone asked.

"I will translate later for Tom," Ani answered in a seductive tone. "In private." A choral response of "Ooo!" filled the room.

"And now," said Grace loudly enough for all to hear, "I believe we have two musicians here to provide us with some dance music. Mr. Solomon Elijah on the saxophone and accompanying him on the guitar, my son-in-law, Bruce!" announced Grace. Everyone clapped as the two musicians took their positions and began to play.

As some of the guests jumped up to dance, Sarah snuck out of the room, hoping no one would notice. But Emmanuel noticed. And after a while, he too left the party room. He found her standing in the kitchen by the sink with her back toward him. Her head bent downward, and her hands were resting on the edge of the sink. She was sniffling.

"There you are!" he said, rushing to her. "My, oh my, what have we here? Tears? What's wrong?" he softly asked as he laid his hand on her shoulder.

Another sniffle, and then another. Sarah wiped her face with her forearm.

He reached for a paper towel from the counter and handed it to her. "Will this do?" he asked.

"Thanks," she laughed between her tears and wiped her face.

"Come. Can't we sit down somewhere?" Emmanuel asked. She nodded. He pulled two chairs from a stack in the corner, seated her first, and then sat down across from her. "I think you should free yourself from these torturous shoes. Can I massage your feet a little?"

She giggled. "Just a little. I'm very ticklish."

Her feet did not tickle as he massaged them on the side where they hurt the most. "That feels good," she said. "Thanks." She pulled back her feet and put on her pumps again.

"Your foot pain isn't why you've been crying, is it?"

"No," she said.

"Do you want to talk about it?"

Her eyes watered afresh. "I—I think I made a horrible mistake," she began. "I should have spoken out against this wedding more strongly. I mean, to Ani, of course. Tom reminds me so much of my dad. He was a loser and very irresponsible, and my mother always had to rescue him. I know in my heart that God uses our mistakes and sometimes turns them around for our good. I also know that God is so much bigger than all our nearsightedness. But today, I'm having a hard time believing that. I'm sorry—maybe I'm just not very rational right now." She paused and heaved a sigh. "I just can't help thinking that if this marriage fails, it will be my fault for not warning Ani ahead of time."

Emmanuel let her cry a bit more and found another tissue to give her. "So why didn't you warn her?"

"Because I was hoping it would be all right. Ani is a strong, smart woman. So far, she's been a good influence on him."

"And you're not so sure about what happens next?"

"I'm not. Now that Tom has Ani, he might relax too much and change back to what he was before. She's strong and smart, but even the strong and smart ones can't change another adult so easily. And I'm worried about the children they're going to have."

"Tom would have to want to change for his own good, not just for Ani," Emmanuel added. "And you never know about how the children would turn out. Look at you—I'm sure glad your parents got together and produced you. Despite their mistakes, you turned out okay!"

Sarah laughed modestly, looking into Emmanuel's compassionate face for a long moment, the longest she remembered ever looking into a man's eyes. They made her feel safe—safer than she had ever dreamed she could feel in the presence of a man.

Just then, Grace's eighty-five-year-old aunt popped her head in through the open door and out again. "Oh my!" they heard her mumble. "*Another* colorful couple." And the woman disappeared again.

Emmanuel and Sarah looked at each other and burst out laughing.

Chapter 27

The wedding was now history. To add feminine touches to Tom's apartment, Ani used finds from estate sales she visited with Grace: a purple bedspread, a new set of dishes, a framed picture of an ocean shore, an area rug, and a bouquet of silk roses in a vase. Fred had brought in a new bookcase as a wedding present, Grace added two decorative pillows to the sofa, and Sarah gave Ani a new rice cooker. Emmanuel gave them a wooden garlic crusher, made in India. Ani now truly felt at home in America.

Well, almost. "Look what I brought home today," Tom announced as he entered the apartment after work. "Can you help me bring it in? It's on top of the car."

Ani peered out through the window. It was a small fir tree. She could not help but laugh. "I thought you didn't care much for Christian traditions," she said.

"I never said I didn't care about *any* of them," he retorted. "Would be fun decorating our first tree together, wouldn't it? I even got some lights and a few decorations to hang up."

"Okay," she said, "as long as you fast Ramadan with me starting next week."

"Ramadan? I forget. Don't you eat only after sunset and before sunrise?"

She nodded.

"Is it really necessary for me to join you in this? I mean, that's not a very good deal, especially since I'd have to do this for a whole month. Why can't you just cook more and let me microwave the leftovers during the day?"

"It's not just the extra work, honey," she replied as she put her hand on his chest and gave him a quick kiss. "I just want you to eat with me, that's all. I miss eating with my family. Now you are my family."

"Wish I had brought the tree earlier so I can enjoy it equal time. But all right. I'll eat with you during the night. Can't promise I'll wake up to eat before sunrise, though."

"You will. I'll see to that!" she said, giggling.

Their first Christmas together was more fun than Ani had expected. Tom surprised her on Christmas morning with a stocking that contained not only chocolates but a key—the second key to his Mustang. "You told me you can drive but didn't dare to do it in the USA because we drive on the wrong side of the road here," he said. "But it's time you learn." And so, with Tom at her side, Ani practiced driving on the "wrong" side of the road. And within one week, he took her to the motor vehicle bureau to get her American driver's license. The written test was not as easy for Ani as she thought it would be. A few rules were different in the USA, but she passed.

Ramadan—her first as a married woman—began. After dark, Tom ate the evening meals with her, but not the other two. He needed his sleep, he said, and he had to work all day. But having at least one meal together with him served to curb Ani's homesickness. Insisting on the fast alleviated the guilt she felt for marrying a non-Muslim. She hoped Allah would forgive her once she could give alms to the poor, but that would have to wait until she got her master's degree and earned a good living. Not that such generous actions guaranteed paradise. But, at least she would try her best to get there.

When the Ramadan month ended four weeks later, she missed having the rest of her family to feast with her and Tom. Fred and Grace could not come; they had left for Florida right after New Year's. Only Sarah and Emmanuel were planning to come to celebrate.

The morning of the feast, which fell on a Saturday, Ani woke

Tom with a kiss. "Hey, Tom, I want to reward you with a special breakfast dish."

"Reward me for what?" he asked sleepily.

"For fasting Ramadan with me. At least part of the time. How about if I make pancakes?"

"Do you know how to make them?" he asked. Just the thought of pancakes gave him the energy to glide out of bed.

"No, no, no. You stay there," Ani said as she covered him with the blanket and pegged a kiss on his lips. "It might take me a while. So you can sleep a bit longer." He playfully grabbed hold of her bathrobe, but she slid away and danced off to the kitchen.

Sometime later, he woke up to a smell he could not identify. His heart sank. What happened to his American breakfast? Yet, in his pajamas with his strands of hair standing upward in total dissymmetry, he ventured into the kitchen. "Are you still making pancakes?"

"Sure am! Want to taste?" she asked, steering a forkful of something into his mouth. Tom made a face.

"Don't you like it?"

"Interesting" was all he could say. He sat down, meekly managing to eat a whole pancake. "What did you put in this?" he asked, trying hard not to betray his dislike for what he was eating.

"Onions, garlic, and some cayenne pepper. Good, isn't it?" she said, chewing happily.

"So, are Emmanuel and Sarah coming over for dinner tonight? If so, what are we going to feed them?"

"I'm hoping you can buy some fried chicken and potato salad on the way home after you play tennis at the indoor club. I will stir-fry some vegetables. They are bringing some ice cream."

"Sounds good."

The American version of Eid feast was, at least, a festive one. The four of them played the Maji game that Sarah brought. Afterward, Tom brought some fresh sodas to Ani and the guests and helped himself to a beer. Sitting down again, he asked, "So what's new with you guys? How is your thesis coming along, Emmanuel?"

"Very well, thank you, Tom," Emmanuel answered. "Everything is going like clockwork. I should be finished by May of this year. Then I must wait around for the professors to review it and interview me before I can graduate, which I hope will be in August."

"Neat, bro. That's neat."

Emmanuel looked at Sarah, who gave him a nod. "Sarah and I have an announcement to make," he said.

Ani gasped. "You do?" she said, clapping her hands together.

"It's not what you're thinking yet," said Sarah quickly. "But go ahead, Emmanuel. Tell them."

"We've gotten to know each other for over a year now, and we want to consider all the angles of a future relationship. Therefore—" Emmanuel stopped, nodding at Sarah to continue for him.

"Therefore," said Sarah, "I am going to leave for South India in September for a nine-month research and teaching assignment at a university for women."

"Nine months? Are you pregnant?" piped Tom.

"No, of course not!" Sarah said, slapping his shoulder. "We think it would be a good idea for me to experience Emmanuel's home territory before we decide on marriage. You do know that he wants to return to India, don't you?"

"Sarah was the one who suggested her living there, not me," added Emmanuel. "And I agree it's a good thing."

"And what happens if you find out Sarah's not cut out for India? Are you going to be able to break up?" Tom asked.

Emmanuel sighed, looking at Sarah. "We'll cross that bridge when we come to it."

"You guys have guts," said Tom, shaking his head. "Waiting so long, I mean."

Ani abruptly excused herself and left the dining area of the kitchen. She had listened to the conversation without saying a word. No one except Sarah had noticed her eyes filling with tears.

Sarah followed her to the hallway. "Ani? What's wrong?"

Ani leaned against the wall and wiped her tears. "You said you'd be there for me if I ever needed to talk. How can you if you are going so far away?"

Sarah put her hand on Ani's shoulder. "I'll have my laptop with me. We'll email each other. And besides, I'll still be here for two more months. By then, your marriage will have all its wrinkles ironed out."

"I hope so," Ani said, smiling between sniffles. "It's just that you are my only sister in America. I will miss you so much."

Ani was sorting the mail the following Monday, throwing several pieces of advertisement into the trash. "Looks like there's a letter for you, Tom," she said as she laid an envelope on the table next to his mug. "I think it's from your mother,"

Tom took a deep breath and held it for ten seconds. "Would you read it first?" he asked, handing Ani the letter. He had not heard from his parents since they canceled coming to his wedding because his father had pneumonia. Tom's preoccupation with marriage adjustment, work, and "moonlighting mission" assignments had prevented him from checking on them. At least that was his excuse. *No news is good news,* Tom consoled himself. His father had probably recovered by now.

Ani cut the envelope open with the keris pin hanging from her necklace. "'Dear Tom,'" she read aloud. "'We are so sorry to have missed your wedding. Dad is doing much better now. We want to see you again and meet your Ani. How about coming to Ohio for a weekend and introducing her to us? Your dad and I have always wanted a daughter. Let us know your schedule.'"

Tom gaped. "She wrote that?"

She returned the letter to him so he could see for himself. "Well, in that case, I can't wait to meet your parents. Especially your mom," she said. "Let's go when my quarter exams are done in March."

"Are you sure about that? You might hate my parents. Especially my mother."

"How can I hate the woman who bore you? She is your mother. We always say in Indonesia, 'Heaven is under a mother's feet.'"

"I thought that grown-ups weren't supposed to need their parents anymore."

"That's a Western point of view. In my culture, parents never let go of their children, and vice versa."

"Except when the children marry non-Muslim Americans," he retorted with sarcasm.

His words felt like gasoline splashed on Ani's face. Perhaps he was right. Maybe her family was not as close and loving as she had always believed. But she had yet to find out for sure.

Chapter 28

A thick February fog had wrapped around Tom's car in the dark as he drove to Solomon Elijah's apartment complex. At one point, he barely missed a ditch along the way.

"How is your cash supply, Tom? For gasoline, for example?" Solomon asked soon after Tom arrived.

"Nil, of course. And my last credit card is pretty much maxed out. I promised Ani I wouldn't charge more than what I can pay off in full when a payment is due."

"Okay, here is some to keep you going to do the job I hired you for," Sol replied, handing him a thick envelope.

Tom opened the envelope. He counted twenty one-hundred-dollar bills neatly packed together. "Thanks," he said casually. But inside, his heart beat as loudly as the grandfather clock ticking in the corner of Solomon's living room. "Just curious—why do you always give me cash?"

Solomon smiled. "As long as the money isn't counterfeit and it's yours, you have nothing to worry about. Remember, this is a secret mission. There must be no paper trails. No one can trace anything if it's in cash. Do what you want with it. But if I were you, I'd put it in a savings account or reinvest it. Or start paying into a retirement fund if you don't already have one. Of course, you could always give it back to me. I have this great lead on an oil drilling project."

"No, thanks."

"Are you sure now?" Solomon's voice sounded half sarcastic, half good-hearted.

"I'm sure," Tom said as he rose from his chair and stretched.

Once in the car, he stuffed the envelope under the seat and sped back to his home. Tomorrow, he would deposit the money into the bank, pay off his credit card, and start a savings account. A few more deposits like this, and he would buy Ani a ten-year-old Ford; perhaps he could even put a down payment on a house. He hoped all of that would give her plenty of reasons to hold on to him forever.

When he had walked from the car to his apartment building, Ani was already asleep. He tiptoed into the kitchen and helped himself to a few beers before going to bed himself.

The sound of shutters beating against the window woke Ani from a deep sleep the following morning. She heard Tom snoring next to her, louder than usual. On her way to the kitchen, she noticed a few empty beer cans in the garbage bag, which did not surprise her. It had become an almost daily occurrence. When she opened the blinds of the kitchen window, she saw about two feet of snow piled up in front of it. The street had been plowed, but not the driveway leading to their apartment.

"Ani, are you still here?" Tom called from the bedroom. "I think I have the flu. I won't be going anywhere today. You can take the Mustang instead of the bus."

"Glad you parked it in the parking garage. It snowed a lot last night. Do you need me to get you anything at the drugstore?"

"No. I have medicine."

Ani drove slowly and carefully. A thick fog closed in all around her so that she could barely see anything ahead. Thankfully it was still early in the morning, and only a few other cars had ventured out thus far. She thought it safer to drive down the middle of the road for fear she might slide into the wall on the right.

Suddenly, blue lights flashed intermittently in the rearview mirror, turning the foggy surroundings into a rhythmic blue. She knew it meant *police car* and immediately veered the car over toward the relatively unplowed side. She hoped she would be able to pull away from the shoulder again, somehow. A blue flashing light appeared in the rearview mirror, leaving no question that it was intended for her. "Police are your friends in America," Sarah had once said when she was stopped for speeding, "especially if you're a woman." But Ani had not encountered one before. She turned off her engine and, with a thumping heart, waited. She rolled down her window halfway when a tall, heavyset African-American officer stood beside the driver's door.

"May I see your driver's license and registration?" he asked.

She quickly opened her purse and fished for her driver's license in her wallet. But where would the car registration be? Would Tom keep it in the ashtray? Or the glove compartment? She tried both but to no avail. Next, she reached underneath the driver's seat. She felt what seemed like an envelope. This must be it! It felt thick, and when she pulled it out from under the seat, she saw that it was marked "Tom Hanson." Without looking inside, she handed him the envelope. "I'm sure it's in there," she said with a smile and all the confidence she could muster.

He opened the envelope and took a peek inside. "Ma'am, I'm going to have to ask you to get out of the car," he said without taking out its contents. "Turn around and put your hands behind your back."

She obeyed, almost fainting as he snapped handcuffs on her wrists. "I don't understand. Why are you doing this?"

"I'm citing you for attempting to bribe an officer of the law. You have every right to remain silent."

When Tom awoke, his head ached, his eyes burned, and he felt a bit dizzy. "This feels worse than a normal hangover," he grumbled to himself as he propped up his head to look outside. It was still foggy. "Ani, are you still here?" he called weakly. Silence. He looked at the clock, which said 9:30 a.m. She had, of course, left at least two hours earlier and taken his car.

He picked up the phone next to him. "Cynthia, I can't come to work today. I'm as sick as a dog. Must be the flu," he said.

"You sure this isn't another hangover?" she asked. Not bothering to wait for an answer, she said, "Okay. I'll reschedule your appointment with Mr. Penelopovich for the beginning of next Monday. See that you get well by then, you hear?" she said briskly and hung up.

Suddenly, Tom remembered that Ani had taken the Mustang, with Solomon's payment under the seat. It was cash as usual, and lots of it. He forced himself out of bed, splashed cold water on his face, and meandered back to the closet to put on his clothes. He would have to take a taxi to the campus, find the Mustang, and then get the envelope from under the seat. *I hope she locked the car door,* he thought to himself.

He went to the kitchen, microwaved a strong instant coffee, and put on his rain jacket. He did not look forward to riding his motorcycle in this weather, especially with a hangover headache. As he opened the front door, his cell phone rang. It registered a number he did not recognize. *Who could this be? Probably an advertising call,* he reasoned. He ignored the phone call and uncovered his Honda bike. His cell phone rang again, showing Cynthia's name once more. He dutifully picked up the receiver and mumbled a grumpy "Yes?"

"Sorry to bother you again, Tom," Cynthia said. "But an officer from the thirty-fifth precinct just called looking for you. He asked you to call him right away. Officer McCauley is his name." She recited the officer's direct number. "He says it's urgent."

"Wait a minute. I need to write this down." Tom went back into the kitchen, fetched a pen and pad from the corner desk. "Can you give it to me again, please?"

Panic gripped him. Could something have happened to his Mustang? Or worse, to the money under the seat? In an instant moment of shame, he realized he was more concerned about the Mustang and the money than for Ani. The hangover was to blame, he rationalized.

He dialed the number Cynthia had given him.

Officer McCauley from the thirty-fifth police precinct answered. "You are returning my call? And who are you?"

"Thomas Hanson, sir."

"Oh, yes. We ask that you come to the station to bail out your wife."

"What?! Are you sure you have the correct Thomas Hanson?"

The officer answered by rattling off Tom's birth date, birthplace, and present address.

"What happened to my wife? Is she all right? I mean, why have you arrested her? What did she do?"

"We can't discuss that over the phone. When you come in, please bring the car registration. She doesn't seem to have it. But that's not why we arrested her. Come to the station, and we'll explain."

"Thanks for coming in, Mr. Hanson," said Officer McCauley, who paced around his office while speaking. "You see, your wife tried to bribe the officer who gave her a ticket for driving in the middle of the road. She was very generous with her money, I might add. But she didn't have the car's registration on her."

"Sir," said Tom, scratching his head. "I find that hard to believe. My wife would never bribe anyone. She's majoring in business ethics."

"Why not? She could be a theology student for all I care. And she's obviously from Asia somewhere, isn't she? I heard they bribe a lot over there."

Tom reddened with anger at the generalization. "Not all Asians do. Did you say she gave you cash? I just got paid last night—in cash. It was in a white office envelope, and I stuffed the envelope under the front seat. She wouldn't have known that that money was even there. She probably thought she was giving the officer the envelope with the registration, which I usually keep under the seat, too. Can you look there?"

The officer stopped pacing and called the arresting officer on the intercom. "Hey, Luke, come in for a sec." The officer entered a minute later. "When the young Asian woman you arrested gave you the money, did she hand it to you in cash as is, or was it in a white envelope?"

"In a white envelope, sir."

"Okay. I want you to go to that car and look under the driver's seat. See if there is another white envelope. Then bring it in."

Tom leaned back and relaxed. He was sure the man would find it. And he did. McCauley finally believed both Ani and Tom and returned both envelopes and the cash to Tom.

"Tom, are you sure your work for Solomon is legal?" Ani prodded when Tom explained the source of the cash on their way home.

"Of course. He's an honest fellow," Tom said.

"Then why is he always paying you in cash?" she asked.

"I have no idea. The less I know, the better, Solomon always said. So I didn't ask."

Chapter 29

Ani sipped her jasmine tea, feeling nostalgic. A brisk March wind was blowing thousands of cherry blossoms against the kitchen window, reminding her of Tom's first kiss under the cherry trees at the Washington Mall the year before. She opened the window screen, scooped up some of the blossoms, and placed them into a glass bowl on the kitchen table.

The apartment phone rang. Ani answered with a warm "Hello."

"Thomas Hanson, please," a woman's voice requested in a mechanical tone.

"He's not here right now. May I give him a message?"

"Am I speaking to Ani Su Li Hanson?"

"Yes, this is she."

"I am calling from the Collins Credit Card Company. You and your husband share a Collins credit card, do you not?"

"I did not know that. I never use a credit card," Ani answered.

"Well, please tell your husband that we had to decline his request to expand the card's credit limit. He has been late in making minimum payments several times this past year."

Ani's throat suddenly felt too dry to answer.

"Mrs. Hanson, are you still there?" the woman asked.

"Y-yes. I understand. But how did my name get on my husband's credit card? I never use it."

"Well, that I don't know."

The blood left her face. "I see. I will tell him," Ani said weakly and put down the receiver, shaking.

Up until that point, she had never felt shame, anger, and fear all at the same time. Tom had lied! He had not only told her that he had paid off all his credit card debts, but now he had also included her name on one of those cards, if not more than one, and asked to raise his debt limit?

With a dramatic clang of pots and pans, she fished out the wok from the cupboard. To make a statement, she decided to cook a lean, skimpy meal that night—a panful of rice with onions and celery, and only half of a cut-up chicken breast. If Tom complained about it, so be it. She'd have a perfect spin-off point for the lecture she was planning to throw at him. While onion slices and garlic chips sizzled in brown oil, Ani rehearsed what she would say and how. Before long, a haze of smoke enveloped her, and the smoke alarm began to shriek. She threw a cover over the wok and moved it to the side.

At that very moment, Tom entered. "What's happening here? Smells awful."

"It's nothing," Ani replied as she opened the back door and windows.

The burned fried rice and Ani's unusually sullen manner over dinner told him that something was bothering her. But he didn't dare ask. "I booked our tickets for Thanksgiving weekend in Cincinnati," he announced instead, using as cheerful a tone as he could muster.

"With what credit card?" shot back Ani.

He slammed down his fork. "What's with you tonight, Ani?"

She rose from the table, picked up her plate, and turned on the faucet in the sink. "We can't go anywhere until your charge cards are paid off!" she said in a maternal tone.

"But honey, that's impossible. When you book a flight these days, you have to use a credit card. I'm planning to pay for it at the end of the month!" *At least I hope so,* he added mentally.

"Well, you can't have booked it with the Collins card. You have reached its limit. So what credit card *did* you use?" she yelped. Not waiting for an answer, she left the kitchen, slamming the door behind her.

The Collins card? Tom felt stumped, much like when his mother used to spank him and he didn't know why. The Collins card company must have called him at home instead of at work. Hadn't he told them to phone his office?

"Ani," he yelled, now following her to the bedroom. "That doesn't mean I won't have the money. I'm expecting a big paycheck next month."

Ani turned around and faced him. "Don't tell me that. They said you had not paid the minimum several times this past year. How do you explain that?"

Tom drew a big sigh. "It's not what it looks like," he whined in defense. "I have only two credit cards now. One for private and one for business. I paid off both of them after I proposed to you."

"And since then, you've accrued debt all over again?"

He scratched his head. "I had to, Ani. The car needed new tires, the dental bill, oh, and I needed a new tennis racket. The old one was bad."

She turned around again, marched off to the bathroom, and locked the door.

Tom let out a big sigh. He wanted to maintain her trust. But how could he tell her some things without lying to her? Not disclosing everything was also betraying her trust. But he felt he had no choice. He needed to defend himself. He pounded on the bathroom door. "Open up, Ani. Don't do this to me."

She gave no reply.

"All right then. I'll—I'll just cancel the flight," he said, hoping she would take him seriously. After all, he reasoned, time with family was a priority, even *his* family. He walked back into the kitchen and finished his dinner alone. *Whatever this thing she has with credit card debts, she'll get over it,* he thought, e*specially when I get paid by Solomon and finally get them all paid off.* But he needed to do something to gain her trust in the meantime. He took out his credit cards from his wallet—all four of them. He cut up three of them with the scissors he found in one of the drawers and laid them on the kitchen table. Then he stuffed the fourth card into his back pocket.

As he was washing the dishes, Ani returned to the kitchen. "Well, congratulations!" she exclaimed when she saw the cut-up credit cards.

He said nothing for a moment. "I can always get another one, you know," he said with a smirk.

"Or you can use a debit card. Don't you have one?"

"Oh, yeah. Somewhere. I'll just have to make sure there's enough in the bank account."

She wrapped her arms around him from the back. "Want me to give you a lesson on microeconomics?" she asked.

He turned around and kissed her. "Yeah, sure. Now?"

"No. In the morning. Before you leave for tennis," she replied and kissed him again, leading him in a slow dance toward the bedroom.

The next evening, after she stashed the dishes into the dishwasher, Ani took out a notebook from her bureau. "Let's write down all your assets and income. All of it. Your average salary again?"

"Four thousand dollars per month net after insurance deductions, etcetera. That's all."

"That's all, you say? That's a hundred times as much as my parents make at home!"

"Yeah, yeah, so I'm rich." His voice was sarcastic. "I know about money value in your part of the world."

"Okay. How much do you still owe?"

Tom squirmed. He didn't want her to know everything. He listed his debts the best that he could remember: his credit cards, his university, his car loan, and a loan from his father.

"Your father? Why did he lend you money?"

"Well, yes. I thought I could pay Dad back with the earnings I made on his investment last year. But it went sour, and I lost all of it."

"And your father still expects you to pay him back?"

"Yep, he sure does. He's a strict businessman."

Ani could not believe what she heard. She instantly thought

of the families back home, where parents saved and saved to send their kids to school, help them establish their careers or businesses, and bought them a home when they married. Parents in her culture never *lent* their children money; they *gave* it. It was their investment in their children's future so that those children could become their caregivers one day.

"Sounds like you gambled, Tom. You didn't invest. Smart investments are diversified, spread out, such as in mutual funds."

Tom hated such lectures. "I know, I know," he said, irritated.

With a small calculator, she added up his monthly minimum payments on his credit cards, car loan payments, and his own university loan. Then she tallied all their other expenses: car insurance, repairs, gasoline, rent, health insurance, income tax, food, household expenses, utility bills, and tennis club membership. She subtracted the total monthly costs from the total monthly income. Only thirty dollars remained. Ani grew pale. "How were you going to pay for the rent next month? And how did you think you were going to help pay for my college expenses? I think we need to cancel that trip to your parents', Tom."

"But I can get another loan until Solomon pays me for the moonlighting expenses. Or he'll give me an advance if I ask him."

Ani slammed her notebook and pen onto the kitchen nook. "I've heard that before. Tom, you are a dreamer, not the sensible, strong man I wish I could lean on." Then she added words that cut even deeper. "You are irresponsible," she screamed, and stomped out of the kitchen.

Irresponsible. That was the same word Tom's mother had used to describe him before he left home. Hearing Ani say it hurt even more. For years, whenever he had tried to prove his mother wrong, one mistake would set him back to her old judgment. It felt like that all over again. The fact that he had poured himself out for Ani, married her, fed her, sheltered her, given her money to pay for her education—all so that she could stay in the United States and finish her education—none of that seemed to matter. And now she accused him of being irresponsible!

"Man, are you ever ungrateful," he bellowed. "I rescued you, and this is the thanks I get?"

She reentered the kitchen. "Rescued me from what?" she screeched. "I didn't marry you for your money or for a visa."

"Oh yeah? Are you sure?" He couldn't imagine why else she would have married him. He got up, fetched his tennis racket and tennis shoes from the hall closet, and left the house, slamming the back door behind him.

A tsunami of anger shattered all the romantic feelings Ani had ever felt. *Ungrateful*, Tom had called her, but her rage was mostly with herself. She had betrayed her religion and her family by marrying a non-Muslim because she was in love with him. And because she loved him, she wanted to help him manage his money. She had tried to teach him but failed. And now, he accused her of being ungrateful?

And then it dawned on her. They both had misjudged each other's motivation for marriage! He thought she would only love and marry him if he helped her financially continue her studies in America! And she thought Tom would only latch on to her as long as he felt she needed him!

No wonder he thought she was ungrateful! In a moment of shame, she realized she had misled him. She had wanted him to believe that she needed rescuing. She had not told him that her cousin Rianto was paying for her expenses for the long haul. Raging through her mind now was the question, how could she prove to him that she loved him apart from his monetary help? She would have to tell Tom about Rianto's financial support, she reasoned. Then she would have to apply to the ASEAN student assistance awards program that Ms. Daniels had told her about. Then she would have to prove to him—somehow—that she loved him—and that she loved him for who he was, not for what he did for her. But how?

For now, she would bake his favorite pineapple upside-down cake. If he regarded it as a mere expression of gratitude, so be it. *Perhaps,* she thought, *it isn't entirely up to me to change his thinking anyway.*

She decided to wait up for him and study until he came home. But when he had not yet arrived by 2:00 a.m., Ani began to worry. *Could he be so angry that he did not want to come home? He's probably out on one of his moonlighting missions,* she thought. She slipped on her pajamas and went to sleep.

A thump at the front door shook her awake. The clock on the dresser said 3:45. She recognized the jingle of Tom's key chain outside and felt relieved. But something was different in the interval of time between the opening of the door and its closing. Not even the footsteps sounded like Tom's; they were heavy, uneven. She heard keys drop onto the floor with a loud jingly thud, then a bang against the shoe shelf in the hallway.

When something or someone fell against the bedroom door, Ani sat up, her heart thumping. "Tom? Are you all right?" she asked.

The door swung open wide, hitting against the chest of drawers. An odor Ani had never smelled before suddenly filled the room. In the reflection of the dresser mirror, she watched Tom stagger toward the bed. He kicked off his shoes and flopped down next to her. A moment later, she heard a snore—an uneven, choking sort of snore.

"You're welcome, Senator," she heard him slur in between snores.

The smell of sweat and whatever it was she couldn't recognize nauseated Ani. She got up, grabbed her pillow from the bed and a blanket from the closet, and carried them into the den. On the way there, she noticed the light on in the kitchen and the cake untouched on the table. Bewildered but too tired to think about it all, she finally dozed off on the couch.

The aroma of strong coffee woke Ani the following morning. The clock next to her said 9 a.m. It was Sunday, a day Tom would typically still be sleeping. It took a moment for Ani to remember why she did not lie in their bed.

"Good morning, princess." Tom's baritone voice droned over her head, more cheerful than usual. She had to cough. A fresh douse of shaving lotion on his face took her breath away.

She opened her eyes. Dressed in an expensive dark gray suit, Tom planted a kiss on her mouth. "Thanks for the scrumptious cake, honey!" he cooed.

"What's that?" she sleepily asked, pointing to the ice bag he put on his head after he straightened.

"Oh, it's for a little hangover. The headache is killing me."

"Where are you going?"

"Solomon's. He owes me some money. We'll need it for spending money on our trip to see my parents."

Chapter 30

The Cincinnati airport buzzed with people. A familiar figure of a short man with a beer belly and scarce, gray hair stepped off the escalator, looking lost.

"Stay here, I see my dad," Tom said as he darted off through the crowd to meet him.

A few minutes later, a curly-red-haired woman in high heels and blue jeans approached Ani. "Are you by any chance Annie Hanson?" she asked. Her face showed middle-age wrinkles around the corners of her mouth, forehead, and temples, and a few more across her neck. She wore a striped purple blazer and a low-cut lace blouse underneath.

Ani instantly recognized the voice. Ignoring the mispronunciation of her name this time, she asked in reply, "Are you Tom's mother, Mrs. Hanson?"

The woman before her laughed. "Yes, but please don't call me that, Annie. It makes me feel so old. I'm just plain Beverly."

"Plain Beverly?"

"Yes, plain Beverly," chuckled her mother-in-law as she hugged Ani. "Welcome to Cincinnati!"

She stood back and looked Ani up and down. "Well, you're a pretty, dainty little thing. I can see why Tom was taken in by you."

Ani tried to smile. Not only did the words "pretty, dainty little thing" sound a bit demeaning, but she did not quite understand the phrase *taken in by you*. Wasn't that passive tense for taking in someone? If so, did she mean he took Ani in like a bum off the street or as a prostitute? She hoped not.

"I see you've found each other!" It was Tom's voice behind them. "Hi, Mom!" he said and gave his mother a stiff kiss on the cheek.

The stocky gray-haired man walked up to them. "Hello, Anne, I'm Andy, Tom's father," he said, extending his hand to her. "You didn't tell us how pretty your wife is, Tom," he added as he turned to his son and, hugging him with one arm, slapped him on the back with the other.

"No one asked," replied Tom tersely, secretly proud of the score he had just landed with his parents. *So far, so good,* he thought. He was sure that all that sweet talk would end early, and he braced himself for whatever would happen next.

The Hanson home shocked Ani. Shabby, old, and dark, oversized furnishings filled every room. Floral wallpaper, peeling off in some places, decorated all its walls. An unpleasant odor which Ani could not identify, but eventually would learn was mold, gave her an instant headache.

"Make yourselves at home. I just need to finish something in the kitchen. But honey," Beverly said, addressing her husband, Andy, "could you please go to the basement and pick out some nice wines and whatever else—you know?"

Within half an hour of their arrival, Ani began to cough and sneeze. Her nose clogged up, and her eyes began to swell. She knew why. Two cats lay around: the multicolored short-haired calico on the sofa and the orange Persian one on top of a bookcase. The dark blue carpet was laden with orange hair. She was allergic to cats! She quickly told Tom, who immediately picked up the cats and took them outside. "Don't worry," he said. "They're in-and-outdoor cats." He quickly went to the medicine cabinet and procured an antihistamine for Ani to take. Then, while his mother was in the kitchen with the radio on, he took the vacuum cleaner and ran it over the carpets, sofa, and chairs. It took 15 minutes. By then, Ani's face and throat had cleared up, and she could breathe and see again.

"Supper is almost ready!" Beverly yelled from the kitchen. "Can you kids set the table, please? And where is Andy?" She opened the door to the basement. "Are you still down there looking, or are you drinking half the stuff?"

"I'm just cleaning up a little glass down here. A wine bottle fell off the shelf," Andy yelled back.

"Oh, no, honey, no need to do that!" Beverly scolded when she saw Ani folding the napkins in a triangle form, the same way Grace had taught her. Beverly yanked them from her, unfolded them, and quickly laid them on top of each plate. "We're not very formal in this house."

"Is there anything else I can do, Plain Beverly?" Ani asked, a bit shaken.

Beverly roared with laughter. "No, honey. And my name is Beverly, not "plain" Beverly. That was a misunderstanding. And as for your offer to help, it makes me feel nervous. I don't like to be rushed or pushed."

"Oh, no, I didn't mean that at all!" Ani quickly replied to save face. In her culture, it would be impolite to show hunger when visiting someone. "I just want to help. We did eat something on the plane, so we're fine."

"You ate?" scolded Beverly. "You ate? Tommy! Why didn't you tell me you had dinner on the airplane? Here I'm going through all this fuss rushing to get your dinner ready."

"We had peanuts, Mother. Peanuts, that's all. A teeny, tiny bag of peanuts. And yes, we *are* hungry."

"Humph!" She turned around, not looking at Ani, who tried hard to fight her tears.

Ani's stomach felt like a rock when they sat down at the table. Not out of hunger so much as out of nervousness. To be polite, she ate a few bites of the salad, the meatloaf, and the mashed potatoes anyway—this time thinking it best not to pull out the *sambal* from her handbag.

"So if Indonesia isn't in India, where is it anyway?" asked Beverly, eyeing Ani more carefully. "It's not in Africa, I gather."

"It's in Southeast Asia," answered Tom for Ani. "Near the Philippines."

"Oh, way down there."

"When stationed in the Philippines," said Andy, "I heard that some people eat dogmeat there. Feed them first with lots of rice, and then roast them. Do you do that, too?"

Ani giggled. "No, we don't in Bandung, where I live. I think they do in Battag, which is far from where I live."

"And don't they run around naked in your country?" pressed Beverly.

"Mom!" cried Tom in a chiding tone.

"Of course, they wear clothes," Andy commented. "Look at Ani. Does she look like she's not wearing clothes?"

Ani laughed. "Actually, in some parts of my country, they used to. But not anymore. And certainly not on Java Island, where most of the population lives, and where I am from."

"See? They are very civilized over there, Mom," argued Tom.

Ani giggled. "The women in most of Indonesia wear more clothes than most women in the United States," she explained.

"Goodness, in that heat over there?" exclaimed Beverly.

"Yes, in that heat."

"No wonder you married Tom. I'm sure you don't want to go back there again, do you?"

Ani looked at Tom for reassurance. It seemed as if she could not say anything right.

Tom came to her rescue. "Well, if she did go back, I'd go there with her. If she got used to the Maryland climate here, I could get used to living over there, don't you think?"

His mother glared at him and said nothing. An awkward silence followed. Andy broke it when he asked, "Is it true that most people in your country are Mohammedans?"

"Muslims or Moslems," Tom corrected. "Mohammed was the name of the prophet and founder of Islam."

"Are you one of them, too, Anne?" the mother asked, stuffing her mouth with a forkful of meat.

Ani nodded and smiled.

"That means she's a heathen," Beverly retorted, looking sharply at Tom. "Haven't you tried to convert her yet, son?"

Tom laughed and shook his head. "Don't go there, Mom. Please don't. I'm afraid you're going to offend Ani with your dogmatic remarks."

"Why not? She can learn."

"It's okay, Tom," interjected Ani, laughing. "I like to learn about other people's religions."

After dinner, Tom joined his Dad watching an "important" ice hockey game on TV while Ani helped Beverly clear the table. "May I help with the dishes?" she asked.

"The dishwasher washes them, hon," replied Beverly.

"But please let me rinse them."

"Well, if you insist. But I will put the dishes into the dishwasher myself. I know just how."

A few minutes later, the dishwasher was running, the pots were cleaned and dried. Beverly climbed onto a step stool to fetch something from the cabinet. It was a small liquor bottle. She plopped it down onto the kitchen counter, took two small glasses from another shelf, and poured some in each glass. Then she sat down on a stool.

"C'mon, Annie, sit with me. We must celebrate this moment. We survived our first meal together, didn't we?" Beverly raised a glass. "Here's to us!"

Ani hesitated. She could smell something strange. It reminded her of something the dentist in Indonesia used to disinfect his instruments. She slowly raised her glass to her lips and pretended to drink. While Beverly turned around to fetch something from the buffet, Ani quickly emptied her glass into the pot of azaleas sitting on the table.

Just then, Tom peered through the opening between the kitchen and dining room. "It's halftime," he announced. "Wanna go for a walk with me, Ani? I could use some fresh air."

"No way will you take my daughter away from me!" cried his mother, slurring her words. Her face was red. "I mean, daughter-in-law," she corrected in a softer tone. She plummeted into the sofa, leaned her head back against a pillow, and closed her eyes.

Stunned, Ani and Tom quietly retreated toward the front door, threw on their jackets, and left for a walk. "Well? What do you think of my wonderful parents?" Tom asked in a sarcastic tone.

Ani said nothing for a moment. "They are your parents, Tom. They made you, didn't they? So they cannot be so bad."

Tom tried hard to make sense of her words; and when he finally did, he had to disagree. But he was too tired to argue with her.

Chapter 31

April Azaleas in myriad colors started to bloom everywhere. A few dogwood trees began to show off their pretty white and pink blossoms as well. Ani was busy preparing for her trip tomorrow to the Embassy of Jordan in the nation's capital to celebrate *Eid al-Adha* or *Kurban*. This annual Muslim feast commemorates that when Abraham was about to sacrifice his son, Allah provided a lamb as a substitute. A fellow student from Jordan and his Saudi friend had invited her and two Malai women to join them. She looked forward to the taste of roasted lamb, even the sight of slaughtered lambs, rams, or goats hanging upside down so that the blood would drain. It would be a festivity that reminded Ani of home.

Baseball season had begun, and as usual on Saturdays, Tom had come home with a caseload of beer a few hours earlier. He plopped down in front of the television and began to watch the Orioles play the Miami Marlins, who had won the World Series the previous year. "Ani, you gotta come here and watch a little with me!" he coaxed with a slur. "Pretty please!"

"You are drunk, and you smell!" she yelled back from the kitchen. "I don't want to be near you." The mother instinct in her wanted to respond to the need, but her disgust far outweighed any caretaking urge.

"Really? Well, if you want to be submissive to your Allah, you should come and sit next to me when I ask you to."

Ani ignored his request. She deeply resented Tom's use of her religion to guilt-manipulate her. The more he pushed, the more she resisted. Non-action might have a more powerful effect than words, she reasoned.

"Muslim arrogance. That's what it is," Ani heard him whine when she did not join him. The words burned sharply, reigniting her wish to get away and celebrate *Kurban* with her Muslim friends. The magnetic pull of her heritage felt more potent than ever.

As Tom opened his eyes the next morning, he watched Ani wrap her long Indonesian batik skirt around her and slip into the lace blouse her aunt had embroidered for her 18th birthday.

"You look pretty. Where are you going today?" Tom asked.

"To Washington to celebrate *Kurban* with friends. It's an important part of my Muslim arrogance," she answered, laughing.

Ani's sarcasm bit hard, partly because he wasn't used to it. "Look. If I said anything that offended you last night, I'm sorry. I was probably a bit tipsy."

"You mean *drunk,"* she replied tersely while putting on her keris necklace. "I'm getting tired of your "I'm sorry's."

Tom sat up in bed, his hair ruffled, his unshaven chin sagging under downward-slanted lips. "Honey, can't you forgive me for what I've done in the past and let me start over? You know, like the boxer Holyfield did when Tyson bit off part of his ear during the boxing match?"

Ani had no idea what he was talking about. She was deaf and blind to current events in the sports world. "Maybe I can forgive you," she retorted. "But my forgiving you does not give you a license to keep doing what hurts me." With those words, she grabbed her purse and jacket and left the bedroom.

"Ani, wait!" he called after her. "Can't you give me a kiss good-bye?"

Climbing into the shiny new Maxima driven by Mohammed the Jordanian, Ani joined the two female students from Malaysia in the back. Loud Arabic music drowned out any conversation. She did not care for the music, but she did not complain. Today, she did not have to play a nagging mother; she could be herself again.

An hour later, they passed a row of blooming cherry trees near the famous presidential monuments in Washington, D.C. Nostalgia moved her to tears. She could not help but miss Tom—the Tom she remembered when they walked under the cherry trees the year before. Those were happier days.

When they arrived at the Jordanian Embassy to participate in the *Kurban* celebration, she felt like Mr. Spock, beamed into another world. A row of headless sheep hung upside-down along the fence of the gardens. About twenty men in long white gowns and turbans sat in a circle, conversing loudly. As Ani walked toward the collective chatter of women and children on the other side of the gardens, the smells, sounds, and sights of this occasion not only triggered pleasant memories of her past, but they also drowned out all the unpleasant ones of her current life.

But not all of the event proved as delightful as she had hoped. *An Arab-dominated event*, Ani inwardly complained. So many subtle things were missing from her Indonesian ways of celebrating this religious ritual. The *krupuks,* for example. Her mouth watered as she thought of these chips made of shrimp, onions, and flour. She remembered how the servants used to slice the dough and lay them out in the sun. As a young girl, she used to sit next to them under an umbrella for hours, waiting for them to dry and shrivel up .

While their driver joined the men on the other side of the courtyard, the three women sat down on a low wall near the edge. "Hummus, anyone?" a server asked, carrying a large plate of round flatbread and a bowl of hummus. Another server brought Ani and each of her friends a small cup of strong coffee.

A Jordanian schoolgirl, about age eight, stopped in front of them. "You look different," she said.

"We *are* different," Ani replied with a laugh.

"Why?"

"We're from another country, far away from Jordan."

"But why do you look different?"

"You mean, our eyes?"

"Yeah. And your skin color."

"Allah made us that way," Ani replied. "He made our parents and our brothers and sisters that way, too. We think it's beautiful. Don't you think so?"

"No, it's ugly," said the girl, giggling as she started to skip away.

Ani's two Malaysian friends jumped off the wall and darted after her. "Watch out, little girl, we're going to get you for this!" they teased.

"Well, that's a challenge to one's self-esteem," commented a young woman with an Arabic accent as she approached Ani. She wore a long black dress and a mauve scarf, and her features reminded Ani of a famous actress whose name she could not remember.

"Oh, not really," Ani said, laughing lightheartedly. "When I was young, my sister and I always made fun of *long nose* people from the Middle East, Europe, and America. So now they are doing it to me."

The woman hopped onto the wall next to Ani. "I'm Fatima—from Jordan, like most everyone else here. And you? Are you from Malaysia?"

"I'm from Indonesia. My name is Ani. Do you live in this house?"

"Yes. My father is an ambassador."

Ani fell silent. She had never been around someone of such a high social standing before. She took a deep breath, enjoying the aroma of lamb roasting over the open fire.

"I can't wait till this is over," sighed Fatima.

"Why?"

"Look at this place. The women are stuck in one area of the house, the men in another. Never eating together. I think it is medieval."

It didn't bother Ani. She felt glad for a break from Tom.

"Isn't this *Kurban* festival fun? Did you know that neither Jews nor Christians do this?" Fatima asked. "The Jews don't do it because their temple was destroyed in the first century, and the followers of Isa don't sacrifice animals because they say that Allah provided the final sacrifice himself."

Ani nodded. "I heard that. But we Muslims believe Isa never actually died on that cross. Allah took him and substituted someone else for him."

"Yes. It's a nice idea," Fatima said.

"Nice idea? You don't believe that?"

"Well, I'm a student of literature. I read the whole *Injil*, and it talks so often about Isa's death that I find it hard to believe that the text was changed in so many places. Christians see his death as Allah's sacrifice for the wrongs of all who believe and ask him for forgiveness. The whole of Christian belief has to do with Isa's death and resurrection. You know, his coming back to life again."

"I see," replied Ani as if she had not heard this before. She was surprised that Fatima even knew the fancy word *resurrection.* "You sound like you are not a Muslim anymore," Ani said, laughing.

Fatima smiled. "I am a traditional Muslim. I follow some of the rituals, but to be honest, I'm not 100 percent Muslim anymore. But I am also not a follower of Isa." She paused as she picked up a small pebble from the wall and threw it on the ground. "I think believing in Isa's death and resurrection is much easier than it is to follow him. For example, he taught that we should be kind to those who do us harm. Mohammed taught the same thing four hundred years later. I doubt if that's even possible. At least, I haven't seen any Christians or Muslims follow this rule, have you?"

"No, I have not seen that," Ani replied. "I do know that Christians believe that when Isa hung on the cross, he asked Allah to forgive the ones who tried to kill him. Isa never defended himself or fought. Some of his followers forgave their enemies, too." She vaguely remembered Grace's pastor's story about Corrie ten Boom, who forgave her Nazi captors. And didn't Tom recently say something about a boxer who forgave his opponent for biting off part of his ear during a fight? "But you're right. Isa's teaching is difficult to follow.

Defense and revenge are pure, natural, human reactions. I don't know how anyone can forgive someone who is trying to harm them."

Just then, several children ran around them, shouting and screeching with laughter. A young schoolboy pushed a smaller boy to the ground. They began to wrestle. A woman with a black veil and long garment scolded them and pulled them apart.

"He pushed me," whined the smaller one.

"He pushed me first," objected the other, who began to charge after the other one.

"A good example of a purely natural, human reaction," Fatima said, laughing.

The rough stones underneath Ani's thighs suddenly felt hard. She remembered something that Sarah had said once. "Not only did Isa teach the opposite of revenge," she had said, "he *did* the opposite." But when Ani was about to tell this to Fatima, the woman jumped off the wall and chased one of the children until they all disappeared. She never saw Fatima again.

On the way back, Ani had her eyes closed while the others in the car chatted away in their respective languages. This gave her time to think. Could she ever forgive Tom for drinking too much? Maybe she could, she decided. But would forgiving him help him in the long run? Probably not. Grace had once said in passing that addicts needed professional help to overcome their addiction. Was Tom addicted to alcohol? She was not sure. Ani felt too ashamed to ask anyone about it, let alone ask for help.

Chapter 32

Tom spent most of the next few evenings out of the house, either working during the day or tending to Solomon's moonlighting missions in the evenings. Whenever he did spend time at home, he sat in front of the television with a beer can in hand. The silence between him and Ani had become customary and even comfortable. It certainly seemed easier to bear than bickering with each other. The less they talked, the less they argued, and the less they argued, the more Ani could concentrate on her studies. And that wasn't all bad.

Ani's burning sensations in her stomach became more frequent. They were so intense one day that she cried out in pain while talking with Grace on the phone.

"Have you gone to a doctor yet?" Grace asked.

"No. I don't know of one."

"Let me take you to a walk-in clinic. I just happen to have time today. I think your student medical insurance would pay for most of it. Then we could go out to lunch together."

Ani eagerly accepted Grace's offer. After an hour in the waiting room, the doctor finally called them in and asked Ani lots of questions.

"What you have, Mrs. Hanson," the young female Korean-American physician concluded, "is most likely an ulcer. We would have to test whether bacteria cause it, and if so, we would have to treat it with an antibiotic. Meantime, you need to avoid eating spicy, fried, and acidic foods. And eat three hours before lying down. Tell me, Mrs. Hanson, have you had a lot of pressure lately?"

Ani looked at Grace. They laughed. "She's a student and

newly married," Grace answered for her. "That should answer your question."

The doctor smiled. "Wow. Two big stressors." She scribbled something on a notepad, tore off the piece of paper, and handed it to Ani. "Here is a prescription that will eliminate the present symptoms within a few weeks or earlier. You must take this pill an hour before you eat in the morning. Eat smaller meal portions and more frequently rather than eating a big meal less often. Also," she added, handing Ani a larger piece of paper, "here is a list of foods you should avoid. Do you eat a lot of spicy food?"

"Does she ever!" Grace piped.

"Well, no hot peppers or spices, no acidic foods like tomato sauce, and no fried foods. Eat just bland, steamed food for a while. Don't drink coffee, black tea, or Coke, either. Is all of that clear?"

Ani nodded. "Is lactose-free milk okay?"

"I think that should be okay. Try to wait at least one and a half hours before lying down or bending down. Do some muscle relaxation and deep breathing exercises, especially before an exam. But even more important, whatever is going on in your life, Mrs. Hanson, try to relax more. You know—like watch a funny movie with your husband so you can laugh together. Can you do that?"

Ani smiled weakly. Laugh with her husband? They hardly watched anything together. Relaxation exercises before an exam? She had learned but forgotten deep breathing and muscle relaxation, both of which worked wonders. "Why do some people have this problem, and others do not?" asked Ani.

The doctor tapped her fingers on her clipboard as if unsure whether to try to explain. Then she finally spoke. "Between the intestine and the esophagus there's like a flexible door called the sphincter, which is supposed to keep any acid from entering back up into the esophagus after you eat. If it doesn't work properly, you get acid reflux, and eventually, even an ulcer. Maybe by the twenty-first century, they will have a permanent fix for this problem. Meantime, make sure you follow my instructions. If you still have a problem in a couple of months, we test you for bacteria. Do you have insurance? The procedure is quite costly."

"Only basic health insurance—another stress factor!" said Ani, laughing.

The doctor did not laugh. "Well, call your medical insurance company and find out, will you? And good luck!"

After stopping to buy the medicine, Grace drove Ani to the Vietnamese soup restaurant on York Road. The waiter placed three dishes of vegetables, noodles, and meats on the table. Using chopsticks and a spoon, the women added these ingredients to their bowls of broth.

Grace wiped her mouth with a napkin and looked at Ani. "How are things between you and Tom these days?" she asked.

"Fine," Ani said quietly, without her usual smile.

"Are you sure *everything* is fine?" Grace asked with a questioning look. "Your face doesn't look like the happy new bride I knew a year ago."

Ani didn't answer. Looking out the window so that Grace would not see her face, she wiped her eyes with the back of her hand The two women ate in silence for a minute. Grace then asked, "If you were back in Indonesia right now, who'd you turn to if you had a personal problem?"

"Probably my aunt Ling. She is much easier to talk with than my mother. Mother is too quick with advice."

"I know what you mean. I had a mother like that, too. I believe it's never good to keep things to yourself. It's okay—no, it is imperative—to talk with someone you can trust. Otherwise, your troubles can get worse." She stopped and laughed. "Oh, dear, I'm giving you advice like your mother! I'm sorry."

"No, that's okay," replied Ani with a smile.

Grace touched Ani's arm. "You don't have to tell me anything right now. I just want you to know I'm here for you in case you want to talk to somebody about it."

Ani blew her nose into a tissue and simply said, "Thanks." Grace's caring, welcoming tone made Ani want to curl into her arms and tell all. But she felt too ashamed to do so. After all, hadn't Grace warned her to be careful about Tom?

Grace reached out for Ani's hand. "I won't be offended if that 'somebody' isn't me," Grace added. "Do you want to know what I do when there's no one I can turn to?"

Ani nodded.

"I cry, and I pray. And sometimes, I ask someone else to pray. Would you mind if I pray for you right now? We followers of Isa do it anytime, anywhere, anyhow we please. Even in a restaurant."

Ani nodded and smiled. "I know."

Resting her hand on Ani's arm, Grace looked up toward the ceiling and closed her eyes. "Thank you, Lord Jesus, for loving us so much. And thank you for caring about my friend Ani. You know all about what she's going through. Would you please lift all of her burdens? Thank you! And would you make her well again in your time? Amen." She stayed in that position for another thirty seconds, moving her lips silently, then looked at Ani with a smile and said, "Phew. Now I feel better myself!"

The pain in Ani's stomach was still there, but she felt she had just experienced a touch of peace she had never felt before. Whoever or whatever was responsible, she hoped for more.

Chapter 33

One day in mid May, Ani began chopping onions and garlic when Tom entered through the back door with a cheery "Hi, honey!" He hadn't greeted her like that in a while, but what surprised Ani more was that he handed her a bouquet of six roses and laid a wrapped meat package on the kitchen counter. "Halal meat for you, my dear," he chirped. "Is it too late for tonight's dinner?"

"No, it isn't," Ani replied as she fetched a vase from the kitchen closet and filled it with water. "What's the rare occasion?"

"To celebrate good news. I paid off every loan and every credit card today. I'm free and clear!"

"Really?" she asked in disbelief as she chopped off the ends of the rose stems with scissors and placed them in the vase on the kitchen table.

"Yup."

"The car loan?"

"Yup."

"All the credit cards?"

"Yep."

"Why, congratulations, Tom. I'm proud of you. You did it!" She pecked a quick kiss on his cheek.

"Thanks," he said, trying hard to look humble. He took off his jacket and sat down on a chair. "But that's not all the news. Guess what's next?" he asked.

"I can't imagine," she said wearily. She wasn't used to good news from Tom. It was more likely to be bad news.

"Next month, I'll be getting an additional five thousand dollars that we could save toward a down payment on a house. We would easily qualify for a mortgage, and the increase of the property value over time would pay far more than the interest. What do you say about that?"

"That's great, Tom. I'm—I'm impressed," she said slowly, still not sure if she could believe him. She turned her back to him as she began to fry the onions in the pan, then the garlic and the meat until they turned brown. She added the sliced celery and carrots, added a small portion of duck sauce, and covered the pan to simmer. With yesterday's leftover rice reheated in a small bowl in the microwave oven, dinner was ready. It took exactly eight minutes.

"I also have good news," she said with a smile. She filled each plate with rice and the meat and vegetable mixture, placed them on the table, and sat down.

"You do? What?"

"Let me eat first, then I'll tell you." She had trained Tom to eat silently with her. It helped her digestion, she had told him. She ate her meal faster than was good for her so that she could tell him the news. "Are you ready?"

He nodded.

"The university offered me a full-time position in the administration, with salary, and with free tuition for the rest of my graduate program! Isn't that exciting?"

Tom's mouth dropped open, his body froze. "C—congratulations!" he let out slowly in a tone that betrayed more disappointment than excitement. He forced a smile. "That's—that's great, honey!" But then his smile faded, and his face turned white.

"What's the matter, Tom? You don't look so happy about it," she said, studying his face. She didn't expect an answer, nor did she need one. She knew that the news robbed him of his role as her rescuer. But this would be her chance—and challenge—to prove to him that she loved him for who he was, not for his money. She hoped he would eventually believe it.

Tom took a deep breath, then another bite of his food, his eyes staring down at the plate. "Well, that's great for you," he finally said. He got up and helped himself to more food at the stove and sat down again. "I guess you won't need me anymore, and when you get that job, you're probably going to leave me, right?"

"Oh, Tom. You got it all wrong. You still think I married you so I could get your financial support and stay in the US to study, don't you."

"Didn't you?" He asked, looking down at his plate.

She said nothing for a while, then sighed and shook her head. She leaned forward and, gently touching his chin, turned his face toward her. "Tom, look at me," she said softly. "I have a confession. I accepted your offer of money because you wanted to be generous, and I saw that it made you so happy and proud. I didn't want to refuse it because I was afraid that your feelings would be hurt if I did not take your help. I fell in love with your generous heart. And I deeply appreciate what you tried to do for me."

He stared at her in disbelief. "Are you saying you didn't need my financial help after all?"

"That's right. I did not really need your help. I allowed my cousin Rianto to pay my expenses so far, just in case you couldn't," she confessed.

"Then why did you bother to marry me? For a visa?"

"No, certainly not for a visa. I eventually want to return to Indonesia, and I told you that before we got married, didn't I?"

"Well. yes, but—, then why did you marry me?"

"I was afraid of losing you."

"But why? Why were you afraid of losing me if you didn't need me?" He shouted the question, combing his hair with his fingers.

"Because I love you! I love you," she said in similar decibels. Her eyes filled with tears by now. "Can't you believe that?"

He could only answer inaudibly. *But if I can't be your hero, Ani, what in me would there be for you to love?*

Ani stared at him, waiting for him to speak. When he didn't, she pushed the chair behind her angrily and said, "If you don't believe that I love you, I can't help you."

She took the empty plates away, poured him coffee from the coffee machine, and sat down again. "I'm sorry, Tom. Maybe I shouldn't have told you about my cousin. Maybe you would have been happier if I hadn't."

"No, no. That's okay," he mumbled. But it wasn't okay. He wished he didn't know. "One more question," he said. "Where is all the money I gave you to use for your expenses if you had help from your cousin all this time?"

She smiled. "I used your money to pay for food, gas, fees, and household expenses. I saved my cousin's money in a CD account for an emergency. The CD is in both our names, but we both have to sign a withdrawal slip if we need to use it. I thought maybe we could use it to buy a better second car."

Tom shook his head. He could not, or would not, believe that she would love him for who he is without his being her hero. Even if she did, he would have to prove to himself that he deserved her unconditional love.

Part III

It was spring. Ani's first semester of graduate school had just ended. Three final exams, a class presentation, and a five-page paper had left her quite exhausted. She had not spoken much with Tom, and on this evening, she was alone once again. He was either with Solomon or out on his moonlighting mission. Ani was packing her suitcase because the following day, she was planning to take the bus to Rhode Island to meet Indri.

The sun had just set behind the apartment building next door. Ani's frugality overruled the need to turn on a light as she hung up Tom's non-smelly suits and jackets and turned the rather smelly pants inside out, tossing them into the laundry basket a few feet away. Barefoot, she suddenly felt something sting her left sole. She looked down and picked it up. "Oh! My old friend, the keris pin," she giggled aloud. "How did you get off my gold chain and onto the closet floor? Well, you're going to Rhode Island with me tomorrow morning."

She picked out one of the golden chains from her jewelry box, slid the pin onto it, placed it into a ziplock bag with her other jewelry, and continued to pack. How could she have allowed it to fall off her necklace? She chided herself. But worse, why had she not even missed it? Surely her troubles with Tom were to blame, she concluded. Never in her wildest imagination could she suspect the real reason why that keris was on the closet floor that evening.

Chapter 34

Everything looked bleak and gray from the bus that snaked its way from Central Station through Manhattan toward Interstate 95. Horns were blowing; people crowded the sidewalks; cars double-parked along both sides of the street—all of it reminded Ani of Bandung. Except there were no motorcycles, motor scooters, or bicycles. Once again, a pang of homesickness gnawed at her sensitive stomach.

The bus passed a large billboard on the side of a skyscraper with the words YOU THINK YOU'RE ALONE? And in the far right corner underneath that question was written, GOD. *Is that true?* Ani asked herself. *Then why does he still seem so far away—despite my fasting and prayer rituals?*

"You sit down, right now!" yelled a loud, deep woman's voice in the back. A child's wail broke loose. "Enough of that, you hear?!" the woman yelled again. The child's crying turned into a whimper. "Stop it, I said! Didn't I tell you we can't go anywhere when you're crying? If you don't stop this minute, the bus driver will stop the bus and make us get out in the middle of nowhere. Then we'll have to walk home and won't get to see Granny. Is that what you want?"

Ani leaned her head against the headrest and almost began to weep for that child. She wondered whether and when the child would ever learn that her mother's words were as meaningless as Tom's countless excuses or her nagging of him.

Tom. A heavy weight of guilt nudged her as she thought of him. Shouldn't she have expressed more gratefulness to the man who had tried to rescue her by giving her all that he had? Shouldn't she have continued to pretend dependence so that he would continue to feel good about himself? *No way,* she concluded. If she had, he would never come to accept his worth on his own, nor take responsibility for it. He would always depend on her to feel good about himself.

At least, that is what she had read in a magazine at the hair salon once. Her head agreed, but not her heart. And between the head and the heart, her stomach burned like coal once again. So far, the bland diet, the medicine, and the relaxation exercises did not seem to work.

"Entering Rhode Island," the sign on the highway announced about three hours later. Soon she would see Indri again.

It was hard to believe—her sweet sister, now married to the wealthy cousin Rianto! The prospect of money and security must have spurred Indri's decision; what else? Ani could not imagine Indri being married to that man any better than if she had married him. She could not help but feel guilty. Perhaps she had not said or done enough to warn Indri not to marry him. Or perhaps, she should have married Rianto to keep Indri from marrying him. Well, maybe not, she admitted.

As the bus approached the Providence bus station, Ani spotted Indri and Rianto walking toward the bus terminal. It had been almost three years since she had seen her sister. How grown-up she looked! *No longer a bouncing teen in sandals!* She was wearing black pants, high-heeled clogs, a hip-length yellow blouse with lace, and a silver belt. Her hair was pinned back into a bun with a purple ribbon holding it in place.

Could Indri still be playful? Ani wondered as she climbed off the bus. Indri greeted her with a bright, open smile and handed her a bouquet of roses. According to Sunda custom, the two sisters did not embrace or kiss. Instead, they held hands for a long time and looked into each other's eyes, laughing in delight.

"You look the same," the younger sister said in the Sunda dialect.

"I do?" Ani replied, grinning. "I don't believe it. You certainly look more grown-up and ladylike than when I left."

"I do?" Indri giggled.

"How is Mother?"

"Very well!"

"How is Father?"

"Doing better."

"What do you mean, doing better? Was he sick?"

Indri looked away.

"Indri," Ani asked again in an anxious voice, "what do you mean?"

"It's nothing to worry about. I will tell you later," Indri answered and looked around for something. "Don't you have a suitcase?"

"Of course. It's over there, next to the bus." Her brown suitcase stood out as the largest among the unloaded bags on the concrete sidewalk. Tucking the roses under one arm, Ani pulled the bag with the other as they walked into the terminal toward where Rianto sat reading a paper. He had not changed, Ani noted. The bald spot on the top of his head glowed with the reflection of the fluorescent lights as he looked up at them with his expressionless eyes. He managed to scramble into a standing position and threw the paper onto the end table.

"Welcome to Rhode Island, sister-in-law," Rianto rasped in the same mechanical voice with which he had proposed marriage to her.

Ani mustered a polite smile. "Thank you, cousin. And congratulations on your marriage to Indri," she said.

He nodded coldly, took her suitcase, and led them to the street, where a gray limousine was waiting. A short, light-brown-skinned Indonesian young man in his 20s ran out from the driver's door, opened the trunk, and lifted her suitcase into it.

Rianto opened the front right door for Ani. "You should sit up front so that you can have a better view," he said in a tone more demanding than inviting. Ani reluctantly obeyed. She would have preferred to sit with her sister in the back.

"I'm Putu from Bali," said the chauffeur next to her with a bucktooth smile. "Have you been to this part of America before?"

"No, I haven't."

"This is the smallest state in America, did you know that?"

"No, I did not know that."

The peach-red clouds danced in the soft ripples of the bay as the limousine crossed over the Hope Bridge to Aquidneck Island. A small fishing boat under the bridge blew its horn.

The silence behind Ani made her feel uneasy. She wished she could at least have eye contact with her sister. They stopped in front of a tall gate of iron. Putu pushed a button on a square box mounted behind the rearview mirror, opening the cast iron gate. The Tudor style "cottage" behind it, with its white gables against the purple, dark sky, reminded Ani of a haunted house in a horror film, or was it a castle in her grandmother's fairy tale book? She wasn't sure.

As Ani climbed out of the car, a cool breeze with a strange aroma of seaweed and salt embraced her. She took a deep breath, then a second and a third. How refreshing and rich the shore air was!

"Are you hungry, Ani? We have dinner waiting inside," asked Indri in Sundanese.

"Who needs to eat when you have this view?" Ani replied in their mother tongue as well. It felt as though her tongue had found its home again.

Putu carried the luggage into Ani's room, with Indri close behind. The house looked to be furnished in American medieval style, or so it seemed, like the houses she had seen in movies. "Did Rianto furnish this?" she asked.

"No," Indri replied. "He bought the house with everything in it, except for the paintings."

They entered a large room with a French door opening to a balcony overlooking the ocean. "You have your own bathroom, toilet, and shower. And look," Indri said as she opened the bathroom door. "The shower is in this large glass box. I get claustrophobic in there, but at least you don't have to worry about slipping on a wet floor when you walk into the bathroom. Oh, and I hope you brought your toothbrush. Putu says that in America, everyone has his own."

"That's right," Ani answered, smiling to herself. *So many things Indri has yet to learn about the American way of life!*

"Come downstairs and have supper now. Putu is a great cook. We cooked together all day for you."

Chapter 35

It was Tom's birthday. Not one phone message waited for him when he came home from work. No email. No letter from his parents, but they usually forgot his birthday, anyway. Ani had been gone for a week. The apartment seemed so empty without her. He realized he missed all of Ani: the mother, the sister, the lover—all of who she was. The fear of losing her pelted him like hail on the head.

But did she miss him? He doubted it. The news that Ani had never really needed his money all this time felt like a betrayal. True, she never asked him for money. She usually paid for their food on her own. But soon she would not need him anymore. She would be earning almost as much money as he and therefore may not want to stay with him. And once she left, he could hear his mother say, "You failed again, Tom." The fear of hearing those words alone drove him to the bottle, even more than the failure itself.

Just as he was about to open a beer bottle from the refrigerator, the doorbell rang. Tom had already taken off his business suit. Shirtless with only Jockeys on, he peered through the peephole: Emmanuel stood there, fishing poles in hand.

"I can see your eye, Tom. Ready to fish for some bass for dinner tonight?" Emmanuel asked through the door. "My fishing gear's in the car. Grab yours and come with me!"

Tom unlocked the door. "Wait a sec while I go into my room to change into my jeans and shoes," Tom said with enthusiasm. "But you can come in and wait if you want." Tom quickly went to his bedroom to put on a pair of jeans and a T-shirt, then grabbed his Orioles cap and a fishing pole from the hallway closet. "My hands are full," he said as he bounced past Emmanuel. Could you lock the door behind you, bro? Just press on the button on the inside knob, and leave the light on in the hallway."

Emmanuel pretended to fiddle with the door, left both inside and outside lights on, and shut the door, leaving it unlocked. He had a reason . . .

They rented a small fishing boat at the dam outside of Baltimore. Tom's fishing license lay secured in his waterproof pouch around his neck. It was the one thing he managed to pay in cash every year.

"Are you enjoying or grieving the distance between you and Ani?" pried Emmanuel.

Tom looked deep into the pond and watched tiny ripples form in the breeze. "I wish I knew myself," he groaned.

"Why are you saying that?"

"She's getting a student assistantship and scholarship money next term. She won't need my help anymore, and I—I don't know who I am without being needed."

Emmanuel remained silent for a while. "Man, Tom. You think Ani married you because she needed your money, or your ability to get her the green card the easy way?"

Tom shrugged his shoulder. "She denies doing that, but I can't believe she would love me for who I am."

"Didn't you ever learn in Sunday school that the God of the universe, the Almighty One who certainly doesn't *need* you because he is all-sufficient and almighty, loved you even before you were born—before you could do anything to please him?"

Tom sneered. "I wish I could believe in that God. He's just an old man with a long stick. Maybe he loved me when I was a cute kid with curly blond hair! But now? I kind of doubt he would love me."

"Why wouldn't he?" laughed Emmanuel. "I don't have curly blond hair, and I know he loves *me*!"

Tom's line jerked just then. "Whoa! I got one," he excitedly yelled as he reeled in whatever tugged on the end of the line. And up from out of the water, dangling on the hook, hung a fat, wiggly bass.

"Looks like the old man with a long stick sent you a birthday present," said Emmanuel, laughing.

Tom managed a humble smile. He had almost forgotten about his birthday. "How did you know it was my birthday?"

"A little birdie told me," was Emmanuel's reply.

When they returned to Tom's place, Emmanuel asked if he could come in and use the bathroom. "Lots of cars are parked here tonight. Someone's having a party," Tom noted. As soon as Tom entered his apartment, a crowd of about 15 people greeted him, singing the "Happy Birthday" song. Turning around, he looked at Emmanuel, who suddenly seemed in no hurry to use the toilet. Tom peered at his group of visitors again. "How did you all get in?"

"Secret insider job!" answered Emmanuel from behind.

The party began. "Pizza is on the kitchen table, everyone; drinks on the coffee table," announced Cynthia, the boss. She turned toward Tom. "My, you're looking glum today. Is turning 30 all that bad, Tom?"

"I'm already 30—really?"

"*Only* 30," corrected Cynthia. "Come on, Tom. Celebrate your youth! You're younger than most of us here."

Emmanuel lifted a glass of punch. "Let's drink to our birthday child, everybody. But I must apologize for this alcohol-free punch. Our boss strictly forbids us to serve any alcohol tonight. She wants us sober and alert in the morning." Ripples of laughter, moans, and a sarcastic "Yeah, sure" reverberated through the living room.

Cynthia added loudly, "Here's to Tom, a thirty-year-old jolly good fellow who is a very efficient computer technician, otherwise imperfect—not always lovable, but very much loved!"

"Amen! Amen!" a colleague started singing to the tune of the spiritual, clapping his hands in rhythm. Others joined in, half singing, half laughing. "Speech, speech!" someone else urged.

Everyone cheered and clapped. When they calmed down, their eyes turned toward Tom.

"Thank you, guys. Thank you very much." He paused a moment. "But I don't think I'm always lovable or a jolly good fellow. And I'm not always a very efficient computer technician," he said slowly, scratching his head. "But it's true! I'm now thirty years old!" Everyone laughed. Something suddenly clicked inside of Tom. For the first time in weeks—no, months—Tom felt light without having had a drop of alcohol.

"Did anyone bring beer?" asked one of the guests.

"There's some beer on top of the fridge and in the laundry room closet. Help yourself," Tom said.

Almost everyone had left by 11:30 p.m. Emmanuel lingered longer to help Tom clean up. Before he left, Emmanuel handed Tom an envelope. "Happy birthday," he said. "Open it later. I gotta go"

A few minutes after his friend left, Tom opened the envelope and pulled out a card with a golden frame. *The Creator loved you before you were born*, it said in gothic print. "Sure," he mumbled, shaking his head. He threw the card onto the coffee table and walked toward the end table to turn off the lamp. Next to it stood a four-foot bookshelf, where Ani's huge scrapbook drew his attention. She had given it to him last Christmas. He pulled it from the shelf, turned the light one notch brighter, and sat down to peruse it again.

You are thoughtful and caring in little things, it began. The words *little things* surprised him. What about the big stuff? Did they not matter to her?

You respect my religion and culture. Well, he thought he did. Lately, he wasn't so sure.

You are a good listener. He was that, at least before he married her.

I enjoy your fun-loving nature. That was also a trait of the past.

When you smile, you smile with your eyes and your mouth. Only Ani would have noticed that.

You are consistent and responsible in your business and work. He was glad she noticed!

You have a wide range of interests and tastes, and you are open-minded. He doubted if Ani knew all of his interests and preferences, but he took it as a compliment.

You have integrity, and I always know where you stand. Not so accurate, he confessed.

You make prompt decisions with consideration of me and my needs. He was not so sure.

You seldom lose your temper, and when you do, you make me laugh, not afraid. True.

You have a great sense of humor. He used to have one.

Tom felt himself reaching for a beer. His body followed. What he was reading made him feel uncomfortable, and he didn't know why. But he read on:

You are strong, and being around you makes me feel secure.
You are very affirming of my strengths and gifts.
You make me feel accepted.
You don't make fun of my accent.
You have good posture, and you walk with resolve.
You have a strong, manly voice, but you can also speak softly.
Your touch is gentle; your words are kind.
You always point out the positive side.
You enjoy competition but don't mind losing once in a while.

Tom couldn't remember having ever read this list before. Could it be that he had assumed she was merely flattering him? Or could it be that she genuinely thought all those things about him? Maybe a few of them were right, but they had become less so lately. He had become distant, inconsiderate, preoccupied, sloppy, and careless. Would she still say all these things? Especially now that he was not needed anymore, and therefore worthless?

The Creator loved you before you were born; the line in Emmanuel's birthday card echoed in his mind. *Why would God love someone before that person became a significant adult?* A thick fuzz formed over Tom's mind as he tried to analyze such irony. "Imperfect and not always lovable," someone had said at the party, "but loved." None of that made any *sense.*

He slammed the scrapbook shut, placed it back on the shelf, and turned off the lamp. His head told him it was bedtime. But suddenly craving for something more potent than beer, he veered toward the kitchen. He knew that behind several empty bottles above the fridge, a pint of vodka was beckoning.

Chapter 36

The sun had already risen when Indri, fully dressed, entered Ani's room with a tray in hand.

"You're still sleeping?!" Indri chided. "Didn't you recite your morning prayers?"

Ani rubbed her eyes and sat up in bed. "What time is it?"

"About six-thirty," Indri said, pulling a rope to the right of the windows so that the curtains folded upward like an accordion. The rays of the morning sun flooded the room.

Ani sat up in bed and took the cup of coffee from the tray. She peered through the French window. The rich dark blue of the Narragansett Bay appeared to flow like a gentle river, glistening in a glass-like calm in the early morning sun. Screeching seagulls flew by. Ani placed the cup on the bedside table, rolled out of bed, and ran toward the open window. "Can we eat breakfast out on the patio?" she asked in Indonesian.

"I don't know," replied Indri. "I'm still new here. I don't know what we're allowed to do."

Ani giggled. "This is your home. You are the lady of the house, and you don't know what you're allowed to do?"

Indri hesitated. Then her eyes lit up. "I guess it's all right. Rianto has gone out for the day. I will ask Putu."

"Oh dear, there's a man in the house. I better get dressed," Ani said with a giggle. She had not felt this free and light in a long, long time. Not thirty minutes later, Ani followed Indri out onto the deck, carrying parts of the breakfast that Putu had prepared for them. But just as she crossed over the threshold, Ani tripped on a loose tile and crashed head-on into the round table a few feet away. The coffee, the cream, and the jam all slid onto the table and combined into a puddle of soup. A few rolls fell onto the tiled floor below. Amazingly, only one cup broke. A roll of giggles and laughter followed.

Putu entered the patio from another door. "I will bring you another tray of food," he said, buck teeth showing. He left and soon returned with a wet rag and a plastic bag for garbage. Indri held the bag for Putu while Ani picked up some rolls from the floor. A seagull flew down and perched on the table, nearing the basket of toast. But Putu quickly shooed it away and covered the basket with a plate. "I will be back with everything shortly, ladies."

Gentle waves crashed against the rocks just fifteen feet down the grassy hill from where they sat. Several seagulls landed on the stone wall that separated the property from the neighbor's, waiting for some food to be thrown to them.

When Putu brought another tray with breakfast and a new pot of coffee, he asked, "May I suggest something? It's a nice day. Why not take a walk on the famous Cliff Walk this afternoon? I will bring you there and pick you up three hours later. You will like it."

Putu dropped them off at the beginning of the Cliff Walk on Memorial Drive. "I will pick you up here again in three hours. Here are two bottles of water for you. Do you have some money with you?"

The women nodded.

As soon as they set out on the Cliff Walk, Ani heard a sound she had not heard in a very long time: a rushing, a crashing, and then a slow rumble. And then again, a rushing, a crashing, and a slow rumble. She peeked between the hedges to her left. Blue and green ocean waves glided toward her below, folding over, crashing against the rocks, exploding into a tall pillar of foam against the blue sky—and after a fall, receding again, dragging pebbles of stone with them.

Ani was instantly in love with this multidimensional beauty—not only its sights, sounds, smells, but also the touch of the breeze that caressed her cheeks. "Oh, Indri, you are so lucky to be here!" And for a very brief moment, she wished she had married Rianto after all. But only for a fraction of a moment.

The two sisters walked in silence for about ninety minutes, taking in the sights of stately mansions on the right, the fragrance of wild rosebushes on the left, and the sounds of seagulls above. The sound of turbulent waves crashing against the rocks accompanied the soothing massage of a warm breeze on Ani's cheeks. After the women passed a Chinese tea house, they walked through a concrete brick tunnel, which provided just the right acoustic for an impromptu Indonesian folk song. When they exited the other end, a cape spread out before them, its tip pointing southward toward the open ocean. A bay lay to its west and a small rocky island to the east.

They sat down on the rocks to rest. Indri opened an umbrella. "Come, Ani. Don't you want to sit under it, too? You have a lighter complexion than I," offered Indri.

"Thanks, no. In America, a suntan is considered beautiful."

"Really?"

"Really. Tell me, sister, tell me about Father and Mother and Rudi. How are they?" Ani asked.

"Father is not well. I wasn't supposed to tell you," Indri began. "He fainted about two months ago. It happened right after Rianto visited us and proposed to me and said he'd take me to America with him."

"What was wrong with him?"

"He had a slight stroke. It was a blessing in disguise, because when the doctor treated him, he discovered that Father has diabetes. So he must take medicine every day and watch what he eats."

"Why didn't anyone tell me this?" cried Ani angrily.

"They didn't want to worry you."

Ani hung her head in shame. As the oldest child, she felt she should have been there when this happened.

"And how is Mother doing?"

"She's exhausted. We can afford only one servant now, and Rudi helps as much as he can. But still—"

"So when will you start attending the School of Design, Indri?" Ani asked. "I sent you the information by email a long time ago, but you never said anything about it."

Indri looked away toward the ocean. "I hope this fall. I am waiting to hear if they will accept me. I hope I can begin soon, before a baby comes."

"Baby already? Oh, Indri. You're too young to have a child!"

"No, I'm not!" answered Indri. "Rianto wants a child before he gets too old."

"If he isn't already too old to make one," Ani teased, picking up and throwing a blade of grass into her sister's face.

"Have you heard what happened to our Chinese neighbors?" Indri asked, obviously eager to change the subject. Ani shook her head.

"Some rioters from the city ransacked their house. They were there alone at the time, and they were beaten badly. Rudi heard them scream, so he went over there and pleaded with the rioters to stop hurting them. It's a good thing that Rudi and I look more brown than you do, and that Father was home. They finally stopped and left the neighbor's house, but only after they broke some of the china and pottery and stole some valuables."

"How are they now?"

"Better. They were badly hurt and afraid for months. They'll open their gate only to us. Mother and I went there every day to nurse them back to health and clean up their house. At least their house was not burned down."

Ani sighed. "I sometimes wish that our mother had married a Chinese instead of our father."

"How can you say such a thing? If we had been born Chinese, we might have been raped and beaten!"

"I know. It's just that I feel so ashamed for our people who make trouble for others of a different race or religion."

"They say that Christians instigated the riots," Indri said coldly.

"I don't believe it," Ani retorted. "Certainly not the ones who follow their founder, Isa. It's more likely that rebels started the riots and then blamed the riots on the Chinese and the Christians."

"Why would they do that?"

"They're just jealous of those who have more means, and they need a scapegoat for their troubles. As I said, it makes me ashamed of our religion."

Indri stared at her sister in disbelief. "But you're still a Muslim, aren't you?"

"Of course, I am. But I live in America now. I'm free to say and believe what I want. And so are you!"

That night, Ani woke up to the sound of a woman's wail. She sat up with a start. Had she been dreaming? No, there it was again. It seemed to come either from the heating vent in the ceiling or the room next to hers. A pang of fear shot through Ani's heart as she recognized the sound, which was the same sound that Indri used to make when their younger brother played a prank on them. Only louder. And there was no giggle or laughter afterward.

Still dressed, Ani ventured into the hall. The crying had stopped, and all seemed quiet. Thirty seconds later, a door opened down the hall from her. She quickly stepped back into her room and closed the door, listening. She could hear the other door slam shut and a man's footsteps pat-patting by her door and down the stairs. Moments later, Rianto's Mercedes' diesel engine started up across the court, and tires screeched. The roar of the motor dissipated into the night.

Ani opened her door. The sound of a sob and quiet wailing came from the room next to hers. *What did he do to my sister?* Ani asked herself. There was only one way to find out.

She knocked gently at Indri's door. No response, just more sobbing. She cracked the door open and whispered, "It's me. Can I come in?"

The sobbing stopped. As Ani tiptoed into the room, she smelled a strong nicotine odor. A small lamp next to the bed shone on Indri's hair as she hid her face behind a blanket. Ani heard another sob and a heave.

"Sister, I'm here now. What happened to you? What did he do to you?" Ani asked, softly touching Indri's shoulder. It was the same question Ani asked Indri once when Indri was only nine years old. At that time, the "he" was a servant in their home who had lured Indri behind the bushes and tried to undress her. Ani told their mother, who instantly fired the servant and told him never to return.

Indri continued to sob quietly. "Careful—he won't be gone long," she managed to say between sobs. "He's gone to buy some cigarettes. He always says that when he's angry."

"Why would he be angry?" Ani asked. She coughed away the smell of smoke, got up, and opened the window. She sat down on the bed next to Indri. "I heard you scream. How did he hurt you?"

Indri slowly turned her face toward Ani and held out her arm. Five round, brownish-black marks were embedded in her raw flesh.

"Ugh!" cried Ani. "Cigarette burns?! Why would he be so angry to do this to you?"

"I showed him the application to the Providence School of Design when he came home. I thought he would be happy. But instead, he—he took it away from me and tore it up. He said—he said I was not—not smart enough to study in America." A surge of fresh tears flowed.

"And then?" Ani prodded, blood rising to her face.

"I reminded him that he promised my father that I could study in America. That's when he—" She stopped and began to weep again, pointing to her arm.

"Do you have any antibiotic ointment? Here?"

Indri shook her head. "I don't want to show this to Putu. Maybe you can ask him."

"I will."

Careful not to touch her arm, Ani gently covered Indri with the blanket and pulled her head close to her chest, cradling her until the tears dried. "It will be okay, you'll see," said Ani. But she wasn't so sure. Ani could not help but felt guilty. If she had married Rianto, this would not be happening. She knew how to stand up for herself. Indri did not.

Ani could not sleep for a long time that night. Fear for Indri's safety deluged her like a wave crashing over the rocks on the shore.

Chapter 37

The morning after his birthday party, Tom woke up with the landline telephone ringing next to his bed. The ringing felt like a rattle of metal balls inside his brain.

"Where are you, Tom Hanson?" The caustic voice belonged to Cynthia. "Still celebrating yesterday's birthday?"

He sleepily looked at the clock next to him. It read 10:05.

"Congratulations," Cynthia continued. "You just lost yourself a five-hundred-dollar bonus commission. Perhaps you now remember that our meeting with the Big Fish was scheduled for 9:30 a.m. this morning?"

He moaned. The Big Fish was to bring the company the highest income since its beginnings. He would be maintaining that company's two hundred personal computers, and he was to sign the contract today.

"I'm sorry, but I woke up with this splitting headache this morning, and I—"

"We both know what *that* means, Tom." The word *that* rattled like a hammer on a metal bar.

"It's your fault, Cynthia," Tom said with a teasing tone. "I heard it was you who planned the birthday party I didn't ask for."

"I beg your pardon? Tom, you didn't drink one drop at the party. What you did after that is way beyond my responsibility."

"I don't know what happened after that. Maybe I got hit on the head and got mugged. Can't you please just let me have me a sick day?"

"Not on your life. If you don't get your butt over here ASAP, you're fired. Do you understand?"

Tom entered Cynthia's office an hour later and sat down on a chair across her mahogany desk. Cynthia, dressed in a gray tailored suit, was sitting sideways, facing the computer. No smiles, no greeting awaited Tom. Instead, Cynthia's eyes were glued to the screen. The long, purple-lacquered nail of her left hand's middle finger pounded in a monotonous *tap tap* on the space next to the keyboard.

Tom scratched his throat to get Cynthia's attention.

"I know you're here," she said coldly without turning to him. Her expression reminded Tom of one she had displayed after a computer crash. It wasn't a pretty one. The contrast between yesterday's and today's Cynthia chilled him to the bone. He wondered whether the love-filled birthday celebration the night before had been just a dream and whether this was the beginning of a nightmare. He leaned forward to take a peek at her computer screen. She quickly held up her hand to stop him, but—too late. He saw what she had not wanted him to see: a screen saver of mere sea monsters gliding slowly from left to right across the screen –not charts with figures or lists with names. She had been dawdling to avoid talking with him!

She turned her swivel chair toward him and glared at him with the iciest look he'd ever seen in a woman's eyes. "Cole took care of your prospective client this morning, Tom. You have no more assignments today."

"Then why did you bother to make me come out here? I told you I was sick."

She lowered her head for a moment, then looked at him again, this time with a momentary expression of compassion. "Tom, I called you here because I suspect you must have indulged in something other than alcohol-free punch after we left you last night. Or perhaps you have a brain tumor that causes these morning headaches after a good night's sleep?"

Tom shook his head. "I don't remember if I had anything after you guys left. Honest. I was tired, and if I had something I shouldn't have, I'm sorry. I won't let it happen ag—"

"Stop it, Tom," she said. "You sing the same tune each time

when you come in late or even call in sick. You've done so at least four times in the past two months, and we just can't put up with that anymore."

"Four times?"

"Yes, four times."

"Maybe I've been overworked, and I—"

"No more excuses, Tom."

"So you're firing me? You could have done that over the phone so I could get more sleep!"

"Not quite." Cynthia swiveled her chair again toward the computer, pushed a few buttons on the keyboard, and finally, the print button. "I'm giving you a new assignment." She handed him a form.

"What's this?" he asked.

"It's a document of a commitment, Tom. Let me explain. We've concluded that your problem is alcohol abuse. A fancier term is substance dependency. In short—" She paused, closed her eyes for a moment, and then continued with a softer, kinder tone. "The board and I decided to give you four weeks off to get you back on track. And here is how," she said, pointing to the form. "It's a treatment program for addicts at the Ridgewood Substance Abuse Treatment and Recovery Center. And because we value your skills and expertise, we're paying for it."

Tom almost fell off his chair. "Oh, for crying out loud, Cynthia. I'm a big boy. I don't need a program to fix me."

Cynthia ignored his statement and continued. "The paper you have in your hand is a form that says you will commit yourself to this 28-day program, plus outpatient care. It's for good and decent professionals like you—people who are in danger of letting the poison of alcohol ruin their health, their marriage, and their career. And I think you are one of them."

Tom shook his head and looked away.

"You mean well when you say you want to stop drinking. Yet

over and over again, you fall back into your habit. And when you do, you miss important appointments, like the one today."

Tom's ears turned crimson. His head bent over the Ridgewood brochure in his hand.

"Your wife is out of town for a couple of weeks, right? This is a perfect opportunity to get this taken care of before Ani leaves you permanently, don't you think?"

He squirmed in his seat. "Why do you think she would leave me permanently?" he asked defensively.

"Oh, Tom," Cynthia said, sighing. "She will if you don't do something about this and if she knows what's good for her. It would be wrong for her to pretend that everything is fine while you're killing yourself and your marriage. Believe me, I know all about it. My mother was an alcoholic before she met my father. She kept waking up with headaches like you. So her first husband packed up his things and left. Never came back again."

Cynthia paused for effect. "After he left, my mother got help and sobered up for good. She found another man and then had me. She was lucky. That's why I think you should get help now before it's too late."

"Boy, you've thought this all through, haven't you?"

"You bet I have, Tom. I know your wife is a treasure. You don't want to lose her, do you?" Cynthia got up, walked to the window, and closed the blinds to block the midmorning sun's rays. Then she sat down again and leaned forward. "There's one more thing, Tom," she said in a gentler tone. "If you don't accept this offer, you are giving me only one alternative, and that is to fire you. Which of the two options would you rather take?"

Tom stared back at her, fighting back the liquid that began to cloud his eyes. "Are you saying I have no other choice?"

"You always have another choice. You can look for a job elsewhere, without our recommendation, or start your own company. We can't force you to accept this offer. But if you want to stay with us, this is our condition."

Tom looked out the window, then at the form. *The nerve of those people*, Tom thought, *controlling me like that. But h*e did not want to lose this job. The company, the clientele, the rhythm, the pay, the bonuses—all felt like an old, comfortable shoe. He usually even liked Cynthia. The idea of starting his own business released a whole new wave of anxiety; neither marketing nor accounting was his forte. He knew it would take years to build up a good clientele elsewhere.

No, he decided; he'd better not give up working for this company. Swallowing his pride and getting admitted to Ridgewood felt safer. He needed to be in good shape to remain Ani's hero. That was still his end goal. Anything to get there would be worth it.

"Who will pay for this again?" Tom asked. "It must cost a fortune."

"The profits you have brought into our company," Cynthia answered. "I must admit, if we lost you, the company would suffer more than I would want to admit. It's also a good tax deduction."

He managed a wry smile. "So this isn't really about saving me. It's about saving the company."

She laughed. "I see it as saving us both."

Saving someone or something outside of himself clinched the deal for Tom. "All right, I'm in," he said, pulling a pen out of his pocket. "Where do I sign?"

"Right here," Cynthia said, showing him where. "I've already taken the liberty of calling the center to see if they have room today, and they do. You can get admitted this very morning."

"This morning?" asked Tom, wincing. "Don't I get to pack first?"

Cynthia looked at her watch. "They want you there before noon, and it's already 11:15. I will arrange for their private shuttle to pick you up from here shortly. But give me your apartment key. I'll ask Emmanuel to bring you some clothes tonight. You'll need them, won't you?"

"Why can't I drive there myself and get them?"

Cynthia gave him a chiding look.

"Never mind," Tom mumbled, not surprised at her distrust. "Here are all my keys," Tom said as he threw the chain on the desk. "Ask Emmanuel to start my car up and run it once in a while, so that the battery won't go dead."

Yes, he was angry. Yes, he felt shame. He felt like a little boy who had been caught and steamrolled over. But after he left Cynthia's office and sat down in his computer cubicle, a calm rolled over him. Cynthia was right, he concluded. Painfully right. And he knew she acted out of "tough love," as he had heard someone coin such action.

But then, panic gripped him. Didn't Cynthia say that the program lasted four weeks? His last and most crucial moonlighting run for Solomon was approaching in two weeks.

Chapter 38

The reception for Rianto and his new bride took place at Shamrock Inn on Newport's Ocean Drive. Wearing a long, peach chiffon gown with the keris pendant clipped to the end of a long gold necklace, Ani felt like a princess at a royal feast. After all, her sister Indri was about to be introduced publicly as the wife of her billionaire cousin.

Minutes before the first guest arrived, Ani and Indri examined the buffet. Everything seemed in place on the two twenty-foot tables laden with hors d'oeuvres of many colors and varieties. Roses and carnations had been entwined in green branches of asparagus and woven in between the dishes in a pattern of symmetrical, continuous waves. On a large round rotating platter, an array of small stuffed tomatoes, halved hard-boiled eggs with spicy yolk fillings, rolled ham, and beef surrounded a basket of Italian bread sticks and crackers.

Ani's mouth watered. She suddenly realized how Americanized she had become. When she first arrived in the USA, she would never have eaten such foods.

Just then, Ani and Indri saw Rianto on the other side of the table, helping himself to several pieces at a time, including the ham.

Ani sighed audibly. "It is hard to be a good Muslim in the United States," she whispered to Indri. Then, reaching over the table, she picked up a rolled ham slice with a toothpick and held it before Indri's face. "Doesn't it say somewhere that when there's nothing else to eat, you can eat what's available?" she asked. "Besides, your husband over there is your model and leader now. You can do what he does, can't you?"

Indri froze. As if in a trance, she took the toothpick between her fingers and guided it toward her mouth. "No!" she suddenly said. "I can't eat this." She dropped the toothpick with the ham onto Ani's paper plate and slipped away.

An hour passed before she spotted Indri again, following Rianto around with a plastic smile on her face and nodding silently at the people he introduced. Ani snaked her way through the crowd. When Indri's eyes met hers, Ani smiled, mouthing, "I'm sorry." The fixed smile on Indri's face slowly turned into a real one, accompanied by a nod. They stood in eye contact for several moments until a fresh array of tuxes and gowns separated their view of each other.

The music stopped. "I would like to make a toast," a rich, loud voice bellowed over the loudspeaker. Everyone turned toward the man on the stage at the other end of the large room. A tall African-looking man with a baton in his hand was adjusting the microphone. Ani jolted. He looked a lot like Solomon, the man who had played the saxophone at her wedding. But then to Ani, all men of African descent looked the same. *And maybe they're all musicians.*

"Can you come up here, Mr. and Mrs. Rianto?" the tall man at the microphone asked in a deep voice.

Ani gasped. Not only did the man look like Solomon, he sounded just like him. She looked again. *If it really is Solomon, what is he doing here of all places?* she asked herelf.

Everyone clapped as Indri and Rianto snaked their way through the crowd, hand in hand. As the couple neared the stage, something dawned on Ani. Hadn't Solomon told her once that he knew a rich guy from Indonesia? Could he have meant Rianto? Why else would Solomon have come from Baltimore to be here? *What a small world!*

But then her heart began to race. What if Solomon blurted out to Rianto and Indri about Ani's marriage to Tom? She hoped that all Asians looked similar in Solomon's estimation and that he would not recognize her. But just in case he did recognize her, she turned around, ducked as low as possible, and wiggled her way through the crowd toward the exit. She stood behind the door in the foyer and listened.

"I would like to make a toast," she heard Solomon's voice boom through the loudspeakers. "Here's to Rianto Rianto, the finest man from Indonesia I have ever met. Well . . . the only man from Indonesia I have ever met."

Everyone laughed.

"And here is to his beautiful, young bride, Indri. To you both, a happy and long, successful life together." Ani imagined he was raising a glass of champagne.

"Thank you very much." It was Rianto's voice. "Thank you all for coming and welcoming us so graciously. My wife tells me that her sister, who is here tonight, will sing for us an Indonesian wedding song. Would you like to hear it?"

Half of the guests, mostly Indonesians, Filipinos, Malaysians, and other Asians, cheered and whistled. The other half were Americans, who showed their approval with a less enthusiastic applause.

"Ani, where are you?" Rianto said as he covered his forehead to block the bright ceiling lights. "I think she is too modest. Can everyone please look for her? She is wearing a peach lace dress, and she has straight, long black hair."

Everyone stirred, turning their heads in different directions. Most of the other women were older and had shorter hair. And no one wore a peach lace dress like Ani.

The rear door of the auditorium opened. "There she is! At the exit!" someone shouted. A spotlight moved around the room and stopped over Ani, who had just entered.

"Ani, come to the front and sing for us. It is your sister's wish," she heard Rianto say. She wished she could just beam up as the characters did in *Star Trek*. But for Indri's sake, she would be brave. Her heart was clapping more wildly than the guests in rhythm to the band's fanfare as she timidly inched her way through the crowd. Rianto gallantly helped her up to the podium and sat down in the first row.

Composure in all circumstances is what her mother had taught her, and she knew how to hide the opposite. She had sung at relatives' weddings many times and always enjoyed the task that defined her role in a crowd. But tonight was different. Her head reeled; her face felt hot, her knees weak. Nevertheless, Ani was a woman who aspired to be in charge of her destiny. Counting on her makeup to cover the redness, she took the microphone and feigned a smile. She would have to sing acapella, she thought. But she was mistaken. Indri had set up the accompanying music on tape with amplifiers, and the music began.

Never mind about Solomon now; just sing for Indri! Ani told herself. She took two long, deep breaths and began to sing to Indri, whose gentle tears formed rivers of rouge on her cheeks. The song itself provided soothing magic—even for the singer herself, and the longer Ani sang, the more relaxed she became.

Halfway through the song, she noticed Rianto's dark and stern stare focusing on her chest. As uncomfortable as it was, she reminded herself to concentrate on her task, turned her eyes away toward the crowd, and continued to sing.

When the song ended, the applause began from the rear and grew into a crescendo from all over the room. "More, more!" a few in the audience cried. She bowed slightly and smiled.

And where had Solomon disappeared? *I must find him before he says anything to Rianto or Indri about my marriage to Tom!*

Chapter 39

The recovery center for adult substance abusers felt more like a three-star hotel to Tom than an institution or a hospital. The attendants, physicians, nurses, and therapists wore regular, informal clothes with official name tags. A comfortable lounge with carpets and curtains, sofas and matching chairs, a television, a pool table, and a Ping-Pong table gave the place the feel of a country club.

"Welcome, Tom. We try to be like a big family here," said Neil, the receiving attendant.

"Will I have to be here for four whole weeks?" Tom asked in a lamenting tone.

"After three weeks here, we'll re-evaluate you. If the therapist agrees, you can then be dismissed and come to an evening program three days a week for at least a month."

"Am I allowed an evening off while I'm here?" Tom asked nervously. "I have an important job I need to do in two weeks from now." It was to be his last rendezvous with a senator.

"I'm sorry, Tom," replied Neil. "You're allowed visitors, but you're not allowed to leave the premises until we release you from the program."

"What is this? A prison?"

"No, but you signed an agreement with us that stated that—"

"Never mind explaining," Tom interrupted grumpily. He would simply have to sneak out when the time came, he surmised.

Emmanuel, the helpful colleague and friend that he was, brought Tom a suitcase full of clothes that evening. One item was the dark gray suit that Tom had explicitly requested. Tom immediately searched for the keris pendant, which he remembered having stuffed into the left trouser pocket after his last rendezvous. But there was no keris on the lapel of his coat. Neither was it in the pockets.

"Are you missing some money?" asked Emmanuel.

Tom ignored the question. "You sure nothing fell out when you put these clothes into the suitcase?" he asked.

"I'm sure. But what exactly are you looking for?" Emmanuel repeated.

"It's sort of like a pendant that almost looks like the old type of tie clasp—not round but long, about this big, and it's in the shape of a sword," Tom answered, showing the length of it with his thumb and index finger. "You might have seen Ani wear one like it on her necklace."

"Vaguely. An ugly thing, if I remember. So why do you need it here? Is it some kind of talisman?"

Tom laughed. "No. I need it to carry out a job ten days from now. In ten days, to be exact." He wiped his brow with a tissue. "It's very important, Emmanuel. You have no idea how important."

"Wait a minute. Aren't you supposed to stay here for three or four weeks?"

"Yeah, I am," Tom said, scratching his head. "While I figure that out, could you please go back to my place and look for the keris pin again? If it wasn't in my coat pocket or on the coat itself, it has to be on the floor somewhere. Oh, and one more thing. I need the charger for my cell phone, and while you're there, please bring me a white shirt, my black shoes, black socks, and a nice tie. I think that should do."

The following morning, Neil escorted Tom to a door marked GROUP THERAPY. "This is the most important part of the program," Neil explained. "But do understand that not all participants come to the recovery center for treatment for alcohol or drug dependency. You'll see what I mean when you listen to their stories."

Tom soon did. A medical doctor said he was there because of burnout. Another had checked in because of an eating disorder. Two others admitted to being addicted to drugs. A professional singer in her twenties said she helped her significant other to remain addicted by rescuing him from financial disaster all the time. "I married Jonathan because he was weak, and I was strong," she told the group. "I wouldn't know who I am without him." *Ah! A soul mate,* Tom thought, remembering his first encounter with Ani. He had thought she was just a lost, needy foreigner then. Look what she turned out to be—someone so strong and independent, she put him to shame. And what was he? A man without significance because she didn't need his rescue anymore.

The first group session lasted 90 minutes. A short, dark-haired Latino in his forties introduced himself. "I'm Ramon, this group's facilitator. I don't lecture; I just make sure you all listen to each other with respect. Once in a while, I might ask some questions, and you are welcome to ask each other questions. I try to make sure you all get a chance to say what's on your mind. All I ask of you is not to repeat anything you hear in here to anyone out there."

It surprised Tom that even he eventually relaxed enough to open up to the group. "I want to be someone special," he confessed when he introduced himself as a workaholic. "I want to prove to my mom and dad, and my wife, that I'm more than just an ordinary guy."

And as he said that, he found himself covering his face, hiding his tears. "I'm sorry," he laughed apologetically.

"Welcome to the human race, Tom," said Ramon in a quiet, reassuring tone. "It's okay to feel that pain. Up till now, you've been trying to drown it in alcohol, but every time you do, it gets worse, doesn't it?"

"I just think that I have to be a hero to earn their regard. The tension is killing me, so I try to numb it. Is that so wrong?"

All eyes were on him. Somber eyes, sympathetic eyes; mouths that had no answer. "Tom, when did your wife start liking you?" asked Ramon.

He shrugged his shoulder. "She smiled a lot. I thought she liked me from the beginning when I first met her."

"Even before you rescued her?"

Tom gave out a short laugh. "Maybe. She used to look at me with those gentle eyes."

"Why do you think she did that even before she needed any rescue?"

Tom scratched his head. "I don't know," he answered slowly, looking at Ramon for an answer. But the therapist just gazed back without expression, waiting. "I have no idea how long she would have liked me the way things were. Because it wasn't long after that—she needed me to rescue her. Or I thought she did. And when I became the rescuer, boy, did I feel good about myself! Is that so wrong?"

Some members of the group moaned. "Lots," said one woman to his left. "How about saying 'I'm valuable even if I don't rescue anyone?'"

Tom shook his head. "I can't believe that."

"Maybe not yet," offered Ramon. "But try saying it anyway. Go ahead, say it."

Tom waited a moment, looking at the group for support. "All right, here goes. I'm valuable even if I don't rescue anyone."

"How was that again?" asked Ramon with a twinkle.

"I can't say it again," Tom said. "It just doesn't sound true."

"Do you know the story from the Bible where Jesus allowed little children to gather around him?" asked Ramon. "Well, are children heroes? Of course not. They hadn't achieved anything, produced anything, or accomplished anything. Apparently, he loved them for who they were. How does that strike you?"

Tom shook his head. "To be frank—that blows my mind. It's making me ask myself why I'm trying so hard to measure up to something, or someone, to feel special or loved."

"Exactly," replied Ramon. "Why do you?"

Tom had no answer.

That night, Tom could not sleep. He turned on the light and began to read the book *The Search for Significance* by Robert S. McGee, which the admissions director had given him to read. It confirmed what he had already learned, that his significance was, first of all, based on God's love and undeserved favor. Would he really *not* have to be rich or rescue others to be significant? Could he just be and do the best he could without having that goal?

I can do good things for others because *I'm special and loved, not* in order *to be special and loved,* Tom concluded. But he wondered if and when the truth of this message would ever sink in deep enough to change his warped thinking.

Chapter 40

Rianto rushed to Solomon, who was standing at the far side of the room. "I need to talk with you," he hissed.

"You have quite a talented sister-in-law," Solomon replied, ignoring his command. "She reminds me of a young lady that I know in Baltimore who sings just like her. In fact, she sang the same song at my friend's wedding."

"That's nice," answered Rianto, who was not listening to a word Solomon said. "Did you notice what my sister-in-law is wearing around her neck?"

"No sir."

"The keris pin, my keris," Rianto hissed. "I told you before there is only one such keris. I had it handmade. It is the same one I gave you to get your courier to wear. How and why do you suppose she is wearing it here? I thought you told me you would pick a non-conspicuous, white male to do the job!"

Solomon shook his head. "I did exactly that. I'm sure what she's wearing is a fake copy or something. How do you know it's yours? Maybe there are others that are similar?"

Rianto shook his head. "Similar, yes, but each one is unique. Mine has two tongues. She is wearing mine, the one with two tongues. I saw it when I was helping her up to the stage."

"Can't you talk to her about it?"

"I will. But I don't see her. If you find her first, please ask her to take it off. One of us better tell her before Senator Johnson gets here."

"Senator Johnson will be here? Oh no! I better make sure he doesn't see me here. He might connect me with you, and he's not supposed to know you're the big donor." As soon as he said this, Solomon darted off to search for the woman who sang while vigilantly checking for the senator's appearance.

He spotted the singer on the other side of the room. *She looks so much like Ani.* But as he started toward her, she slipped out through one of the side doors.

Ani was heading for the women's restroom, where she thought she could hide from Solomon. Just as she passed a supporting column, a strong black hand grasped her elbow from behind. It was Solomon's.

"Sorry to be so rough on you, Annie," he said, saying her name the American way. "But I need to talk with you. It's urgent."

"You're Solomon, right?"

"Yes! It's been a while since the wedding. I didn't recognize you at first. Small world, isn't it?"

"Solomon, please don't tell anyone here that I'm married to Tom. None of my family, not even Indri, know about it. They must not know!"

Solomon laughed. "Rest assured. I won't say anything as long as you—" Solomon paused, his dark brown eyes piercing the pendant on her necklace. "As long as you give me that pretty thing you're wearing on your chain."

"What?" she protested with a caustic laugh. She grasped the keris pendant. "It's my family emblem. I can't give you that!"

"Hmm," he said, eyeing the emblem. "Two tongues on a dragon's mouth. What does that represent?"

"You're wrong. It has only one tongue."

"Are you sure? I'll bet you two million dollars that the one you're wearing has two, not one."

"You're drunk and seeing double," she laughed.

He shook his head. "I don't drink on the job. I swear it has two."

"It does not!" She instinctively slid off her necklace and held it out between him and her. "See?" she said. "It has only—" She paused and gaped as she scrutinized it herself. "Oh, my goodness. It *does* have two tongues. How did that hap—? Why it's, it's—"

"It's what?"

"It's not mine to give you," she said, paling. "It *is* Rianto's. He must have given it to Indri, and somehow it ended up with my things. I must give it back to Indri. I can't give you this. Isn't there something else I can do in exchange for your silence?"

"Not really. You see, when Rianto helped you up to the stage, he noticed you were wearing his pin. He asked me to get it from you before—"

"Before what?"

Solomon swallowed and shifted. "Never mind. Just do me a favor for now. Please take it off and put it in your purse. Just don't wear it here. I can't explain why right now. That's the only favor I ask of you in exchange for my keeping my mouth shut about your marriage to Tom."

"What? Your marriage? Are you married?" asked a woman with an Indonesian accent from behind them. Indri. "Who is Tom?"

Solomon quickly assessed the embarrassing situation for Ani and excused himself.

Indri moved closer to Ani and switched from English to Indonesian. "I don't understand much English, but I am sure I heard this man say something about you being married."

"You didn't understand correctly," said Ani, laughing nervously. As soon as she lied, she felt nauseous. "I—I need the ladies' room," she said and darted for the restroom, Indri following behind.

When Ani emerged from her stall to wash her hands and face, Indri was there, waiting with a stern look just like that of their mother when she was cross.

"You always get sick when you lie!" Indri said. "So, are you going to tell me the truth?"

"All right, I'll tell you. But first, I have to ask you something.

Do you see this pendant?" Ani asked, taking it off her chain. "Did Rianto give you one like this?"

Indri looked at it closely. "No, but I saw this strange thing somewhere. Oh yes. On a large painting in our house."

"Never mind then." Ani put it into her little purse. "As for my marriage to a man named Tom, it's true. But please, promise not to tell anyone, especially not Mother and Father."

Indri nodded. They found a two-seater sofa in the room adjoining the restroom and sat down.

"When Uncle Lee fell ill," Ani began to explain, "I knew he could not support my education here anymore. Tom is a friend of the band leader, Solomon. He offered to marry me so I could stay here and study. But I said no. Meantime, Rianto offered to pay for my education, so I stayed. A few months later, I fell in love with Tom."

"The same Tom?"

"Yes. And I married him. That's much better than what you did," Ani added.

"What do you mean? What did I do?"

"You married an old man for his money, didn't you?"

"Yes, but our parents approved of my marriage. You know they never would approve of yours," Indri retorted.

"Maybe so, but would they have approved of your marriage if they knew what Rianto would be doing to you every night?"

Indri's eyes welled with tears. "No. But please, promise not to tell them!"

Ani drew a big sigh. "Let's make a deal," she pressed. "If you don't tell our parents about my marriage to an American, I won't tell them about Rianto's cruelty to you."

"Okay," Indri answered sheepishly. Then they shook hands as Americans do when they agree on something.

To Ani, their "deal" was only a temporary one, knowing that Rianto's cruelty to Indri was far worse than her marriage to an American. However, it would buy her time. And Rianto's keris pin would be her bargaining tool.

Before they left the powder room, Ani fished out the keris pin from her little purse. "Is this yours?" she asked Indri.

Indri looked at it and shook her head. "Isn't it the same ugly head that is on the painting in Rianto's house?"

"Yes, it is. But this is a long story. Don't worry about it." Ani slipped the keris pin back into her little purse. "I will tell you about it another time."

"Can we go back to the party now?" Indri asked.

"You go ahead," replied Ani. "Do you mind if I ask Putu to take me home early? I'm very tired."

Rianto spotted Solomon near the stage and approached him. "Is Ani still wearing my keris pin?"

"No. She took it off at my request when she realized it was yours. She put it into her purse and says she plans to give it back to you tonight."

"Good," Rianto mumbled. "That will help. How did she explain that she is wearing my keris pendant and not hers?"

"Some mix-up, she says," Solomon replied. "Something about another pin."

"What other pin?" Rianto scowled. Suddenly, a surge of self-doubt overcame him. Did he not receive Ani's package with his keris pin in the mail before giving it to Solomon to hand to the courier? If so, how did Ani end up with it?

Solomon was worried. Not only about Ani returning the keris pendant to Rianto, but also that Tom would get it back in time for his next rendezvous with a senator. He pulled out his cell phone and dialed Tom's number. The voice mail answered as it had for the third day in a row. *That is so unlike Tom,* Solomon thought. *Where could he be?*

"Well, well. Solomon Elijah, what a small world to find you here!" A deep, distinguished male voice chuckled from behind.

Solomon turned around. He saw that the voice belonged to

Senator Johnson. "Bert! What in the world are you doing here on this fine occasion?"

"It's my business to show up at large social events like this," replied the senator. "Prospective voters for the next time around, you see. And you? What are you doing here?"

"I play the sax and lead a jazz band that plays for fancy parties," Solomon replied as casually as he could muster. "It's sort of an extra source of income for me. And just like you, I see this kind of thing as a good way of making important connections."

The senator patted Solomon on the shoulder. "Great minds think alike, eh?"

A photographer came by just then, lifting the camera to their faces. But in the nick of time, Solomon lifted his elbows and blocked his face. The last thing he needed now was a public connection between him and the senator—any senator.

Chapter 41

The rays of a half-moon were dancing in the gentle waves of low tide. Now dressed in jeans and a T-shirt, Ani rested on a lounge chair on Rianto's patio and tried to answer the question, *What was Rianto's keris doing on the floor of our bedroom closet? How could I have not noticed before that I was wearing his?*

Not that it was her style to keep chiding herself. She would typically correct her mistake and get on with life as before. But this time, she didn't. In her estimation, Rianto did not deserve to get his keris back, even if it was her mistake that she had it in her possession. She wondered if the keris was valuable enough to him that she could use it as a bargaining tool to rescue Indri from his abusive grip.

A rush of cool breeze caused Ani to shiver. Her stomach not only growled, it burned as it always did when she had not eaten for several hours. She suddenly realized she had not taken one bite of the delicious spread of hors d'oevres at the reception. The full moon was hiding behind a cloud just then, and it was pitch dark. She almost stumbled over some wood while looking for the back door. When she finally found it, it was locked. She knocked gently, hoping that Putu would be there to open. She heard the door unlocking and saw the knob turning. When the door opened, Rianto stood there, still dressed in his white tuxedo, his face as stern as ever.

"Oh, you were outside all this time?" he asked. "We thought you had gone to bed!"

"I needed time to think," she stammered, shivering partly from the cold, partly out of nervousness.

"You left the reception quite early. Did you have anything

to eat?" Rianto asked, closing the door behind her. His words of concern surprised her.

She shook her head. "Can I help myself to something from the refrigerator?" she asked.

"Suit yourself." He followed her into the kitchen, sat down on a stool, and watched her microwave some of the rice and leftover *dingdong*. "You can make some tea as well if you like."

Why is he so polite? Ani wondered with a feeling of unease. The memory of his icy stares at her chest earlier in the evening still haunted her. Then it dawned on her. He was waiting for his keris pin! But she decided to wait until he asked for it. She took the heated bowl of rice out of the microwave oven, sat down two stools away from him, and began to eat.

"I hear you are married to an American?" Rianto asked after she started eating.

She almost dropped her sticks. "Who told you that?" she asked, laughing and choking at the same time. She guessed that Indri had let the cat out of the bag. Indri simply could not keep a secret.

"That is not an answer to my question. I can see you have lost your manners in America. I am your elder cousin and your sponsor, and expect more respect."

Ani lowered her head toward the bowl of rice, shoveling more of it into her mouth. She did not know what else to say.

"I assume you married an American to get a permanent visa. Your parents would never approve. They probably don't know, am I right?"

She looked up at his cold, glassy eyes, then looked back down at her rice bowl. Her silence could mean yes or no, so she said nothing and left the interpretation up to Rianto.

"Your parents asked me to watch out for you in this country. I promised to tell them how you are doing and what you are doing here," Rianto said.

Ani felt her stomach turn. He would surely tell her parents all he knew. And if they heard about her marriage to Tom—she dared not think about it.

"I noticed you were wearing my keris tonight," Rianto continued. "What I want to know is, how in the world did you get it?"

Ani hung her head. "Maybe I sent you mine by mistake."

"Is that how well you keep in touch with your family heritage?" he asked in a stern voice.

And what about you? she wanted to ask. *Why didn't you notice before that you were missing it?* But she controlled her tongue. After all, he was older than her. Much older. "I will give yours back as soon as you give me mine," she said with as much assertiveness as she could muster.

Rianto guffawed. "I don't have yours. I never had it. You see, you sent me back the one you are wearing today. I am sure of that, because I inspected it, took a photo of it, and gave it to someone else a few months ago to use for my business transactions."

"That's impossible," she stammered. "Why would I have it then?"

"You should know. Maybe you stole it."

Ani's mouth dropped open. "Why would I steal yours if I have my own?" she said with raised voice. "Honest, cousin. I just don't know how I got yours. I am sorry. I really don't know," she repeated with tears welling. She wiped her eyes, got up, and washed her bowl and spoon.

Rianto rose from his chair. "Fine," he said resolutely. "Just give me back my keris pin, and we will forget about how you got it," he demanded. "If you're right and I find yours when I get back to Indonesia, I will bring it back to you. But I'm sure that's not the case. Meantime, I will need mine for my business." He held out his hand, palm upward. "So give it to me. Now," he commanded with a sterner voice than ever.

She turned from the sink and faced him squarely. "Okay. I will give your keris pin to you on one condition."

"Name it."

"Stop hurting my sister. She told me what you do to her. And I saw the cigarette burns on her arm. If you hurt her again, I will tell my parents and make sure she leaves you."

Rianto cracked a second-long smile, but his eyes remained icy cold. "Very well. As long as your sister behaves herself, I will not hurt her."

Blood rushed to Ani's face. "What do you mean, 'behaves herself'? Does she hurt you?"

He turned away. "You don't understand."

"It doesn't matter how she behaves," Ani retorted. "You are stronger than she. You have no right to hurt her."

"All right. All right. I promise not to hurt your sister anymore."

"Good." Ani slowly took out the gold necklace from her purse and slipped off the keris pin. "Here," she said, handing it to him.

Rianto scrutinized it, then, without thanking her, gave it back to her. "Can you do me a favor? Give it to Solomon tomorrow morning when he comes here to take you back to Maryland. Solomon needs the keris pin for a very important job he is doing for me."

"What? Why is he taking me to Maryland? I don't have to be back until a week from now. I thought you knew that."

"I had a change of plans. Indri is coming with me to Maine for a week. We leave at six in the morning." He fished a fat envelope from his coat pocket and threw it on the table. "Here is some spending money for you in addition to the tuition money I send directly to your college."

Ani hesitated. She did not really want to take the money. But then, she thought, why not? She would save the money for a day when she needed it. "Thank you," she mumbled. "Will I be able to see Indri and say good-bye to her in the morning?"

"I will tell her to knock on your door before we leave."

As Ani began to ascend the stairs, Rianto moved in front of her and blocked her with his arm. "Tell me," he seethed. "Why did you turn down my marriage proposal?"

Had she not been afraid of him, she would have given him

several reasons. But of course, she could only give one. “I told you. I want to continue my studies and have a career, and you told me you wanted a wife to stay at home with your children. Excuse me, cousin. I’m very tired and would like to go upstairs now,” she said, trying to push past him.

He grabbed her arm so firmly that she let out a short scream. A door opened upstairs. “Is everything okay?” Putu’s high-pitched voice called from the loft.

“Yes, everything is all right,” Rianto answered in a gruff voice, letting go of his grip.

Ani quickly ducked under his arm and ran upstairs.

Chapter 42

"I hear from Ramon that you've had some breakthrough, Tom," Ridgewood's director of therapy, Andrew, said as he leafed through several typed pages on his desk. He kept reading in silence as Tom looked out the window and watched the branches of a large chestnut tree sway in a gentle breeze.

"I think I may still have a lot of it only up here," Tom said, pointing to his head. "I just hope it will sink into my mouth, hands, and feet by the time I get back out there."

Andrew stopped reading and looked at Tom. "How will you know it's done that?"

"When I don't feel the need for alcohol anymore, I guess," Tom replied.

"Any idea what will have to happen so you won't ever feel the need for it again?"

"I guess a train would have to roll over me and kill me," Tom joked.

Andrew did not laugh. "That's right. As long as you're alive, you'll feel that thirst—maybe less often as time goes by, but it will come. There will always be pain from time to time, pain you want to drown out. The good news is, you're healthier when you feel the thirst than when you don't feel it."

"Huh? How so? I hoped this place was going to make that thirst go away."

"No one ever said it would. You see, my question was a trick question. You might feel the need for alcohol again and again, but the feeling of the need is not the same as actually needing it. Can you say that? The feeling of the need is—"

"The feeling of the need is not the same as actually needing it," repeated Tom thoughtfully.

"How was that again?" coaxed Andrew.

Tom repeated it, a bit annoyed at being treated like a child.

"Do I detect a negative feeling just now?"

"Yeah. I felt like I did with my nagging mother. Boy, I hate that feeling."

"Good."

"What's good about it?"

"It's good that you recognize its roots—you know—when it all began. The more you recognize that, the easier it is for you to deal with the urge to use alcohol when it comes up again. It's a good start."

"Start to what?" asked Tom.

"Your sobriety. You'll see."

"So I've just started?"

Andrew smiled. "Yes. But it's a good start, Tom. Congratulations."

"Does that mean I can leave early?"

"We'll talk about that tomorrow. Oh, I forgot something!" Andrew handed Tom a small brown bag. "Your friend Emmanuel came by while you were in a group session this morning. He said he did not find what you asked him to bring, but he brought you your cell phone cable."

Tom raced to his room, attached the cable to his cell phone, and plugged it into the wall socket. As soon as the phone was partly charged, he listened to his messages. There was a brief message from Ani wishing him well on his birthday. It felt good to hear her voice again. Then he realized that she did not even know where he was. She didn't have to know. At least not yet. It was more important to call Solomon right now and tell him about the missing pin.

But Solomon did not answer.

Meanwhile, Ani entered her room in Rianto's mansion. She locked the door behind her, her heart racing, and fell onto her bed. She had just survived a battle with the man who resembled the head of his two-tongued keris. Shuddering at the thought of having worn his horrid keris pin for a whole long evening without noticing it was his, she also wondered how she had obtained it in the first place. And where was hers? None of it made any sense.

She started packing her clothes and getting ready for bed. When she tucked her toothbrush and toothpaste into her toilet bag, something pricked her index finger. She turned the bag upside down and shook it. Two lipsticks fell out, the powder box, an eyebrow pencil, an eyelash brush, a mascara tube, and a pen. Then, after she pulled out a tissue and gave the bag another shake, something metallic tumbled out onto the dresser. It was a keris pendant with only *one* tongue sticking out of its grotesque head. Her very own precious keris! "How could I have lost you and misplaced you?" she chided half aloud to herself. "And how in the world did I get both keris pins in my possession?" These questions raged louder than the waves of the incoming tide, so loud that she did not hear the muffled cries of her sister in the room near hers.

"Sorry, Ani, but Rianto and Indri already left for Maine," announced Putu when Ani came downstairs the following morning. "They said to give you their regards."

Ani flushed with anger and said nothing.

"And there's a tall black man in the living room who says he is to take you to Maryland with him."

Ani nodded, gulping down the coffee Putu had placed in front of her. "So is it true that you are married to an American?" asked Putu, who refilled her cup.

Ani groaned, irked that Indri had lost no time gossiping behind her back once again. "What if it were true?" she asked grumpily.

"The worst that could happen is a free trip home if someone reported a false marriage so you can stay in the US."

"Why would anyone do that?"

"So is it true?" he asked with a smile.

She did not smile back. "It's none of your business, Putu."

He shifted toward the kitchen sink and cleaned a pan. Turning back toward the table, he faced Ani. "Why are you leaving so soon? You should stay here because your sister needs you." His concerned look gave credence to his words. "Rianto is—well, he's not nice to her, you know."

"I know," she said quietly. "Do you have any idea how I can help her?"

"Not yet, but I think you shouldn't leave the area until you can figure it out," Putu said. "I have a close friend who has a room for you. She's from Trinidad and a graduate student at Brown University. Why not stay in the area a bit longer until you can figure out how to help her?"

Ani thought for a moment. "How much will she charge?"

Putu laughed. "I see you have lived in America too long," he teased. "Kameela is her name. She's from Trinidad, not an American! She's hospitable and generous. She wouldn't charge you a cent. I'll tell this man that I will bring you to the bus station after you run some errands in the area. How's that?"

"Let me tell him myself." She excused herself and looked for Solomon in the living room.

Half an hour later, Putu drove Ani over Hope Bridge toward Providence in silence. Ani watched the setting three-quarter moon peek in between the mist over the western sound. She sighed. *Why do bad things happen in such a beautiful environment?* She vaguely knew the answer to such a fundamental question but did not have the mental energy to think of it.

Putu stopped his car in front of a brown brick row house. A tall, slender, East Asian young woman wearing tight jeans and a bright orange T-shirt came bouncing out the front door and hugged Putu.

She nodded as she listened to Putu, then smiled and waved at Ani, who was still in the car. Ani got out of the car to meet the woman.

"Hi, Ani. I'm Kameela," said Putu's friend with a melodic West Indian English accent as she shook Ani's hand. "Putu tells me you need a place to stay for a few days. You're welcome to stay with me. Why don't you and Putu first come in? I just made a fresh pot of tea."

"I don't want to impose," Ani protested.

"Oh, it's no trouble at all," Kameela said warmly. "I'm house-sitting here for the summer. The owners trust me completely and tell me I can bring anyone over that I want to. And, since you're a friend of Putu, I trust you!"

The aroma of curry greeted them as they entered the foyer. While Putu carried Ani's suitcase up the stairs, Kameela ushered Ani into the living room and offered her a seat on the red leather sofa. A moment later, Kameela returned with a multicolored teapot in one hand and two mugs in the other. "Let's see," she chimed musically. "You are Indonesian, and Indonesians don't drink tea with milk and sugar, do they?"

"How do you know that?" Ani asked with a smile of surprise.

"I have a few Chinese friends who drink only plain tea, and Putu tells me you are half Chinese."

Ani nodded. "Your accent sounds Asian-Indian. Why is that?"

"My father is a first-generation Brahmin from India," Kameela replied, pouring tea into Ani's mug. "But I grew up in Trinidad. I came here to study at Brown University a few years ago."

"What do you study?"

"Law. I'm doing an internship right now. And you?"

"Business administration in Maryland. How did you meet Putu?"

"We met at a party for international students who study at colleges all over the Providence area."

"Putu is a student? I didn't know that."

Kameela chuckled. "He never told you? He's at URI, studying culinary arts and hotel management," Kameela continued. "I needed to consult an Indonesian to help me with my internship project involving an artifact from Java. But I soon learned that Putu is from Bali and has little knowledge about anything in Java. Even in Java, there are many different cultures, right?"

Ani nodded in agreement. "I'm from West Java, where the Sundanese people live."

"Interesting. That's one of the largest people groups in Indonesia, isn't it?"

"Yes."

"Putu, do you want some tea with us?"

"I would rather have coffee. I'll get some a little later." He sat down on the far side of the table and unfolded the Providence Journal.

Kameela turned back to Ani. "Putu suggested you might be able to help me with my internship project," she began. You see, I'm helping the FBI with an investigation of several US senators who have received sizable monetary gifts from a wealthy donor we think might be from Indonesia. I have reason to believe that this very generous donor is giving away these gifts to persuade some of our senators and representatives to vote according to their agenda. Nothing wrong with that, except that our elected government officials aren't supposed to receive any gifts from foreigners while they're in office. So my job is to track and prove which ones did receive those gifts so we can prosecute them."

"What makes you think that the donor is from Indonesia?" Ani asked, peering at Putu to see if he was listening. He seemed not to be.

"May I show you why we think so?" asked Kameela. Without waiting for Ani's answer, she got up and walked toward a desk in the kitchen. "Let me show you some photos of someone who met with one of the senators," she said. She returned a few moments later and placed a large folder on the table. Opening the folder, she pulled out a five-by-seven-inch photo that showed the back of a man's head with brown curly hair. Facing him was a slightly taller man with broad shoulders, brown eyes, and a bald head.

"Now, please have a close look at the next picture," Kameela instructed. "Note that it is dated and timed within the same hour as the first photo." The second one zeroed in on the chest of the man facing the bald man. It showed a keris pin on the lapel of a dark gray suit—and the keris had two tongues, like Rianto's.

"We need to find the man who is wearing this pin. So here's one more photo," Kameela said as she pulled out another and laid it on the table. "Can you tell if this is an Indonesian's hand?"

Ani looked closely at the photo taken on the same date and a minute later. It magnified the right hand of the man handing a slip of paper across the table.

"Well? Is it the hand of an Indonesian?"

Ani shrugged. "What do you think, Putu? Is this an Indonesian hand?"

Putu peered over the newspaper. "No," he replied. "I think it's a white man's hand. The fingers are too long, and it has hair on the back."

As Ani looked at it more closely, she paled. Just below the nail of the man's thumb was a nickel-sized, dark brown birthmark—just like Tom's. A moment later, blood rushed back into her face. She now understood why and how the two-tongued keris had found its way into her toilet bag and onto her necklace.

Chapter 43

"Well, whoever the Indonesian is, he probably could have hired someone else to meet with the senators," Kameela said as she gathered the photos into her folder. "If we found the man who wore that pin, and if we could get him to testify, we could nail the senators who took the bribes."

Ani felt dizzy. She now realized how she had ended up with both Rianto's keris pin and her own at the same time. Tom must have worn the keris on his lapel as part of the moonlighting assignment for Solomon. It must then have fallen off his jacket when he hung it up in the closet. That's where she had found it before going to Rhode Island. No wonder both Solomon and Rianto seemed so anxious to get the pin from her when they saw it on her necklace! And no wonder Rianto arranged for Solomon to pick her up and bring her back to Baltimore!

Poor Tom. Does he know what he has been doing? Probably not. Either way, Tom would have to turn himself in and testify, she decided. His testimony would lead to the FBI's questioning Rianto, which would most likely lead to Rianto's deportation.

When Ani woke the following morning, the sun had not yet come up. She recited her morning prayer, got dressed, and went downstairs. Kameela called her into the kitchen, where she was preparing breakfast. "Come, Ani. I'm making some eggs and toast. Do you like bacon?"

"That's pork, right?"

"Actually, no. There's some halal turkey bacon in the freezer, already made. The owners of this home are Muslim, too."

"Thank you. I will try it. How can I help?"

"Just sit here," her hostess said, pointing to one of the stools around the butcher block island. Ani was able to view the whole kitchen from there: Over the island hung an array of pots and pans. A shelf with about 20 mugs hung on the wall to the right of the stove, and to the left, a set of black kitchen utensils. Kameela set a teapot and two colorful mugs on the table. Then she quickly scrambled some eggs while toasting two slices of bread.

"I know you like spices, and I have some from Trinidad. Would you like to try them?" she asked. Ani nodded with a smile; she had not brought her usual *sambal* sauce.

"Kameela," Ani began after she finished eating, "I think I know the person who is wearing the keris pin." I don't think he has any idea what he's doing is wrong or illegal. He is a very honest person. I also know the person who hired him to do it, and that person is Rianto's friend or partner."

"Oh wow," Kameela said, gaping and holding her hand to her mouth. "Looks like we hit the jackpot! Can you tell me who they all are?"

"I would rather ask the man in the picture first and see if he admits it. And if he does, I hope he will report to the FBI himself. Can I have a copy of the last photo you showed me? I'd like to show it to him."

"Sure. I'll make a copy on campus this morning. Wow, this is so exciting!" Kameela said, jumping up to put the plates into the dishwasher. "It's all coming together. Glory be!"

The doorbell rang. "I bet it's Putu," said Kameela. "Can you get the door, Ani?"

Ani looked through the peephole. She could see Putu's face up against the other side and opened the door. But it was not just Putu who waited at the door. Indri popped out from behind him! Both women gave out a loud burst of surprise. "What are you doing here?" they asked each other.

"Don't talk at the door, ladies. You two visit together while I run some errands," Putu said. "But later, I am driving Indri to the doctor's office. Can you come with us, Ani?"

While Kameela excused herself to study in her room, the two sisters sat on the sofa facing each other. "I had pain here," Indri began, pointing to her genital area. "So we came home yesterday evening. He wants me to see a doctor. He also said you had to go back to Maryland."

"No, I did not have to go. He commanded me to go. But Putu talked me out of it. He said I should stay and make sure you are all right. Tell me, sister. Are you all right? You look so pale and sad."

Indri shook her head and burst into tears. "Do you—do you hurt when you s-sleep with your husband?" she asked her older sister.

"Never. Why? Do *you*?"

Indri nodded, wiping her tears. "Every time. A lot."

Ani sat next to Indri on the sofa and put her arms around her. "I'm not surprised to hear that. I heard you crying during the night. Does he force you to have sex?"

Indri nodded again. "He grabs me and does it quickly, without warning. Is that how it's supposed to be? Or am I doing something wrong?"

"No, you are not doing anything wrong, sister," Ani said, tears streaming down her cheeks. "Rianto is doing it all wrong. He is abusing you. I know this is hard, but if you want to save your life, you must leave Rianto and go to Maryland with me. This cannot go on."

"But we're married! Isn't that how all husbands do it?"

"No, dear sister. If he forces you and it hurts, it's called rape. Normal sex is a wonderful thing. It's not supposed to be painful, except maybe the first time a little. And he is also hurting you physically. That is not only illegal in this country, it is dangerous!"

Putu drove them to a gynecological clinic in Providence. Ani asked to tag along in the examination room in case Indri needed a translator.

"Indri, it seems you have numerous abrasions in your vagina," said Dr. Eisenstein, the female gynecologist who examined Indri. "That must hurt a lot. How long have you been feeling pain during intercourse?" the doctor asked. Ani began to translate, but Indri motioned she understood the question.

"Since the first time three months ago, every time," Indri said quietly in Indonesian. Ani translated.

"Does he force you to have sex? No foreplay, no pleasure?"

Indri looked at Ani to translate the question. She still did not understand. "Only hurts," Indri quietly said, shrugging her shoulder.

The doctor got up and went to her desk, typing something into her computer. Then she got up again and sat across from Indri. "Your vagina looks like your husband is raping you. That is why it hurts. It not only hurts you, but it is also illegal. You need to rest for a while; do not let your husband touch you until you are healed inside."

Ani translated. Indri began to weep. "How can I stop him?" she asked.

The doctor looked at Ani. "Your sister must get to a safe place, Ani. Can she go home with you? Or should I arrange a women's shelter?"

"She can come home with me," Ani said. "But what should we tell her husband?"

"Nothing," replied the doctor. "I must report him to the authorities. The police will deal with him and go from there. Is the man in the waiting room her husband?"

"No, he is Indri's chauffeur," Ani explained.

"Good. That makes it easier. She must not go back to her husband, that's for sure. Oh, and what's that?" the doctor asked when she saw the burn marks on Indri's arm. After Ani told her, she said, "Another reason why I must report this man. He's dangerous!"

After the two women thanked Dr. Eisenstein and left her office, they climbed into Putu's car. "Please take us both back to Kameela's," Ani said. "And then bring us Indri's personal things—all of them. She's going to Maryland with me in the morning."

"No problem," he said with his bucktooth smile. "But what should I tell the boss when he returns from Maine?"

"Tell him the truth. Indri wanted to go to Maryland to be with her sister. Don't you, Indri?" Ani asked, looking at her sister. Indri nodded and shrugged her shoulder, looking more afraid than relieved.

"Maybe I will lose my job, but it is worth a try," Putu said.

"What?!" Ani said, hitting him on his shoulder from the back seat. Indri is your boss when Rianto is away, is she not? Or did Rianto tell you she is not allowed to give you orders?"

Putu smiled his toothy smile again. "You are right. I'm Indri's servant when her husband is gone," he said.

When the bus rolled into the Baltimore midtown station the next day, it was easy to pick out Grace Osterhouse's white, round face in the crowd. The welcoming hug and smile from Grace felt like home to Ani.

"And who is this pretty young lady?" asked Grace when she laid eyes on Indri.

"Grace, meet my sister, Indri. Indri, this is Grace."

"So what's going on, Ani? How come Tom couldn't come and get you?" Grace asked as soon as they buckled up in the car. "Not that I minded; don't get me wrong."

"Tom is at a place called Ridgewood. Do you know what that is?"

"Oh—the substance abuse rehab center! How wonderful!" replied Grace. "It's about time!"

"Do you—I mean you knew about—?"

"Honey, we knew for some time that he had a problem. We're so proud he finally got some help. Hey, why not both of you come over to my house for a couple of days? It's still your vacation, isn't it, Ani? That would give us a chance to get to know Indri a little better, too. And if she wants, she can stay longer."

When Ani woke up the following morning, she could not remember where she was at first. A warm but dry breeze from the partially opened window caressed her cheeks. Indri was still asleep when Ani joined Grace and Fred for breakfast on the patio. A few dogwood blossoms had fallen on the wrought iron table and decorated their placemats. Ani told them about the villa by the sea, the party, the ocean walks, and then she stopped and gave a big sigh.

"What was that sigh all about?" responded Grace. "Don't tell me your vacation wasn't all rosy posy."

"It wasn't," said Ani, bursting into tears. Then she began to tell them about Indri's plight. But that was all.

Grace touched Ani's arm. "Under these circumstances, as well as your own, I think it would be better if Indri stays with us for a while, especially after Tom gets back, don't you think? If she wants to, of course."

"Oh, thank you, Grace!"

"Whenever you're ready, I'll bring you to your place and get your car—with jumping cables in case it's dead by now. You want to visit Tom at the rehab, don't you?"

Chapter 44

Ani's heart thumped with trepidation as she arrived at the Ridgewood Rehab Center. It seemed like a pleasant place, more like a hotel than an institution, Ani mused. But would Tom be happy to see her?

She cautiously peeked through the slightly opened door of the patients' lounge, expecting lunatics with wild eyes charging at her. Instead, she was surprised to see about fifteen well-dressed men and women ranging from age twenty to seventy calmly socializing with each other. Some were watching TV; others were playing chess or cards. One man was typing on a laptop.

But where was Tom?

Ani opened the door wider. Just then, she saw Tom enter the lounge from the other side. He wore his white tennis T-shirt and looked as handsome as ever. Heart racing, she quickly closed the door again and continued to watch him through the square glass on the door. She suddenly realized how much she had missed that blue-eyed, sandy-haired husband of hers—the Tom she thought she knew.

Taking a deep breath, she opened the door again and ventured inside, slowly walking toward Tom. She watched him sitting down on a sofa in the middle of the room and picking up a magazine to read. As she neared, she saw him looking around in the opposite direction and wiggling in his seat. Perhaps he could smell her perfume, she thought, or a subconscious magnet drew him, but he turned to stare in her direction. And when she noticed his face turn toward her, she could not help but blush as she once did a long time ago. She saw his face light up, then he threw down the magazine and jumped up from the chair. And when she heard his familiar voice chime, "Ani!" with the same warmth she had heard in the distant past, she melted and ran toward him.

She let him hug her and plant a kiss on her lips. "Did you get my email yesterday?" she asked as soon as he let go of her.

"No, I didn't. I don't have access to a computer here. I guess Emmanuel told you I was here."

She nodded. "Can we go outside and talk where it's quieter?" They walked through a double door into a large courtyard. A warm early-summer breeze blew a pleasant scent of rhododendron blossoms in their direction as they sat down on a bench and faced each other.

"I'm sorry I missed your birthday," Ani said. "Emmanuel told me he threw a party for you."

"Yeah." He laughed. "That was a big surprise. Cynthia knew from my records that I was turning thirty. She quietly organized everything with Emmanuel's help."

"So, what do they do for you here?"

"Mostly talk, then detox, and more talk."

"What's detox?" Ani asked.

"In my case, it means no alcohol of any kind for 28 days. To clean the body from the poison. Sometimes being here is boring. Other times, it's embarrassing. But it's starting to feel good, you know. I had forgotten how good life can be without booze."

"Without who?"

Tom laughed. "Alcohol, I mean."

Ani looked at him suspiciously. "And you remember now?"

"Yeah, except—" He paused a moment and looked down, then up at her again. "Except I miss you. I miss us together." He paused. "I miss the old days, Ani."

She smiled weakly, fighting tears as she looked into his eyes. She saw an old sparkle flicker for a moment—like the one she noticed when she saw him for the first time. But it was just a flicker.

"Did you have a good time with your sister?" he asked.

"Yes and no. But it's a long story."

"Tell me everything. We're free until five tonight. Can you stay that long?"

She nodded and began to tell him all the good things about her time with her sister at the beautiful villa by the sea. While she told him about Putu from Bali and his friend Kameela, she often checked to see if he was listening. She could see his gentle eyes look into hers with genuine interest, his head nodding occasionally. *He is a good listener*, she concluded, something she had not been able to relish in him for a long time.

And then, she told him that Solomon had been there, too.

"You're kidding! Solomon? What a coincidence! Let me guess. He was leading his band and playing the saxophone."

Ani nodded, got up and stretched, then sat down again. "Tom, I have something important to talk with you about," she said with a grave face. She reached inside her purse, fished out a large envelope, and held it out to him. "Have a look, please!"

Divorce papers? Tom wondered, shaking inside as he grasped its contents. But no. A few large photographs were in his hand instead. He quizzically examined the first, then the second.

"Does anything in those pictures look familiar to you?" Ani asked.

He nodded weakly. "I see a photo of a keris pin, like yours."

"Hmm. Are you sure? Take a close look at the keris on my necklace," she said, holding it up close to his face. "Do you see any difference between this one and the one on the photo?"

He looked at it, then at the one in the photo. "Oh, yeah! The one on the photograph must be a female, and yours is a male."

"What gives you that idea?"

"Yours has only one tongue. The one on the photo has two," Tom said, laughing.

"Very funny," she giggled. "Now, look at the other photographs and tell me what you see."

He obeyed. "I see the chest of someone wearing a two-headed

keris pin, like the one I—" He stopped short, almost forgetting that what he was about to say was confidential.

"Okay. Now look closely at this person's hand," Ani said, ignoring what he had just said.

"It's holding a piece of paper with numbers on it. And—and, oh my!" he cried, "That's—that's my hand!"

"Really?" Ani asked, feigning ignorance. "You sure?"

"How—where in the world did you get these photos, Ani?"

She calmly slid the photos back into the envelope and stuffed it back into her handbag. "I'll tell you after you tell me how you got that keris pin you were wearing."

He cringed. For the first time in days, he wished he could have a big mug of beer. *Bad, bad,* he chided himself. He should have suspected that a mission that had to be kept secret might be shady. "Solomon gave it to me to wear as identification," he finally answered. "But I don't know if it belongs to him or someone else."

"Do you have any idea who Solomon works for?" Ani asked. Her head was burning with what she knew and he didn't know.

He shook his head.

"No idea at all?"

"None."

"I see. Do you know where the keris pendant is now?"

"I wish I knew. I asked Emmanuel to get it and bring it to me, but he couldn't find it. It's probably somewhere in the closet at home. I thought it was in my gray trousers, but it wasn't. I need it for my next assignment, Ani. Could you look for it again?"

"What happens if we don't find it by then or if you don't show up?"

His forehead wrinkled as he looked at the treetops towering above the high wall of the complex. "I'd lose lots of money, I guess. Enough to put a huge deposit down on a house that I wanted to buy for you."

Ani gulped. She, too, had dreamed of owning a house one day. "That's a lot of money!"

"Yep, it sure is," Tom said. "But how did you get these photos? And why are you showing them to me?"

Ani got up, walked over to the rhododendron tree, and picked a blossom. She took off her sweater as she walked toward the bench and sat down again. "I know where the keris is," she announced calmly. "But I will tell you a few other things first."

Chapter 45

"First of all, the keris you are wearing on that photo belongs to a man named Rianto," Ani explained.

"Wait a minute," Tom said. "Did you say Rianto? Isn't he the billionaire from Asia somewhere that was written up in *Forbes* magazine last month?"

"That's him. He is from Indonesia."

"How in the world did Solomon get the keris pin from Rianto?"

"Solomon works for Rianto. And Rianto is my cousin. That's why I know this keris. It looks similar to mine, doesn't it?" She pointed to hers hanging on a gold chain around her neck.

"So why did Rianto give it to Solomon to let me use it for an ID?"

"He knew that Congress members were not allowed to receive gifts from foreigners. So he hired Solomon, who hired you to meet with these senators so that they could give you a deposit slip, which you turned in to Solomon, and so on. Do you know anything about why Solomon or Rianto needed those deposit slips?"

"I have no idea. He always said the less I know, the better. So I didn't ask."

"Well, I know more than you do. Solomon would use the account number on the deposit slips to transfer money from Rianto's account into the congressmen's and women's accounts electronically," Ani explained. "Once the FBI has proof that the donor of these gifts is Rianto, who is a foreign citizen, a lot of Congress members will be in trouble."

Tom's face turned pale. "How about Solomon and me? Are we in trouble?"

"Maybe. Maybe not. That depends on who will talk."

Tom shook his head and combed through his hair with his fingers. "So, where and how did you get these photos?"

Ani sighed. "A long story of coincidences. A friend of Rianto's servant showed them to me, asking if I could identify the owner of the keris pin, because she knew it was Indonesian."

"And how did you know this keris pin belongs to Rianto?"

Ani thought a moment. She wasn't sure if she should tell him. But she decided it would not hurt if he knew. "Rianto gave that same pin to me when he proposed to me, not long before you proposed to me."

"No way! He proposed to you? He's one of the richest men in the world, and you turned him down, or did he change his mind?"

"I turned him down."

"For me?"

"Well, not exactly for you. Mostly for my education, which he refused to allow. I already knew you at the time. He had a lot more money than you, but my education was more important to me than money."

Tom had to laugh. "Oh, man! You meant to tell me you gave up a billionaire to marry me so you can have an education?"

"Not exactly. You thought I married you because I needed you. Turns out that Rianto paid for my education anyway. Got it?"

Tom sank back into the chair and shook his head. "So, if you didn't need me, why did you marry me?"

"Because I love you," she said. "Can you finally believe it now?"

His face relaxed. "I think I finally believe you. You are sublimely unique, Ani Sunatu Hanson!"

Ani smiled, her glistening eyes looking deeply into Tom's. She wished she could freeze this moment. The old magic between them had returned—just enough to ignite the old chemistry. He reached out for her hand; she gave it to him. The touch alone would suffice for now.

Tom wanted to hug her, but then he remembered a burning question. "So, where is the keris pin now?" he asked nervously.

"Solomon has it. That's another long story. I gave the pin back to Rianto when I told him I would not marry him. He then at some point gave it to Solomon to use as an ID for the job. Solomon hired you to wear the pin for this job. I found it on the closet floor the evening before I left for Maryland, and because it was a little dark, I didn't notice it was not mine. I found out at Rianto and Indri's reception. I gave it back to Rianto, who then gave it back to me to give it to Solomon, who happened to be at the reception leading a band."

"STOP! I think I lost you. You sure Solomon has it?"

"I'm sure. I gave it to him. I think he wants to bring it to you any day now. But you shouldn't—"

"Ani, listen. I have only one more rendezvous to do for Solomon, and then I'm finished with this moonlighting mission. I swear. See, I'm getting this huge bonus reward, which is how I would get that down payment. Wouldn't you want that?"

Ani shot up from the bench, her body stiffened, and with a flushed face she shouted, "I don't believe this—you want to do another illegal delivery? The FBI already has photos of you. Do you want to land in jail and lose everything?"

"Oh, come on, honey. No one can prove I did anything wrong. Besides, no one's getting hurt, and no one's hurting anybody!"

She sat down again, shook her head, and with tears said, "I wish that were true, Tom."

"Huh? What do you mean? Who's hurting whom?"

Ani waited several seconds before she answered. "The man who profits the most from your moonlighting mission is hurting my sister."

"Who? Solomon?"

"No. Rianto."

"How is he hurting your sister? Why?"

Amid sobs and broken sentences, Ani told him the rest of the story.

Tom pulled her to himself and stroked her head. "That's horrible, honey. Truly horrible." He let her cry for a while, then dried her tears with his handkerchief. "But why doesn't your sister just call the police?" he asked.

Ani shook her head. "Indri is his wife. She is dependent on him for her visa and livelihood. And she's new to this country. Even if she knew English well enough, she would never have the courage to call the police."

"Why don't *you* report him then?"

Ani sighed. "Because he's also our cousin. If he gets into trouble because we report him for abusing Indri, we shame not only him but the whole family, including ourselves. We must hold up the family honor. It is the Indonesian way. I know that's hard for some Americans to understand. But if *you* report to the FBI that Rianto is behind all these illegal gifts to the senators, he would be sent back to Indonesia without us shaming him."

"What good would that do for your sister? Wouldn't she have to go back to Indonesia, too?"

Ani shook her head. "I hope not. She wants to study here. She will be safer with us."

"With us?!" he guffawed, shooting up from a sitting position. "You mean—live with us? Good grief! I suppose you'll let her sleep between us on the double bed? I can't believe that your family's honor is more important than your husband's need for privacy."

Ani playfully hit him on the arm. "I can't believe that your need for privacy is more important than my sister's safety. Don't worry, she can sleep on the sofa."

He sat down again. With his elbows on his knees, he pulled on his left hand's knuckles, one by one. "It's not the privacy that bothers me so much," he continued in a lower tone. "It's losing the bonus if I don't finish the job."

For a tiny moment, Ani could not help but feel sorry for Tom. But then she collected herself and gently touched his shoulder. "Remember, I loved you when you were in debt. "I still love you as you are. You don't have to get rich for me. More important to me than all the money in the world is my family, including you!"

He said nothing, staring grimly at the ground. His head told him she was right, but his body did not follow. He suddenly felt thirsty for a beer, but there was none around. Instead, he kicked some walkway gravel into the manicured lawn beside it. The material world he had tried to build up was crumbling. Would he ever fully be able to grasp the idea that he was significant without it? During the last ten days, he had caught a glimpse of that possibility. But it kept eluding him. It had not seeped down into his stomach, as his counselor would say.

Ani got up and grabbed her purse. "I tell you what," she said in a tone like that of a judge delivering the final verdict. "*You* decide what's more important. But if you don't cancel out on Solomon on Friday and report all you know to the FBI, I'll have to report it myself. Do you understand?"

Then she left, hoping he would be not only the man she loved but also her hero.

Chapter 46

That night, Ani dreamed she was sleeping in the big family bed with her sister next to her. A large scorpion crept on top of Indri. She tried to shout, "Tom, help!" but she had no voice. When she woke in a cold sweat, she felt shame. She instantly knew that the dream was about her inability to persuade Tom to rescue her sweet sister.

Wide-awake a few minutes later, Ani asked herself whether she could ever forgive Tom if he chose not to turn himself in. She would have to do the dirty work for him, hurting him and her pride in the process. Just as Ani prostrated herself on the prayer rug the next morning, she heard the sound of scurrying footsteps in the hall. They stopped at her door. "Ani," Grace called. "Can you come right away? It's urgent."

With a pounding heart, Ani rushed out into the hall and followed Grace into the master bedroom. Half on, half off the bed, Fred hung over the side, groaning loudly. His mouth was open, and he was drooling badly.

"Help me pull him back to bed, Ani. Then call the ambulance for me, will you? He must have had a stroke," said Grace with a trembling voice. He was a heavy man, and the women had no easy time getting him back into bed.

Ani had no idea what the word "stroke" meant. She rushed to the kitchen phone and dialed 911. "Please send an ambulance. A man here cannot talk or move. We think he had a—uh, a struck."

"STROKE!" Grace yelled from the bedroom.

"Uh, yes, a stroke," Ani corrected. "The address? Just a minute." She found a printed envelope addressed to Grace lying near the telephone and read off the address. Twenty minutes later, the ambulance arrived. The paramedics brought in a stretcher and proceeded to lift Fred onto it.

"You can follow us to the hospital if you like," the men suggested to Grace as they wheeled Fred out to the ambulance.

Grace kissed Fred on the forehead. "See you in the hospital, my dear." Then she turned to Ani. "I don't think I'm up to driving. Would you drive me there, Ani?"

"Sure. I have to wake up Indri first. Can we bring her along?"

Once they arrived at the hospital, the women had to wait a good three hours before the neurologist appeared in the waiting room. "It's good you brought him in right away when you noticed something was wrong, Mrs. Osterhouse," he said. "You were right. Your husband had a stroke. It affected his left arm and face—also his speech, but we have high hopes for his recovery. We immediately put him on medication, and he's resting quietly. Tomorrow, we want you to come and let the physical therapist teach you how to mobilize his arm and leg. A speech therapist will start working with him, too."

"Can we see him now?" asked Grace.

"You'll have to wait until we get him into a regular room. Meanwhile, I suggest you get yourselves something to eat in the cafeteria."

Sitting by a sunny window in the cafeteria, the three women ate scrambled eggs and a doughnut. "Can you explain something to me, Grace?" Ani asked after they finished eating.

"Yes, dear?"

"Do you remember when I first met you? I thanked you and asked how I could repay you? You said, 'I'm the one who owes a debt' or something like that. You promised you would explain what you meant someday. Can you explain this now?"

Grace took a sip of her coffee and began to tell her story.

"About fifty-one years ago, when I was fifteen years old, I was asked to watch Candy, the neighbor's ten-year-old daughter. About an hour after her parents left, a school friend invited Candy and me to go to the fair. I knew Candy would love it there, and I thought the fair would be so much more fun than sitting inside the house."

Grace drew a deep breath and then continued. "I don't remember exactly how, but at one point, Candy let go of my hand and ran off into the crowd. We searched everywhere and called for her, but we could not find her. We finally talked to a police officer. They got a search party going right away. You can imagine how the family suffered, and how I suffered," Grace said with tears in her eyes.

"That night, they found a body by the swamp near the fair. It was Candy's."

"No! That's awful!" Ani cried, reaching over and touching Grace's arm to comfort her.

"Candy loved the geese and enjoyed feeding them. She probably fell in, and no one heard her screaming because the noise of the fair was much louder." She blew her nose with a napkin. "I was devastated. And, of course, her parents were even more devastated. You can imagine the guilt I felt."

"Did they blame you?"

"Not verbally. But I felt guilty anyway. I vowed I would work like a slave so that I could pay them a few thousand dollars. And I told them so, over and over again. But they'd only say, 'no money could ever replace our daughter.' And every time they would say those words, I'd feel even worse. So week after week, I baked them a cake with chocolate marzipan frosting, decorated it real fancy, and brought it to them. I did that for three years."

"How nice of you. Did you feel any better then?"

"No, I didn't. But I kept doing it week after week. One day, their older son came home from Korea, where he'd been serving in the Army. He was about twenty-two years old by then, and I was eighteen. I'll never forget that day. I brought a cake to them as usual, and there he stood at the door and said in a kind voice, 'Why are you still baking a cake every week?' I said, 'You know why.' With a twinkle in his eye, he said, 'I know. But don't you know that my parents forgave you a long time ago? They don't hold it against you anymore.'"

Grace wiped a tear. "'But why,' I asked, 'why would they want to forgive me?' 'Because God forgave them when they asked him to,' he answered. I asked him, 'What had they done wrong?' 'Nothing in particular,' he answered. 'Nothing horrible. But they missed the mark of God's standard, which is much higher than anybody's.'"

Grace sighed and looked out the window. "That's when it finally sank in. The whole family had forgiven me, and I couldn't believe it all that time!"

"That is amazing. But I don't understand something, Grace," said Ani. "If God forgave you, and the family forgave you, why do you still think you have to repay a debt?"

Grace's eyes froze as she looked at Ani. "Oh, my goodness!" she said, gasping. "Why would I think that indeed?! Come to think of it—I've burned myself out, trying hard to pay a debt that God has already paid. I've known in my head that he did, but my body hasn't followed," she added with a chuckle.

Grace closed her eyes for a few seconds and took a deep breath. She opened them again and smiled. "But I still want to help others, of course—not out of guilt or to repay a debt. From now on, I will do kind deeds when they're helpful—but out of gratefulness, because God forgave my debts. Does that make better sense, Ani?"

Ani smiled and nodded. "It makes much more sense!"

"Thanks, Ani, for bringing that to my attention."

"But what about the son who told you that the family forgave you? Where is he now?"

"Oh, don't you know?" she asked. "He's the dear man we brought to the hospital this morning."

Chapter 47

Tom's group had a new leader the day after Ani visited. His name was Duke. "Who needs to talk first today?" he asked.

Several in the group pointed to Tom. "You seem nervous today," said Javier, the fifty-year-old Puerto Rican who plunked down his 350-pound bulk onto the sofa next to him.

"How can you tell?" asked Tom.

"You look stone-faced and spacey. Your wife was here yesterday, wasn't she? You looked like a puppy dog with its tail hanging after she left!"

"Want to talk about it, Tom?" asked Duke.

"Okay, I have a question," Tom replied, stroking his hair with his fingers. "I heard the psychologist's lecture about codependence the other day. You know, how trying to rescue someone dependent on alcohol or drugs sometimes enables the addict to do more of it. But in church, they taught us to be helpful, love others, and be kind. I feel like a villain when I don't rescue someone who's in trouble, especially someone I care about personally. You know, a relative, for example. How can I tell if my helpfulness is a dysfunction—you know, what they call "codependence"?

"Anyone want to give their thoughts on that?" asked Duke.

"Yeah," said Jamie, the forty-year-old woman who had been a medication addict. She turned to face Tom. "If Bobby over here was trying to choke me in front of you, would you jump and try to stop him, or ask yourself, oops—that might be codependence?"

Everyone laughed, including Tom. "I'd jump, of course."

"But why would you jump?" Duke asked. "Are you sure you

wouldn't do it just so that you'd look good in the eyes of everybody here?"

"Nah. I'd do it even if nobody else were around watching!"

"So...you'd do it for her, not for you, right? But if you do kind things for others to feel good about yourself, or if you look for others to depend on you so that you feel good about yourself, that's codependency. You need to be needed. And then what happens is the other person you're close to depends on you even more, and so on. It's an addiction in itself."

"But it's okay to do kind things when they're needed, right?"

"Yeah, of course. But it's not okay when your kindness enables an addict to continue self-destructive and unhealthy behavior, making that person depend on you even more."

Tom nodded.

"So, is Javier correct? Does your question have anything to do with your wife's visit last night?" asked Duke.

Tom lifted his arm to scratch his head but then dropped it again. "Yeah, it does. She wants me to save her sister from her husband, who's abusing her. I have some evidence that this guy is also involved in something illegal. If I report to the authorities what I know about the situation, this guy would have to return to his country, my sister-in-law could stay here with us and be safe, but I would lose a lot of money. Wouldn't I be codependent if I report him?"

They all looked at each other and laughed. "Not necessarily," commented Javier. "It's true that you don't have to be a rescuer or macho to be an okay guy. But that doesn't mean you have to be a jerk or a wimp, either." The others laughed and nodded in affirmation.

"Javier's right," commented Duke. "Reporting a bad guy to save his wife from abuse is not codependency. But if this becomes a pattern for you—like for example, if she keeps getting hitched with abusers, and if you end up rescuing her every time because it's the only way you feel good about yourself, then I might label you as a codependent. Because you might be enabling her to become continuously dependent on you. And that's neither good for her nor you."

That night, Tom thought hard about what Duke had said. *I don't have to be macho to be an okay guy. But that doesn't mean I have to be a wimp, either!* As he wrote these words into his journal, an idea crossed his mind. What if he could kill two birds with one stone?

First, he would call Solomon, asking him to bring him the keris pin. Then, he would ask Ravi to bring him his white shirt, tie, black shoes, and gray socks. He would need them—and a ride from Ravi—for his last moonlighting mission.

Chapter 48

It was Saturday, and Ani still had not heard from Tom. She had told him that if he did not report to the FBI by Friday (yesterday), she would have to report the whole operation in his stead. Blood rushed to her cheeks as she realized that perhaps he was not the hero she hoped he would be. She felt ashamed of him. And for the first time, she wished she had never married him.

But she would wait until Monday, a business day, before she would contact the FBI.

She decided to go home and check her mail. As she entered her apartment, she smelled beer. The trash bin was full of beer cans and on top of it, an empty liquor bottle. Because tomorrow would be the garbage pickup day, she tied the trash bags, tossed them into the large garbage bins, and pulled them to the curbside. She then opened the windows, vacuumed and dusted, and after she closed the windows again, she dropped onto the couch and flicked on the television with the remote. Maybe something funny and light would help her relax and feel at home, she hoped.

After a commercial, Mary Randall, the newscaster, appeared on the screen. "Late last night," she began, "a man in a dark gray suit without any identification was found beaten and badly wounded in the parking lot of Mirror Lake Pub just outside Columbia, Maryland. He was rushed to St. Agnes' emergency room and is in critical condition."

Ani barely listened. Every evening news brought something similar. She wanted something light and funny and was about to change channels. But the next words grabbed her attention: "At the same location within the same hour, the FBI arrested Senator Norman O'Conner of Kentucky for allegedly receiving an illegal monetary donation from a banker from Indonesia. At this point, it is unclear as to whether the two incidences are related."

Ani grew pale. Could they be talking about Tom? Did he manage to leave Ridgewood, meet the senator at the pub, and then—? She turned off the television and dialed Tom's cell phone. His voice mail immediately answered, meaning that he was talking on the phone or he had turned it off. He must be the one they admitted to St. Agnes' emergency room, she concluded.

She fetched her purse and put on her jacket. Vaguely remembering the location of the hospital, she drove in the direction of downtown Baltimore. Luckily, she soon spotted the entrance to the St. Agnes emergency room and parked in the nearby underground garage. Once inside, she found her way to the intensive care unit of the emergency wing, casually snuck behind a few other people, and entered through a door marked NO VISITORS ALLOWED. *Tom has to be here somewhere*, she thought. The nursing staff seemed too busy to notice her.

Most of the rooms had a name posted on the outside of the door. None bore Tom's name. But a shield on the last doorpost displayed the word "UNKNOWN." The door was ajar; the room was semi-dark, so Ani tiptoed in. A patient with a bloody bandage on his head and face lay in the hospital bed. All sorts of plugs and contraptions hung from his body and head. She sneaked closer and saw that his eyes were closed. A deep groan sounded from underneath the bandages and contraptions.

She saw a plastic bag in the corner of the room and looked inside. Tom's dark gray suit was in it, his pale blue shirt, a tie she had bought him for Christmas, and his black shoes. Trembling from shock and anger, she sank into a chair nearby and waited for the patient to open his eyes.

A few minutes later, the door to the hospital room opened and a nurse came in. "Ma'am, are you this man's wife?"

Ani nodded.

The nurse checked the connections to the machines. She turned to Ani. "I'm glad you're here," she said. "Your husband is in very critical condition. To be honest, we're not sure if he'll make it. He suffered heavy trauma to his head. Tell you what. Can you fill out some papers for us? He did not have any ID on him when they brought him in, and he couldn't talk." She handed Ani a pad with a stack of forms and then left the room again, closing the door behind her.

Ani could barely concentrate on filling out the forms the nurse had given her. Did he have accident insurance? Yes, he did. Hospital and doctors' bills were phenomenal in this country. Did he have a life insurance policy? She was not sure. They had talked about one once, but she wasn't sure if he had been paying for one.

Rage welled up in her. The feeling was so strong that she wanted to run from the room and never look at Tom again. Could she ever forgive him for going against her principles and advice? No, she decided. Even if Tom died here in this hospital room, she could never forgive him.

She went into the hallway, drank from a water fountain, and then returned to the room to finish filling out the form. Her eyes fell on the picture of a crucifix hanging on the wall above the bed. As many times before, she shuddered at the sight, asking herself, *how could Christians believe that Allah would allow his holy prophet to die such a cruel death? And how can they believe that the Creator-God became a man so that he would die as a sacrifice for their sins? And even if he did die that way, why do Christians use such an object for décor?*

Suddenly, new questions etched their way into Ani's mind: *What if Isa did die to pay for our sins by his death? What if he really is the Creator-God who came to earth as a man?* If he was, he could not only hear her prayer, but he could also forgive her as he forgave those who nailed him to the cross. And could he not also help her forgive Tom?

She got up and paced the room for a long time. How long, she could not remember. Finally, when she reached the point of exhaustion, she stooped at the bedside and sank to her knees. "Oh, Lord Isa," she said aloud with eyes closed as she had seen Grace do when she prayed. "In case you can hear me, can you forgive me for not forgiving Tom? And will you help me to forgive him?"

As if in a trance, or perhaps in her imagination, Ani suddenly saw herself in a fog. As the fog gradually lifted, she could see a man with long hair and a beard, standing behind a glass door. When she looked more closely, she noticed scars on his bare feet and his hands. A torn cape revealed a wound on his side. She instantly recognized who it was from paintings she had seen at the Baltimore Museum of Art. But she was not afraid when she heard him knock gently on the glass door. His eyes seemed kind and patient. She felt safe.

In her imagination, she opened the door to let him in. As soon as he entered, she fell on her feet and buried her head in her hands. Then she heard him say, "Daughter, I forgive you. I paid for all your sins. And don't worry. I will help you to forgive."

Something deep inside her made her body heave. She began to weep as she had never wept before. A calm swept over her like a warm, soothing wave in slow motion. She did not remember how long she remained kneeling beside the bed.

Suddenly, she heard a deep groan, and then the words, "Ani? Is that you?" The voice was hoarse and the words garbled.

"I'm here, Tom. I'm here!" she said. Tears started to flow again, but this time they were tears of joy and relief.

When the patient's eyes opened a bit, she saw they were dark brown—not blue like Tom's. *Could the oxygen have changed the color of his eyes?* she wondered.

"Ani, I'm not Tom," the man in the bed said in a hoarse whisper.

"What?!" Ani gasped. She peered at his face more closely. Then she noticed a shiny black strand of hair between all the bandages on his head and face. "Oh, my goodness! You're—you're Emmanuel!"

"Ah-hum," Emmanuel said weakly.

"But the news said—it sounded like it said—but Tom's clothes are here. Where is he?"

"At Ridgewood," Emmanuel began, pausing every few words to breathe. "I convinced him to let me take his place."

"You did? Oh, Emmanuel. Then what happened? Do you know who did this to you and why?"

"No idea. I think it happened right after I met with Tom's contact," he said, belaboring each word. "When I was leaving the bar, someone came from behind and tackled me to the ground. I don't remember anything after that. Where am I now?"

"You're in the hospital, all bandaged up. That's why I didn't recognize you. Oh, I'm so sorry!" Ani said through tears.

"It's not your fault, Ani,"

She then thought of the keris. "Did they take anything?"

"Not sure," he said, his words becoming slurry. "You can check my suit pockets. My wallet should be in it."

She walked over to the bag and checked the suit. The pockets were empty. "Nothing," she said. She then checked the lapel of the coat. "Do you know what happened to the keris pin on the lapel of Tom's coat?" she asked.

Emmanuel said nothing for a moment. "What do you know about that?" he asked cautiously.

"Everything. The keris had an important part in this assignment."

Emmanuel groaned again and adjusted his arm. "Before I left the bar," he said, his words becoming even more slow and slurry, "I gave the deposit slip and the keris pin to an FBI agent in the bar's restroom, just as Tom told me to do."

"He told you to do that? Oh, wow," she exclaimed, letting out a sigh of relief. Tom must have tipped off the FBI before Emmanuel got there! "But look what happened to you!" she said, fighting fresh tears.

"It's not Tom's fault," Emmanuel replied, closing his eyes. "It was my choice. I told him if he would not let me do it, I would tell the rehab staff."

"But why? It wasn't your responsibility to stop him, was it?"

"No. But I think it was wrong for him to leave the program. He was doing well there. If he left early, he would lose everything. Maybe his job. Maybe you." He started coughing a dry cough, then closed his eyes.

Ani wanted to say "thank you" and give him a big hug. But instead, she asked, "Should I call Sarah and tell her to come home from India?"

"No," he said, breathing unevenly and faster. "You mustn't worry her." He opened his eyes again and looked at Ani. "But in case I die—"

"You will not die. You can't die!"

"Whether I die or not, promise me one thing."

"What?"

"Don't be too hard on Tom. He wants to be your hero. And he doesn't want to lose you."

Ani nodded quietly. "But *you* are the *real* hero, Emmanuel. You shouldn't have done what you did."

Emmanuel closed his eyes again. His breathing became less shallow and more even as he fell asleep. A nurse entered and checked the machines connected to his head and body.

"He woke up and talked with me!" Ani told her. "But he is not my husband, after all. His first name is Emmanuel. The reason that I thought he was my husband is a long story. I don't know his last name, but I know someone who does." She pulled out Grace's business card from her purse. "Here is a mutual friend's name and phone number. She can tell you more about him."

The nurse took the card. "Thank you. But you shouldn't be in this room if you're not even his wife," she said coldly.

"Right. But he's a very close friend of my husband, and he doesn't have any family here. Can't you let me stay a few more minutes? Please?"

The nurse shook her head. "You've been here longer than you

should have, Miss. But I'll give you one more minute, that's all," she said as she turned to leave the room.

Ani lightly laid her hand on Emmanuel's bandaged arm and closed her eyes. She took a peek at Emmanuel's face and saw he was breathing deeply and regularly. "Lord Isa," she prayed, "Please don't let him die! Make him well again." Then she left the room. As Ani walked down the long hall toward the hospital exit, she suddenly realized that, although she had not eaten all day, the usual, nagging pain in the pit of her acid stomach was not there anymore.

Chapter 49

When the person who would and should have been lying in that hospital bed heard what had happened to his friend, he was beside himself. Both guilt and shame felt like steel on top of his head for a long, long time, mellowing him more than he had ever been mellowed. Forever grateful to Emmanuel, he did everything he could to help with the latter's recovery as well as the finances involved. Emmanuel eventually recovered, finished his thesis, and returned to his beloved India, where he joined Sarah, his soon-to-be bride.

When Solomon heard of the details of the last mission's rendezvous, he hung up before he could speak—not just for shock, but also out of shame. Deep down he knew he was at fault for what had happened to Tom's friend. Although Solomon did not receive all the money originally promised to him by Rianto, he did make good on the promised pay to Tom. As destiny would have it, none of the three men were ever found out or arraigned for their involvement in the money scheme.

Rianto, however, did not fare as well.

One month and a day after Indri joined Ani in Baltimore and the final rendezvous for Solomon's moonlighting mission took place, Putu and Rianto were seated in the Newport Creamery on East Main Road in Middletown, Rhode Island. "What time did you say these people were coming to talk with me?" Rianto asked nervously.

"Around noon. They should be here any minute."

"I still do not understand why they want to meet here."

Putu nodded. "I am sorry, sir. I'm not sure, either."

Just then, the main door of the restaurant opened. "Ah, they're here!" said Putu, waving at Kameela, who had just entered the restaurant. Following her were a chubby Caucasian man and a tall, slim Black man, both in dark suits.

"You must be Mr. Rianto. I am Kameela Prempradan," Kameela said warmly, extending her hand. "I have heard so much about you."

But Rianto barely touched her hand while looking at the men behind her. He turned to the Black man. "And you are—?"

"I'm John Hagely, sir. And this is Roy Wimber. We're here to bring you to the state prosecutor's office for a visit with him. He's looking forward to meeting you, sir."

Showing no sign as to whether he understood their intent, Rianto asked coldly, "Would you like me to order something for you before we go?"

"Oh, that won't be necessary," Mr. Hagely answered.

Rianto looked at Putu. "You all right with that?" he asked. Putu nodded and mouthed the word *okay.* Then, picking up his briefcase, Rianto leaned over next to Putu's ear while eying Kameela. "She looks nice, Putu. Don't lose her!" he whispered as he turned to follow Mr. Hagely, the shorter Mr. Wimber close behind.

Kameela and Putu watched through the window and waited until John Hagely's car was out of sight. Kameela shouted, "Yippee!" and grabbed Putu by the hand. She pulled him from his chair and danced a happy dance with him. "We did it! We did it!" she chimed.

"So what's going to happen now?" asked Putu after they both sat down again.

"Are you sure that Rianto will cooperate?"

"Ninety-nine percent sure," replied Kameela. "If he doesn't agree to sign an affidavit saying that he was responsible for the gifts to the senators, they will arrest him for spouse abuse. I think he would prefer to sign the confession, don't you?"

Putu nodded. "Will they escort him to the airport?"

"Of course. But Rianto will probably call you first and ask you to bring him a suitcase with his personal things. His flight to Jakarta leaves at 6:00 p.m.

"I already have his suitcase in the trunk. Want to have lunch with me before all that happens?"

"Sure."

While they were eating, Kameela remarked, "You know, I feel for the guy. He probably has no idea that you know what's behind his sudden departure. To save face, he'll probably make up some lame excuse as to why he needs to go back to Indonesia so suddenly."

Putu nodded and sighed. "He's good at keeping his life private. I'm just relieved that Indri is safe. But what will happen to her now?"

"She will stay with Ani and most likely study art in Maryland."

"But who will support her?"

"The FBI will get Rianto to transfer a big chunk of his account to a new account in Indri's name."

"Good. And what about the villa? Will I lose my job and a place to live?"

Kameela touched his hand. "No, my friend. You won't. At least not yet. Since Rianto's lease on the house won't expire until next year in June, you have a job and a place to live until next May. Indri must pay your salary out of her account. And believe me, she will have plenty. But you will need to ship Rianto's personal belongings to him in Indonesia. And eventually, you'll have to sell all the furniture in the house and send the money to Indri."

"Where should I go after next May?" Putu asked.

"Hmmm. I'm sure you'll think of something!" she said with a suggestive smile.